D0707982
1798

57

£ 2.25

Jain Barrie Stewart.

3

The current carried me on (see page 199)

TALES FROM
THE ARABIAN NIGHTS

——many a sheeny summer morn
Adown the Tigris I was borne,
By Bagdad's shrines of fretted gold,
High-wall'd gardens green and old.

TENNYSON.

Thomas Nelson and Sons, Ltd.
London, Edinburgh, New York
Toronto, and Paris

CONTENTS

LIST OF ILLUSTRATIONS

TALES FROM THE ARABIAN NIGHTS

SCHEHERA-ZADE'S TASK

THE Persian sultan, Schah-riah, having discovered that his wife was disloyal to him, took a savage vow to marry a new wife every night and command her to be executed in the morning. This cruel oath was put into operation, to the great consternation of the families from which his unhappy brides were drawn.

The grand vizier, who was entrusted with the task of selecting the brides, had two daughters. The elder was called Schehera-zade, and the younger Dinar-zade. Schehera-zade had a degree of courage beyond her sex. She had read much, and was possessed of so great a memory that she never forgot anything once learned. Her beauty was only equalled by her virtuous disposition, and the vizier was passionately fond of so deserving a daughter.

As they were conversing together one day, she made a request of her father, to his very great astonishment, that she might have the honour of becoming the sultan's bride. The grand vizier endeavoured to dissuade his daughter from her intention by pointing out the fearful penalty of an immediate death attached to the favour which she sought. Schehera-zade, however, persisted in her request, intimating to her father that she had in her mind a plan, which she thought might be successful in making a change in the intention of the sultan, and in putting a stop to the dreadful cruelty exercised towards the inhabitants of the city.

"Yes, my father," replied this heroic woman, "I am aware of the danger I run, but it does not deter me from my purpose. If I die, my death will be glorious; and if I succeed, I shall render my country an important service."

The vizier was most reluctant to allow his beloved child to enter on so dangerous an enterprise. But at length, overcome by his daughter's firmness, he yielded to her entreaties. Although he was very sorry at not being able to conquer her resolution, he went to Schah-riah, and announced to him that Schehera-zade herself would be his bride on the following night.

The sultan was much astonished at the sacrifice of the grand vizier. "Is it possible," said he, "that you can give up your own child?"

"Sire," replied the vizier, "she has herself made the offer. The dreadful fate that hangs over her does not alarm her; and she resigns her life for the honour of being the consort of your majesty."

"Vizier," said the sultan, "do not deceive yourself with any hopes; for be assured that, in delivering Schehera-zade into your charge to-morrow, it will be with an order for her death; and if you disobey, your own head will be the forfeit."

"Though I am her father," replied the vizier, "I will answer for the fidelity of this arm in fulfilling your commands."

When the grand vizier returned to Schehera-zade, she thanked him; and observing him to be much afflicted, consoled him by saying, she hoped he would be so far from repenting her marriage with the sultan that it would become a subject of joy to him for the remainder of his life.

Before Schehera-zade went to the palace, she called her sister, Dinar-zade, aside, and said, "As soon as I

He was charmed with her beauty.

shall have presented myself before the sultan, I shall entreat him to suffer you to sleep near the bridal chamber, that in the morning I may see you without delay and enjoy for the last time your company. If I obtain this favour, as I expect, remember I shall awaken you to-morrow an hour before daybreak, and you must come in and say, 'My sister, I beg of you to recount to me one of those delightful stories you know.' I will at once begin to tell one; and I flatter myself that by these means I shall free the kingdom from the fear in which it lies."

Dinar-zade promised to do what her sister required.

Within a short time Schehera-zade was conducted by her father to the palace, and was admitted to the presence of the sultan. He was charmed with her beauty; but perceiving tears in her eyes, he demanded the cause of them.

"Sire," answered Schehera-zade, "I have a sister whom I tenderly love—I earnestly wish that she might be permitted to pass the night in an apartment adjoining ours, that we may see each other again in the morning, and once more take a tender farewell. Will you allow me the consolation of giving her this last proof of my affection?"

Schah-riah having agreed to it, they sent word to Dinar-zade. On the morrow Schehera-zade awoke about an hour before day, and called to her sister, who soon came into the royal chamber. After greeting each other, Dinar-zade said, "My dear sister, if you are willing, I entreat you to relate to me one of those delightful tales you know. It will, alas, be the last time I shall receive that pleasure."

Instead of returning an answer to her sister, Schehera-zade addressed the sultan, and said, "Will your majesty permit me to indulge my sister in her request?"

"Freely," replied he.

Schehera-zade then began as follows:—

THE STORY OF THE MERCHANT AND THE GENIE

THERE was formerly a merchant, who was possessed of great wealth in land, merchandise, and ready money. Having one day an affair of great importance to settle at a considerable distance from home, he mounted his horse, and with only a small bag behind him, in which he had put a few biscuits and dates, he began his journey. He arrived without any accident at his destination ; and finishing his business, set out to return.

On the fourth day of his homeward journey, he felt so troubled by the heat of the sun, that he turned out of the road, in order to rest under some trees, by which there was a spring. He alighted, and tying his horse to a branch of a tree, sat down on the bank of the spring to eat some biscuits and dates from his little store. When he had satisfied his hunger, he amused himself with throwing about the stones of the fruit. Afterwards he washed his hands, his face, and his feet, and repeated a prayer, like a good Mohammedan.

He was still on his knees, when he saw a genie, white with age, and of a great stature, advancing towards him, with a scimitar in his hand. As soon as he was close to him, he said in a most terrible tone, " Get up, that I may kill thee with this scimitar, as thou hast caused the death of my son."

He said these words with a dreadful yell. The merchant, alarmed by the horrible figure of this giant, as well as by the words he heard, replied in trembling accents, " How can I have slain him ? I do not know him, nor have I ever seen him."

" Didst thou not, on thine arrival here, sit down, and take some dates from thy wallet ? " asked the giant ; " and after eating them didst thou not throw the stones about on all sides ? "

" That is all true," replied the merchant ; " I do not deny it."

" Well, then," said the other, " I tell thee thou hast killed my son ; for while thou wast throwing about the stones, my son passed by. One of them struck him in the eye, and caused his death, and thus hast thou slain my son."

" Ah, sire, forgive me," cried the merchant.

" I have neither forgiveness nor mercy," added the giant ; " and is it not just that he who has inflicted death should suffer it ? "

" Yet surely, even if I have inflicted death," said the merchant, " I have done so innocently, and therefore I entreat you to pardon me, and suffer me to live."

" No, no," cried the genie, still persisting in his resolution, " I must destroy thee, as thou hast done my son."

At these words, he took the merchant in his arms, and having thrown him with his face on the ground, he lifted up his sabre, in order to strike off his head.

Schehera-zade, at this instant, perceiving it was day, and knowing that the sultan rose early to his prayers, and then to hold a council, broke off.

" What a wonderful story," said Dinar-zade.

" The conclusion," answered Schehera-zade, " is still more surprising, as you would confess, *if the sultan would consent that I should live another day, and in the morning permit me to continue the relation.*"

Schah-riah, who had listened with much pleasure to the narration, determined to wait till the morrow, intending to order her execution after she had finished her story. He arose, and having prayed, went to the council.

The grand vizier, in the meantime, was in a state of cruel suspense. Unable to sleep, he passed the night lamenting the approaching fate of his daughter, whose executioner he was compelled to be. Dreading, therefore, in this melancholy situation, to meet the sultan, how great was his surprise to see him enter the council chamber without giving him the horrible order he expected!

The sultan spent the day, as usual, in regulating the affairs of his kingdom, and on the approach of night, retired with Schehera-zade to his apartment.

On the next morning, the sultan did not wait for Schehera-zade to ask permission to continue her story, but said, "Finish the tale of the genie and the merchant. I am curious to hear the end of it."

Schehera-zade immediately went on as follows *:—

When the merchant perceived that the genie was about to execute his purpose, he cried aloud, "One word more, I entreat you; have the goodness to grant me a little delay; give me only one year to go and take leave of my dear wife and children, and I promise to return to this spot, and submit myself entirely to your pleasure."

"Take God to witness of the promise thou hast made me," said the other.

"Again I swear," replied the merchant, "and you may rely on my oath."

* So, night after night for a thousand and one nights she told new stories, and by that time the sultan had not only become ashamed of his cruelty but had learnt to love the brave and clever woman, with whom he lived happily until the end. Some of the stories are related in this book.

Then the genie left him near the spring, and disappeared.

The merchant, as soon as he reached home, related faithfully all that had happened to him. On hearing the sad news, his wife uttered the most lamentable groans, tearing her hair, and beating her breast; and his children made the house resound with their grief; while the father, overcome by affection, mingled his tears with theirs. The year quickly passed away. The good merchant having settled his affairs, paid his just debts, given alms to the poor, and made provision to the best of his ability for his wife and family, tore himself away amidst the most frantic expressions of grief; and, mindful of his oath, arrived at the destined spot on the very day he had promised. While he was waiting for the genie, there appeared an old man leading a deer, and the newcomer, after a respectful salutation, inquired what brought him to that desert place. The merchant satisfied the old man's curiosity, on which the latter expressed a wish to witness his interview with the genie. They had scarcely finished speaking when another old man, accompanied by two black dogs, came in sight, and having heard the tale of the merchant, determined also to remain to see the event.

Soon they perceived, towards the plain, a thick vapour of smoke, like a column of dust raised by the wind. This vapour approached them, and then it suddenly disappeared, and they saw the genie, who, without noticing the others, went towards the merchant, with his scimitar in his hand; and taking him by the arm said, "Get up, that I may kill thee, as thou hast slain my son."

Both the merchant and the two old men, struck with terror, began to weep and fill the air with their lamentations. The old man who conducted the deer, seeing the genie lay hold of the merchant, and about to murder him without mercy, threw himself at the monster's feet, and, kissing them, said, "Lord Genie,

I humbly entreat you to suspend your rage, and hear my history, and that of the deer which you see ; and if you find it more wonderful and surprising than the adventure of this merchant, whose life you wish to take, may I not hope that you will at least grant me one half part of the blood of this unfortunate man ? "

After meditating some time, the genie answered, " Well, then, I agree to it."

THE HISTORY OF THE FIRST OLD MAN AND THE DEER

THE deer, whom you, Lord Genie, see here, is my wife. After I married her we lived together thirty years, without having any children. At the end of that time I adopted into my family the son of a slave woman. This act of mine excited against the slave mother and her child the hatred and jealousy of my wife. She availed herself, during my absence on a journey, of her knowledge of magic, to change the slave and my adopted son into a cow and a calf, and sent them to my farm to be fed and taken care of by the steward.

Immediately, on my return, I inquired after the child and his mother. " Your slave is dead," said she, " and it is now more than two months since I have beheld your son; nor do I know what is become of him."

I was very much affected at the death of the slave; but as my son had only disappeared, I flattered myself that he would soon be found. Eight months, however, passed, and he did not return; nor could I learn any tidings of him. In order to celebrate a holy festival, which was approaching, I ordered my steward to bring me the fattest cow I possessed, for a sacrifice. He obeyed my commands. Having bound the cow, I was about to slay her, when she lowed most sorrowfully, and tears fell from her eyes. This seemed to me so extraordinary, that I could not but feel compassion for her, and was unable to give the fatal blow. I therefore ordered her to be led away, and another brought.

My wife, who was present, seemed very angry at my compassion, and opposed my order.

I then said to my steward, "Make the sacrifice yourself; the lamentations and tears of the animal have overcome me."

The steward was less compassionate, and sacrificed her. On removing the skin we found hardly anything but bones, though she appeared very fat. "Take her away," said I to the steward, truly chagrined, "and if you have a very fat calf, bring it in her place."

He returned with a remarkably fine calf, who, as soon as he perceived me, made so great an effort to come to me, that he broke his cord. He lay down at my feet, with his head on the ground, as if he endeavoured to excite my compassion, and to entreat me not to have the cruelty to take away his life.

"Wife," said I, "I will not sacrifice this calf. I wish to favour him."

She, however, did not agree to my proposal; and demanded his sacrifice so obstinately, that I was compelled to yield. I bound the calf, and took the fatal knife to bury it in his throat, when he turned his eyes, filled with tears, so persuasively on me, that I had no power to execute my intention. The knife fell from my hand, and I told my wife I was determined to have another calf. She tried every means to induce me to alter my mind. I continued firm, however, in my resolution, in spite of all she could say, promising, for the sake of appeasing her, to sacrifice this calf the following year.

The next morning my steward informed me that his daughter, who had some knowledge of magic, wished to speak with me. On being admitted to my presence, she told me that, during my absence, my wife had turned the slave and my son into a cow and calf; that I had already sacrificed the cow, but that she could restore my son to his natural self, if I would give him to her for her husband, and allow her to punish my wife as her cruelty deserved. To these proposals I gave my consent.

The damsel then took a vessel full of water, and pronouncing over it some words I did not understand, she threw the water over the calf, and he instantly regained his own form.

"My son! my son!" I exclaimed, and embraced him with transport; "this damsel has destroyed the horrible charm with which you were surrounded. I am sure your gratitude will induce you to marry her, as I have already promised for you." He joyfully consented; but before they were united the damsel changed my wife into this deer, which you see here.

My son long ago became a widower, and is now travelling. Many years have passed since I have heard anything of him. I have, therefore, now set out with a view to gain some information of him; and as I did not like to trust my wife to the care of any one during my search, I thought proper to take her along with me. This is the history of myself and this deer. Can anything be more wonderful?

"It is so marvellous a history," said the genie, "that I grant to you a half of the blood of this merchant."

As soon as the first old man had finished, the second, who led the two black dogs, also made request to the genie for a half of the merchant's blood, on the condition that his tale exceeded in interest the one that had been just related. The genie signified his assent, and the old man began.

THE HISTORY OF THE SECOND OLD MAN AND THE TWO BLACK DOGS

GREAT Prince of the genies, you must know that these two black dogs, which you see here, and myself are three brothers. Our father, when he died, left us one thousand sequins each. With this sum we all embarked in business as merchants. My two brothers determined to travel, that they might trade in foreign parts. They were both unfortunate, and returned at the end of two years in a state of abject poverty, having lost their all. I had in the meanwhile prospered, and I gladly received them, and gave them one thousand sequins each, and again set them up as merchants. My brothers frequently proposed to me that I should make a voyage with them for the purpose of traffic. Knowing their former want of success, I refused to join them, until at the end of five years I at length yielded to their repeated requests. On consulting about the merchandise to be bought for the voyage, I discovered that nothing remained of the thousand sequins I had given to each. I did not reproach them. On the contrary, as my capital was increased to six thousand sequins, I again gave them each one thousand sequins, and kept a like sum myself, and concealed the other three thousand in a corner of my house, in order that if our voyage proved unsuccessful, we might be able to console ourselves and begin our former profession. We purchased our goods, embarked in a vessel, which we ourselves freighted, and set sail with a favourable wind. After sailing about a month, we arrived, without any accident, at a port, where we landed, and had a most profitable sale for our merchandise. I, in particular, sold mine so well, that I gained ten for one.

About the time that we were ready to embark on our return, I accidentally met on the sea-shore a female, of great beauty, but very poorly dressed. She accosted me by kissing my hand, and entreated me most earnestly to permit her to be my wife. I stated many difficulties to such a plan; but at length she said so much to persuade me that I ought not to regard her poverty, and that I should be well satisfied with her conduct, that I was quite overcome. I directly procured proper dresses for her, and after marrying her in due form, she went on the vessel with me, and we set sail.

During our voyage, I found my wife possessed of so many good qualities, that I loved her every day more and more. In the meantime my two brothers, who had not traded so advantageously as myself, and who were jealous of my prosperity, began to feel very envious. They even went so far as to conspire against my life; for one night, while my wife and I were asleep, they threw us into the sea. I had hardly, however, fallen into the water, before my wife took me up and transported me into an island.

As soon as it was day she thus addressed me: "You must know that I am a fairy, and being on the shore when you were about to sail, I wished to try the goodness of your heart, and for this purpose I presented myself before you in the disguise you saw. You acted most generously, and I am therefore delighted in finding an occasion of showing my gratitude, and I trust, my husband, that in saving your life, I have not ill rewarded the good you have done me; but I am enraged against your brothers, nor shall I be satisfied till I have taken their lives."

I listened with astonishment to the discourse of the fairy, and thanked her, as well as I was able, for the great kindness she had conferred on me. "But, madame," said I to her, "I must entreat you to pardon my brothers."

I related to her what I had done for each of them, but my account only increased her anger.

"I must instantly fly after these ungrateful wretches," cried she, "and bring them to a just punishment. I will sink their vessel, and send them to the bottom of the sea."

"No, beautiful lady," replied I; "for heaven's sake, moderate your indignation, and do not execute so dreadful an intention; remember they are still my brothers, and that we are bound to return good for evil."

No sooner had I pronounced these words, than I was transported in an instant from the island, where we were, to the entrance of my own house. Then I opened the door, and dug up the three thousand sequins which I had hidden. I afterwards went to my shop, opened it, and received the congratulations of the merchants in the neighbourhood on my arrival. When I returned home, I perceived these two black dogs, which came towards me with a submissive air. I could not imagine what their actions meant, but the fairy, who soon appeared, satisfied my curiosity. "My dear husband," said she, "be not surprised at seeing these two dogs; they are your brothers."

My blood ran cold on hearing this, and I inquired by what power they had been transformed into that state.

"It is I," replied the fairy, "who have done it, and I have sunk their ship. For the loss of the merchandise it contained, I shall recompense you. As to your brothers, I have condemned them to remain in this form ten years, as a punishment for their perfidy."

Then informing me where I might hear of her, she disappeared.

The ten years are now completed, and I am travelling in search of her. "This, O Lord Genie, is my history. Does it not appear to you of a most extraordinary nature ?"

"Yes," replied the genie, "I confess it is most wonderful, and therefore I grant you the other half of this merchant's blood;" and having said this, the genie disappeared, to the great joy of the merchant and of the two old men.

The merchant did not omit to bestow many thanks on his liberators, who, bidding him adieu, proceeded on their travels. He mounted his horse, and returned home to his wife and children, and spent the remainder of his days with them in tranquillity.

THE HISTORY OF THE FISHERMAN

THERE was formerly an aged fisherman, so poor that he could barely obtain food for himself, his wife, and his three children. He went out early every morning to his employment; and he had imposed a rule on himself never to cast his nets more than four times a day.

On one occasion he set out before the night had disappeared. When he reached the sea-shore, he cast his nets and drew them to land three times in succession, feeling assured each time from their resistance and weight that he had secured an excellent draught of fish. Instead of which, he only found on the first haul the carcass of an ass; on the second, a big wicker basket filled with sand and mud; and on the third, a large quantity of heavy stones, shells, and filth. It is impossible to describe his disappointment and despair. The day now began to break, and he threw his nets for the fourth time. Again he supposed he had caught a great quantity of fish, as he drew them with as much difficulty as before. He nevertheless found none; but discovered a heavy vase of yellow copper, shut up and fastened with lead, on which there was the impression of a seal. "I will sell this copper vase to a metal-worker," said he, with joy, "and with the money I shall get for it I will purchase a measure of corn."

He examined the vase on all sides, and he shook it, but could hear nothing; and yet the impression of the seal on the lead made him think it was filled with something valuable. In order to find out, he took his knife, and got it open. He then turned the top downwards, and was much surprised when nothing came out. He set it down before him, and while he was attentively observing it, there issued from it so thick a smoke that he was obliged to step back a few paces. This smoke, by degrees, rose almost to the clouds, and spread itself over both the water and the shore, appearing like a thick fog. The fisherman, as may easily be imagined, was a good deal surprised at this sight. When the smoke had all come out from the vase, it collected itself, and became a solid body, and then took the shape of a genie of gigantic size.

The genie, looking at the fisherman, exclaimed, " Humble thyself before me. I intend to kill thee."

" And for what reason, pray, will you kill me ? " answered the fisherman. " Have you already forgotten that I set you at liberty ? "

" I remember it very well," the genie responded ; " but that shall not prevent my destroying thee, and I will only grant thee one favour."

" And pray what is that ? " said the fisherman.

" It is," replied the genie, " to permit thee to choose the manner of thy death. I can treat thee no otherwise, and to convince thee of it, hear my history—

" I am one of those spirits who rebelled against God. Solomon, the prophet of God, commanded me to acknowledge his authority, and submit to his laws. I proudly refused. In order, therefore, to punish me, he enclosed me in this copper vase ; and, to prevent me from forcing my way out, he put on the leaden cover his seal, on which the great name of God is engraven. This done, he gave the vase to one of those genies who obeyed him, and ordered him to cast me into the sea.

" During the first century of my captivity, I swore that if any one delivered me before a hundred years were passed, I would make him rich. During the second century, I swore that if any one released me, I would discover to him all the treasures of the earth. During the third, I promised to make my deliverer a most powerful monarch, and to grant him every day any three requests he chose. These centuries passed away without any deliverance. Enraged, at last, to be so long a prisoner, I swore that I would, without mercy, kill whoever should in future release me, and that the only favour I would grant him should be, to choose what manner of death he pleased. Since, therefore, thou hast come here to-day, and hast delivered me, fix upon whatever kind of death thou wilt."

The fisherman was in great distress at finding the genie thus resolved on his death, not so much on his own account as for his three children, whose means of living would be greatly reduced. "Alas!" he cried, "have pity on me; remember what I have done for thee."

"Let us lose no time," cried the genie; "your arguments avail not. Make haste, tell me how you wish to die."

Necessity is the mother of invention; and the fisherman thought of a stratagem. "Since," said he, "I cannot escape death, I submit to the will of God; but before I choose the sort of death, I conjure you, by the great name of God, which is graven upon the seal of the prophet Solomon, answer me truly a question I am going to put to you."

The genie trembled at this adjuration, and said to the fisherman, "Ask what thou wilt, and make haste."

"Dare you, then, to swear by the great name of God that you really were in that vase? This vase cannot contain one of your feet. How, then, can it hold your whole body?"

"I swear to thee, notwithstanding," replied he, "that I was there just as thou seest me. Wilt thou not believe me after the solemn oath I have taken?"

"No," declared the fisherman, "I shall not believe you unless I see it."

Immediately, the form of the genie began to change into smoke, and extended itself, as before, over both the shore and the sea; and then, collecting itself, began to enter the vase, and continued to do so, in a slow and equal manner, till nothing remained without. The fisherman at once took the leaden cover, and put it on the vase. "Genie," he cried, "it is now your turn to ask pardon. I shall throw you again into the sea, and I will build, opposite the very spot where you are cast, a house upon the shore, in which I will live, to warn all fishermen that shall come and throw their nets, not to fish up so evil a genie as thou art, who makest an oath to kill the man who sets thee at liberty."

The genie tried every argument to move the fisherman's pity, but in vain. "You are too treacherous for me to trust you," declared the fisherman; "I should deserve to lose my life if I put myself in your power a second time."

"One word more, fisherman," cried the genie; "I will teach you how to become as rich as possible."

The hope of being no longer in want at once disarmed the fisherman. "I could listen to thee," he said, "were there any credit to be given to thy word. Swear to me by the great name of God that you will faithfully perform what you promise, and I will open the vase. I do not believe that you will dare break such an oath."

The genie did as he was bidden; and the fisherman took off the covering. The smoke instantly ascended, and the genie resuming his usual form, kicked the vase into the sea. "Be of good heart, fisherman," cried he, "I have thrown the vase into the sea only to observe whether you would be alarmed. To show you that I intend to keep my word, take your nets and follow me."

They passed by the city, and went over the top of a mountain, whence they descended into a vast plain, and continued till they came to a lake, situated between four small hills.

When they arrived on the borders of the lake, the genie said to the fisherman, "Throw your nets and catch fish."

The fisherman saw a great quantity of fish in the lake; and was surprised at finding them of four different colours—white, red, blue, and yellow. He threw his nets and caught four fish, one of each colour. As he had never seen any similar to them, he could hardly cease admiring them; and judging that he could dispose of them for a considerable sum, he expressed great joy.

"Carry these fish to the palace," said the genie, "and present them to the sultan, and he will give you more money than you ever handled in all your life. You may come every day and fish in this lake, but beware of casting your nets more than once each day. If you act otherwise you will repent. Therefore, take care. This is my advice, and if you follow it exactly you will do well." Having said this, he struck his foot on the ground, which opened and swallowed him up, and then closed.

The fisherman resolved to observe the advice of the genie in every point, and never to throw his nets a second time the same day. He went back to the town, and presented his fish at the sultan's palace.

The sultan was much surprised when he saw the four fish brought him by the fisherman. He took them one by one, and observed them most attentively; and after admiring them a long time, he said to his grand vizier, "Take these fish, and carry them to the cook. I think they must be as good to eat as they are beautiful; and give the fisherman four hundred pieces of gold." The fisherman, who was never before in possession of so large a sum of money, could not conceal his joy, and thought it all a dream, until he applied the gold in relieving the wants of his family.

As soon as the cook had cleaned the fish which the vizier had brought, she put them on the fire in a frying-pan, with some oil; and when she thought them sufficiently done on one side, she turned them. She had hardly done so when, wonderful to relate, the wall of the kitchen opened, and a young lady of marvellous beauty appeared. She was dressed in a satin robe, embroidered with flowers, and wore a necklace of large pearls, and gold bracelets set with rubies, and held a rod in her hand. She moved towards the frying-pan, to the great amazement of the cook, who remained motionless at the sight, and striking one of the fish with her rod, she said, "Fish, fish, art thou doing thy duty?"

The fish answering not a word, she repeated her question, when the four fish all raised themselves up, and said very distinctly, "Yes, yes, if you reckon, we reckon; if you pay your debts, we pay ours; if you fly, we conquer, and are content."

As soon as they had spoken these words, the damsel overturned the frying-pan, and went back through the open wall, which immediately closed, and was in the same state as before.

The cook, having recovered from her fright, went to take up the fish, which had fallen on the hot ashes; but found them blacker than coal, and not fit to send to the sultan. At this she began to cry with all her might. "Alas," said she, "what will become of me? I am sure, when I tell the sultan what I have seen, he will not believe me, but will be enraged with me!"

While she was in this distress, the grand vizier entered, and asked if the fish were ready. The cook then related all that had taken place, at which he was much astonished; but without speaking a word of it to the sultan, he invented an excuse which satisfied him. He then sent directly to the fisherman for four more fish, and the fisherman promised to bring them the next morning.

The fisherman set out before it was day, and went to the lake. He threw his nets, and drawing them out, found four more fish, like those he had taken the day before, each of a different colour. He returned directly, and brought them to the grand vizier by the time he had promised. The minister took them, and carried them to the kitchen, where he shut himself up with only the cook, who dressed them before him. She put them on the fire as she had done the others, when the grand vizier witnessed an exact repetition of all that the cook had told him.

"This is very surprising," he cried, "and too extraordinary to be kept secret from the sultan's ears. I will myself go and inform him of this prodigy."

The sultan being much astonished, sent for the fisherman, and said to him, "Canst thou bring me four more such fish?"

"If your majesty will grant me till to-morrow, I will do so," answered the fisherman.

He obtained the time he wished, and went again, for the third time, to the lake, and caught four fish of different colours at the first throw of his nets. He took them to the sultan, who expressed the greatest pleasure at seeing them, and ordered four hundred more pieces of money to be given to the fisherman.

As soon as the sultan got the fish, he had them taken into his own cabinet, with all that was necessary for frying them. Here he shut himself up with the grand vizier, who put the fish on the fire in the pan. As soon as they were done on one side, he turned them on the other. The wall of the cabinet immediately opened; but, instead of the beautiful lady, there appeared a black man of gigantic stature dressed in the habit of a slave, and holding a large green staff in his hand. He advanced to the frying-pan, and touching one of the fish with his rod, he cried out in a terrible voice, "Fish, fish, art thou doing thy duty?"

At these words all the fish lifted up their heads, and answered, "Yes, yes, we are; if you reckon, we reckon; if you pay your debts, we pay ours; if you fly, we conquer, and are content."

The fish had scarcely said this, when the black man overturned the frying-pan into the fire and reduced the fish to coals; and having done this, he retired fiercely, and entering into the aperture in the wall, it closed, and the wall appeared just as it did before.

The sultan being convinced that these fish signified something very extraordinary, and having learnt from the fisherman that he caught them in the lake situated in the midst of the four small hills, not more than three hours' journey from the palace, commanded all his court to mount horses and set out for the place, with the fisherman as a guide.

The sultan halted on the side of the lake, and, after observing the fish with great admiration, demanded of his courtiers if it were possible that they had never seen this lake, which was within so short a distance of the city. They all said they had never so much as heard of it. "Since you all agree, then," said he, "that you have never heard of it, and since I am not less astonished than you are at this novelty, I am resolved not to return to my palace till I have found how this lake came here, and why all the fish in it are of four colours."

Having thus spoken, he ordered his court to encamp, and his own tent and the tents of his household were pitched on the borders of the lake.

When night came, the sultan retired to his tent, and talked with his grand vizier. "My mind," said he, "is much disturbed. This lake, suddenly placed here; this black man who appeared to us in my cabinet; the fish, too, whom we heard speak—these things so excite my curiosity, that I cannot conquer my impatience to be satisfied. I shall go quite alone from my camp, and try to solve the mystery. I order you to keep my departure a profound secret. Remain in my tent, and when my officers and courtiers present themselves at the entrance to-morrow morning, send them away, and say I have a slight indisposition, and wish to be alone; and day by day make the same report till I return."

The grand vizier endeavoured to turn the sultan from his design; but in vain. The sultan was resolved. He put on a suit fit for walking, and took his scimitar; and as soon as he found that everything in the camp was quiet, went out alone.

He bent his course towards one of the small hills, which he mounted without much difficulty. He then came down to a plain, on which, when the sun rose, he perceived a grand palace, built of polished black marble, and covered with fine steel, as bright as crystal. Delighted with having so soon met with something worthy his curiosity, he went to the front of the palace, and stopped before one of the doors, which was open. He waited some time, but seeing no one, he was exceedingly surprised. "If there be no one in this palace," said he to himself, "I have nothing to fear; and if it be inhabited, I have wherewith to defend myself."

At last he entered, and when he was in the porch, he called out as loud as he could. There was no answer. This silence increased his astonishment. He passed on to a spacious court, and could not discover a living creature. He then entered and walked through some large halls, the carpets of which were of silk, and the door-curtains of the richest shawls of India, embroidered with gold and silver. Farther on, he came to a superb saloon, in the middle of which was a large fountain, with a lion of massive gold at each corner. Water issued from the mouths of the four lions, and as it fell, appeared to break into a thousand diamonds and pearls.

The castle was surrounded by a garden full of all kinds of flowers and shrubs, and furnished with a multitude of birds, which filled the air with the sweetest notes, nets being thrown entirely over the trees to prevent the birds from escaping.

The sultan wandered a long time from room to room, where everything was grand and magnificent. Being tired with walking, he sat down on a verandah, which faced towards the garden, when suddenly a plaintive voice, accompanied by the most heart-rending cries, reached his ears. He listened attentively, and heard these melancholy words: "O Fortune, thou hast not suffered me long to enjoy a happy lot! Cease to persecute me, and by a speedy death put an end to my sufferings."

The sultan immediately rose, and went towards the spot whence the voice issued, and drawing the door-curtain aside, saw a young man very richly dressed seated on a sort of throne, raised a little from the ground. Deep sorrow was impressed on his countenance. The sultan approached, and saluted him. The young man bent his head very low, but did not get up. "My lord, I should rise to receive you, but am hindered by sad necessity. You will not therefore, I trust, take it ill."

"I feel myself highly honoured, sir," replied the sultan, "by the good opinion you express of me. Whatever may be your motive for not rising, I willingly receive your apologies. I come to offer you my help. But inform me the meaning of the lake near this palace, where the fish are of four different colours; tell me how, also, this palace came here, and why you are thus alone."

Instead of answering these questions, the young man began to weep bitterly, and lifted up his robe, so that the sultan perceived he was a living man only to his waist, and that thence to his feet he was changed into black marble.

"What you show me," said the sultan, "fills me with horror. I am impatient to learn your history, with which I am persuaded that the lake and the fish have some connection. Pray, therefore, relate it; for the unhappy often experience relief in telling their sorrows."

"I will not refuse your request," replied the young man, and narrated the following story:—

THE HISTORY OF THE YOUNG KING OF THE BLACK ISLES

This is the kingdom of the Black Isles, of which my father, named Mahmoud, was king. It takes its name from the four small mountains which you have seen. Those mountains were formerly isles. The capital where the king my father resided was situated on the spot now occupied by the lake you have seen. On the death of my father, I succeeded him on the throne and married a lady, my cousin. We lived happily together for five years, when I began to perceive that the queen no longer loved me.

One day, after dinner, while she was at the bath, I lay down to sleep on a sofa. Two of her ladies came and sat, one at my head and the other at my feet, with fans in their hands to moderate the heat and to prevent the flies from disturbing me. They thought I was asleep, and spoke in whispers ; but as I only closed my eyes, I heard all their conversation.

One of them said to the other, " Is not the queen wrong, not to love so amiable a prince ? "

" Certainly," replied the other ; " and I cannot understand why she goes out every night and leaves him. Does he not perceive it ? "

" How should he ? " resumed the first ; " she mixes in his drink, every evening, the juice of a certain herb, which makes him sleep all night so soundly that she has time to go wherever she likes ; and when at break of day she returns to him, she rouses him by the smell of some scent she puts under his nostrils."

I pretended to awake without having heard the conversation.

The queen returned and we supped together, and before we went to bed she presented to me the cup of water, which it was usual for me to take ; but instead of drinking it, I approached a window that was open, and threw it out without her perceiving what I did. I then returned the cup into her own hands, that she might believe I had drunk the contents. We soon retired to rest, and shortly after, supposing that I was asleep, she got up and said, " Sleep, and mayest thou never wake more." She then dressed herself and left the chamber.

As soon as the queen was gone, I dressed in haste, took my scimitar, and followed her so quickly that I soon heard the sound of her feet before me. I walked softly after her and she passed through several gates, the locks of which fell off upon her pronouncing some magical words. The last gate she opened was that of the garden. She entered and I stopped. Then looking after her as far as the darkness of the night permitted, I saw her go into a little wood, whose walks were guarded by a thick hedge. I went thither by another way, and concealing myself behind the hedge of one of the paths, I perceived she was in the company of a man, with whom she offered to fly to another land. Enraged at this, I drew my scimitar and struck him, and he fell. I retired in haste and secrecy to the palace. Although I had inflicted a mortal wound, yet the queen by her enchantments contrived to preserve in her lover that trance-like existence which can neither be called death nor life. On her return to her chamber, she was absorbed in grief, and when the day dawned, requested my permission to build a tomb for herself, in the grounds of the palace, where she would continue, she told me, to the end of her days. I consented, and she built a stately edifice, and called it the Palace of Tears. When it was finished, she caused her lover to be conveyed thither, from the place to which he had been carried the night I wounded him. She had hitherto prevented his dying by potions which she had administered ; and she continued to convey them to him herself every day after he came to the Palace of Tears. After some time, I went myself to the tomb which the queen had built, and hearing her address the inanimate body in words of passionate affection, I lost all patience, and drew my scimitar and raised my arm to punish her.

" Moderate thy rage," said she to me, with a disdainful smile, and at the same instant pronounced some magic words ; and added, " By my enchantments, I command thee to become half marble and half man."

Immediately, my lord, I became what you see me : a dead man among the living, and a living man among the dead.

As soon as this cruel sorceress had thus transformed me, and by her magic had conveyed me to this apartment, she destroyed my capital ; she annihilated the palaces, public places, and markets ; and reduced the site of the whole to the lake and desert plain you have seen. The fishes of four colours in the lake are the four kinds of inhabitants, of different religions, which the city contained. The white are the Mohammedans ; the red, the Persians, who worship fire ; the blue, the Christians ; and the yellow, the Jews. The four islands that gave a name to this kingdom became four hills. The enchantress, to add to my affliction, comes every day, and gives me on my naked back a hundred lashes with a whip.

When he came to this part of his narrative, the young king could not restrain his tears, and the sultan was himself greatly affected. " No one, prince," said he, " could have experienced a more extraordinary fate than yourself. One thing only is wanting to complete your history, and that is, for you to be revenged; nor will I leave anything untried to accomplish it."

The sultan having informed the prince who he was, and the reason of his entering the castle, consulted with him on the best means of obtaining a just revenge; and a plan occurred to the sultan, which he at once communicated, but the execution of which they deferred till the following day. In the meantime, as the night was far advanced, the sultan took some repose. The young prince, as usual, passed his time in continual watchfulness, for he was unable to sleep since his enchantment. The hopes, however slight, which he cherished of being soon relieved from his sufferings, constantly occupied his thoughts.

Next morning the sultan arose with the dawn and prepared to execute his design. He proceeded to the Palace of Tears and found it lighted with a great number of torches of white wax, and perfumed by a delicious scent issuing from several censers of fine gold. As soon as he saw the couch on which the inanimate form of the lover was laid, he drew his scimitar, destroyed the little remains of life left, and dragging the body into the outer court, threw it into the well. After this, he lay down on the couch, placed his scimitar under the covering, and waited to complete his design.

The queen arrived shortly after in the chamber of her husband, the king of the Black Islands. On her approach, the unfortunate prince filled the palace with the lamentations, and begged her in the most affecting tone to take pity on him. She, however, ceased not to beat him till she had completed the hundred stripes. She next went to the Palace of Tears. "Alas!" cried she, addressing herself to the sultan, whom she took for her lover, "wilt thou always, light of my life, preserve this silence? Utter at least one word, I conjure thee."

The sultan then, lowering his voice as if in great

weakness, spoke a few words. The sorceress gave a violent scream through excess of joy. "My dear lord," she exclaimed, "is what I hear true? Is it really you who speak?"

"Wretched woman," replied the sultan, "art thou worthy of an answer?"

"What!" cried the queen, "dost thou reproach me?"

"The cries, the tears, the groans of thy husband," answered the supposed lover, "whom you every day beat with so much cruelty, prevent my rest. I should have long since recovered the use of my tongue, if you had disenchanted him. This, and this only, has been the cause of my silence."

"Well, then," said she, "I am ready to execute your commands. Would you have me restore him?"

"Yes," replied the sultan; "make haste to set him at liberty, that I be no longer disturbed by his moanings."

The queen immediately went out from the Palace of Tears; and taking a vessel of water, proceeded to the apartment where the young king was. "If the Creator of all things," said she, throwing the water over him, "hath formed thee as thou now art, do not change; but if thou art in that state by virtue of my enchantment, reassume thy natural form, and become the same as before."

She had hardly concluded when the marble limbs of the prince became flesh and he rose, with all possible joy, and returned thanks to God. "Go," said the enchantress, addressing him, "hasten from this palace, and never return on pain of death."

The young king, yielding to necessity, without replying a word, retired to a remote place, where he awaited the appearance of the sultan. Meanwhile the enchantress returned to the Palace of Tears, and supposing that she still spoke to her lover, said, "I have done what you required."

The sultan, disguising his voice as before, answered in a low tone: "What you have yet done is not sufficient for my cure. You have destroyed only a part of the evil, but you must strike at the root."

"What do you mean by the root, dear heart?" answered she.

"Understand you not that I allude to the town, and its inhabitants, and the four islands, destroyed by thy enchantments? The fish every night at midnight raise their heads out of the lake, and cry for vengeance against thee and me. This is the true cause of the delay of my cure. Go speedily, restore things to their former state, and at thy return I will give thee my hand, and thou shalt help me to arise."

The enchantress, inspired with hope from these words, cried out in a transport of joy, "My heart, my soul, you shall soon be restored to your health."

Accordingly she went that instant, and when she came to the border of the lake, she took a little water in her hand, and scattered it about. She had no sooner done so, and pronounced certain words, than the city instantly appeared. The fish became men, women, and children—Mohammedans, Christians, Persians, and Jews—freemen or slaves; in short, each took his natural form. The houses and shops became filled with inhabitants, who found everything in the same state as it was previous to the change. The officers and attendants of the sultan, who were encamped where the great square happened to be, were astonished at finding themselves on a sudden in the midst of a large, well-built, and inhabited city.

But to return to the enchantress: as soon as she had completed this change, she hastened back to the Palace of Tears. "My dear lord," she cried on entering, "I have done all you have required of me; arise, and give me your hand."

"Come near, then," said the sultan.

She did so. He then rose, and with a blow of his

scimitar slew her. This done, he left the Palace of Tears, and returned to the young king of the Black Isles. "Prince," said he, "rejoice; you have now nothing to fear; your cruel enemy is dead. You may henceforward dwell peaceably in your capital, unless you will accompany me to mine, which is near. You shall there be welcome, and have as much honour and respect shown you as if you were in your own kingdom."

"Potent monarch, to whom I owe so much," replied the king, "you think, then, that you are near your capital?"

"Yes," said the sultan, "I know it is not above four or five hours' journey."

"It is a whole year's journey," said the prince. "I do, indeed, believe that you came hither from your capital in the time you mention, because mine was enchanted; but since the enchantment is taken off, things are changed. This, however, shall not prevent my following you to the ends of the earth. You are my liberator; and to show you my gratitude as long as I live, I shall freely accompany you, and resign my kingdom without regret."

The sultan, extremely surprised to understand that he was so far from his kingdom, replied, "It is no matter; the long journey to my own country is sufficiently repaid by acquiring you for a son; for since you will accompany me, as I have no child, I will make you my heir and successor."

At the end of three weeks the sultan and the young prince began their journey, with a hundred camels laden with riches from the treasury of the young king, followed by fifty men-at-arms on horseback, perfectly well mounted and dressed. They had a pleasant journey, and when the sultan, who had sent messengers to give notice of his coming, and to explain the reason of his delay, drew near to his capital, the principal officers, whom he had left there, came to receive him. The inhabitants, also, crowded to meet him, and welcomed him with every sign of joy.

The day after his arrival the sultan assembled his people, and declared to them his intention of adopting the king of the four Black Isles, who had left a large kingdom to accompany and live with him ; and when he finished speaking he bestowed presents on all, according to their rank and station.

The sultan did not forget the fisherman, and made him and his family happy and comfortable for the rest of their days

THE STORY OF PRINCE AHMED AND THE FAIRY PERIE BANOU

THERE was a sultan of India who, after a long reign, had reached a good old age. He had three sons and one niece, the chief ornaments of his court. The eldest son was called Houssain, the second Ali, the youngest Ahmed. The name of his niece, their cousin, was Nouronnihar. This niece, the daughter of a favourite brother who had died young, had been brought up in the palace from her childhood, and was remarkable for her wit and for her beauty. The sultan, on her arriving at the proper age, was consulting about a neighbouring prince with whom she might form an alliance, when he found that all the three princes, his sons, loved their cousin and wished to marry her. This discovery caused him great grief—not from any disappointment of his own plans for his niece, but from the discord which this mutual passion for their cousin would cause to his sons.

He spoke to each of them apart, and showed the impossibility of one princess being the wife of three brothers, and the troubles they would create if they persisted in their purpose. He did all he could to persuade them to abide by a declaration of the princess in favour of one of them; or that all should agree to resign their claims to her hand, that she might marry a stranger. But as he found them equally obstinate, he sent for them all together, and said, " My sons, since I have not been able to persuade you in this matter, and as I have no wish to use my authority, to give the princess your cousin to one in preference of another, I have thought of a plan which will please you all, and preserve harmony among you, if you will but hear me and follow my advice. I think it would not be amiss if you were to travel separately into different countries, so that you might not meet each other; and I promise my niece in marriage to him who shall bring me the most extraordinary rarity. I will give each of you a sum suited to your rank, and for the purchase of the rarity you shall search after."

The three princes cheerfully consented to this proposal, as each flattered himself fortune might prove favourable to him, and give him possession of the Princess Nouronnihar. The sultan gave them the money he promised, and issued orders for the preparations for their travels. Early next morning they all went out at the same gate of the city, each dressed like a merchant, attended by a trusty officer habited as a slave, and all well mounted and equipped. They proceeded the first day's journey together; and at night when they were at supper, they agreed to travel for a twelvemonth, and that day a year later to meet again at the khan where they were stopping; so that as they had all three taken leave together of the sultan, they might return in company. The next morning by break of day, after they had embraced and wished each other good success, they mounted their horses and each took a different road.

Prince Houssain, the eldest brother, who had heard of the extent, power, riches, and splendour of the kingdom of Bisnagar, bent his course towards the Indian coast; and after three months' travelling with different caravans, sometimes over deserts and barren mountains, and sometimes through populous and fertile countries, arrived at Bisnagar, the capital of the kingdom of that name, and the residence of its king. He lodged at a khan appointed for foreign merchants, and soon learned that there were four principal bazaars where merchants of all sorts kept their shops, on a large extent of ground, in the centre of the city.

Prince Houssain went to one of these bazaars on the next day. It was large, divided into several vaulted avenues, and shaded from the sun, but yet very light. The shops were all of the same size and proportion; and all who dealt in the same sort of goods lived in one avenue.

The number of shops stocked with all kinds of merchandise—as the finest linens from several parts of India; silks and brocades from Persia; porcelain from Japan—surprised him very much; but when he came to the shops of the goldsmiths and jewellers, he was in a kind of ecstasy at beholding such quantities of wrought gold and silver, and was dazzled by the lustre of the pearls, diamonds, rubies, emeralds, and other precious stones exposed for sale.

After Prince Houssain had passed through that quarter, street by street, a merchant perceiving him go by much fatigued, invited him to sit down in front of his shop. He had not been seated long before a crier appeared, with a piece of carpet on his arm, about six feet square, and offered it at forty purses. The prince called to the crier, and when he had examined the carpet, told him that he could not comprehend how so small a piece of carpet, and of so indifferent an appearance, could be held at so high a price unless it had something very extraordinary in it which he knew nothing of.

"You have guessed right, sir," replied the crier; "whoever sits on this piece of carpet may be transported in an instant wherever he desires to be."

"If the carpet," said he to the crier, "has the virtue you attribute to it, I shall not think forty purses too much."

"Sir," replied the crier, "I have told you the truth,

and with the leave of the master of this shop we will go into the back warehouse, where I will spread the carpet, and when we have both sat down, and you have formed the wish to be transported into your apartment at the khan, if we are not conveyed thither, it shall be no bargain."

On this proposal they went into the merchant's back-shop, where they both sat down on the carpet; and as soon as the prince had formed his wish to be transported into his apartment at the khan, he in an instant found himself and the crier there. After this convincing proof of the virtue of the carpet, he counted to the crier forty purses of gold, and gave him twenty pieces for himself.

In this manner Prince Houssain became the possessor of the carpet, and was overjoyed that at his arrival at Bisnagar he had found so rare a curiosity, which he never doubted must of course gain him the possession of Nouronnihar, as his younger brothers could not meet with anything to be compared with it. By sitting on this carpet, it was in his power to be at the place of meeting that very day; but as he would be obliged to wait there for his brothers until the time they had agreed upon, he chose to make a longer abode in this capital.

When Prince Houssain had seen all the wonders of the city, he wished to be nearer his dear Princess Nouronnihar, and having paid all the charges, and returned the key of his apartment to the owner of the khan, he spread the carpet, and as soon as he had formed his wish he and his officer whom he had brought with him were transported to the inn at which he and his brothers were to meet, and where he passed for a merchant till their arrival.

Prince Ali, the second brother, who had designed to travel into Persia, after he had parted with his brothers, joined a caravan, and in four months arrived at Shiraz, the capital of that empire.

On the next morning after his arrival, while the merchants opened their bales of merchandise, Prince Ali took a walk into that quarter of the town where is the bazaar of the jewellers, in which they sold precious stones, gold and silver works, and other choice and valuable articles, for which Shiraz was celebrated.

Among the criers who passed backwards and forwards with samples of several sorts of goods, he was not a little surprised to see one who held in his hand an ivory tube, about a foot in length, and about an inch thick, which he cried at forty purses. At first he thought the crier mad, and asked him what he meant by asking forty purses for that tube which seemed to be a thing of no value.

The crier replied, " Sir, you are not the only person that takes me for a madman on account of this tube; you shall judge yourself whether I am or not, when I have told you its peculiar power. By looking through this tube, you will see whatever object you wish to behold."

The crier presented the tube to him, and he looked through, wishing at the same time to see the sultan his father, whom he immediately beheld in perfect health, sitting on his throne, in the midst of his council. Next, as there was nothing in the world so dear to him, after the sultan, as the Princess Nouronnihar, he wished to see her; and instantly beheld her laughing, and in a gay humour, with her women about her.

Prince Ali wanted no other proof to persuade him that this tube was the most valuable article, not only in the city of Shiraz, but in all the world; and believed that if he should neglect to purchase it, he would never meet with an equally wonderful curiosity. He said to the crier, " I am very sorry that I have entertained so wrong an opinion of you, but I hope to make amends by buying the tube, and I will give you the price you ask."

On this the prince took the crier to the khan where he lodged, counted him out the money, and received the tube.

Prince Ali was overjoyed at his purchase; he persuaded himself that, as his brothers would not be able to meet with anything so rare and admirable, the Princess Nouronnihar must be the recompense of his fatigue and travels. He now thought only of visiting the court of Persia, and of seeing whatever was curious in Shiraz, and when the caravan took its departure he joined the party of merchants with whom he had travelled, and arrived happily without any accident or trouble at the place appointed, where he found Prince Houssain, and both waited for Prince Ahmed.

Prince Ahmed took the road to Samarcand, and the day after his arrival went, as his brothers had done, into the market, where he had not walked long before he heard a crier, who had an artificial apple in his hand, offer it at forty purses. He stopped the crier, and said to him, "Let me see that apple, and tell me what virtue it possesses, to be valued at so high a rate."

"Sir," replied the crier, giving it into his hand, "if you look at the mere outside of this apple, it is not very remarkable; but if you consider its properties, you will say it is invaluable, and that he who possesses it is master of a great treasure. It cures all sick persons of every disease, and even if the patient is dying, it will help him immediately, and restore him to perfect health; and this merely by the patient's smelling it."

"If one may believe you," replied Prince Ahmed, "the virtues of this apple are wonderful, and it is indeed invaluable; but how am I to know that there is no error in the high praises you bestow on it?"

"Sir," replied the crier, "the truth is known by the whole city of Samarcand. Ask all these merchants you see here, and hear what they say. You will find several of them will tell you they had not been alive this day had they not made use of this excellent remedy."

While the crier was detailing to Prince Ahmed the virtues of the artificial apple, many persons gathered round them, and confirmed what he declared; and one amongst the rest said he had a friend dangerously ill, whose life was despaired of, which was a favourable opportunity to show the apple's power; on which Prince Ahmed told the crier he would give him forty purses for the apple if it cured the sick person by smelling it.

"Come, sir," said the crier to Prince Ahmed, "let us go and make the experiment, and the apple shall be yours."

The experiment succeeded; and the prince, after he had counted out to the crier forty purses, received the apple. He then spent his time in seeing all that was curious at and about Samarcand; and having joined the first caravan that set out for the Indies, he arrived in perfect health at the inn, where the Princes Houssain and Ali waited for him.

When Prince Ahmed joined his brothers, they embraced with tenderness, and complimented each other on the happiness of meeting together in safety at the same place they had set out from. Houssain, as the eldest brother, then said, "Brothers, we shall have time enough hereafter to describe our travels. Let us come to that which is of the greatest importance for us to know, and not conceal from each other the curiosities we have brought, but show them, that we may ourselves judge to which of us the sultan our father may give the preference. I will tell you that the rarity which I have brought from the kingdom of Bisnagar is the carpet on which I sit. It looks but ordinary, and makes no show, but its virtues are wonderful. Whoever sits on it, and desires to be transported to any place, be it ever so far distant, is immediately carried thither. On my return here I made use of no other conveyance than this wonderful carpet, for which I paid forty purses. I expect now that you should tell me whether what you have brought is to be compared with this carpet."

Prince Ali next spoke. " I acknowledge, brother," said he, " that your carpet is a most surprising curiosity. But you must allow that there may be other rarities at least as wonderful. Here is an ivory tube, which appears to the eye no more a prodigy than your carpet. It cost me forty purses, and I am as well satisfied with my purchase as you can be with yours ; for on looking at one end of this tube you can see whatever object you wish to behold. I would not have you take my word," added Prince Ali, presenting the tube to him. " Take it, and make a trial of it yourself."

Houssain took the ivory tube, and wished to see the Princess Nouronnihar, when Ali and Prince Ahmed, who kept their eyes fixed on him, were extremely surprised to see his countenance suddenly express extraordinary alarm and affliction. Prince Houssain did not give them time to ask what was the matter, but cried out, " Alas ! princes, to what purpose have we undertaken such long and fatiguing journeys, with the hopes of being recompensed by the hand of the charming Nouronnihar, when in a few moments that lovely princess will breathe her last ! I saw her in bed, surrounded by her women, all weeping and seeming to expect her death. Take the tube, behold yourselves the miserable state she is in, and mingle your tears with mine."

Prince Ali took the tube out of Houssain's hand, and after he had seen the same object, with the deepest grief presented it to Ahmed, who also beheld the sad sight which so much concerned them all.

When Prince Ahmed had taken the tube out of Ali's hands, and saw that the Princess Nouronnihar's end was so near, he addressed himself to his two companions, and said, " Brothers, the Princess Nouronnihar, whom we all equally loved, is indeed just at death's door ; but provided we make haste and lose no time, we may preserve her life. This apple which you see cost the same sum as the carpet and the tube ; but it has this surprising power—its smell will restore to life a sick person, whatever be the malady. I have made the experiment, and can show you its wonderful effect on the person of the Princess Nouronnihar if we hasten to assist her."

" If that be all," replied Prince Houssain, " we cannot make more dispatch than by transporting ourselves instantly into her chamber by means of my carpet. Come, lose no time, sit down ; it is large enough to hold us all."

As soon as the order was given, the Princes Ali and Ahmed sat down by Houssain, and as their interest was the same, they all framed the same wish, and were transported instantaneously into the Princess Nouronnihar's chamber.

The presence of the three princes, who were so little expected, alarmed the princess's women and guards, who could not comprehend by what enchantment three men should be among them ; for they did not know them at first : and the guards were ready to fall on them, as people who had got into a part of the palace where they were not allowed to come ; but they quickly found out their mistake.

Prince Ahmed no sooner saw himself in Nouronnihar's chamber than he rose off the carpet, and went to the bedside, and put the apple to her nostrils. The princess instantly opened her eyes, and sitting up, asked to be dressed, as if she had awakened out of a sound sleep. Her women presently informed her that she was obliged to the three princes her cousins, and particularly to Prince Ahmed, for the sudden recovery of her health. She immediately expressed her joy at seeing them, and thanked them all together, but afterwards Prince Ahmed in particular. As she desired to dress, the princes contented themselves with telling her how great a pleasure it was to them to have come soon enough to contribute each in any degree towards relieving her from the imminent danger she was in, and what ardent prayers they had offered for the continuance of her life; after which they retired.

While the princess was dressing, the princes went to throw themselves at the sultan their father's feet; but when they came to him, they found he had been previously informed of their unexpected arrival by the chief of the princess's guards, and by what means the princess had been so suddenly cured. The sultan received and embraced them with the greatest joy, both for their return and the wonderful recovery of the princess his niece, whom he loved as if she had been his own daughter. After the usual compliments, the princes each presented the rarity which he had brought: Prince Houssain his carpet, Prince Ali his ivory tube, and Prince Ahmed the artificial apple; and after each had commended his present, as he put it into the sultan's hands, they begged of him to pronounce their fate, and declare to which of them he would give the Princess Nouronnihar, according to his promise.

The Sultan of the Indies having heard all that the princes had to say in favour of their rarities remained some time silent, considering what answer he should make. At last he broke silence, and said to them in terms full of wisdom, "I would declare for one of you, my sons, if I could do it with justice. It is true, Ahmed, the princess, my niece, is obliged to your artificial apple for her cure; but let me ask you, whether you could have contrived to cure her if you had not known by Ali's tube the danger she was in, and if Houssain's carpet had not brought you to her so soon? Your tube, Ali, revealed to you and your brothers the illness of your cousin; but you must grant that the knowledge of her illness would have been of no service without the artificial apple and the carpet. And as for you, Houssain, your carpet was an essential instrument in effecting her cure; but consider, it would have been of little use if you had not been acquainted with her illness by Ali's tube, or if Ahmed had not applied his artificial apple. Therefore, as the carpet, the ivory tube, and the artificial apple have no preference over each other; but on the contrary, as each had an equal share in her cure, I cannot grant the princess to any one of you; and the only fruit you have reaped from your travels is the happiness of having equally contributed to restore her to health.

"As this is the case," added the sultan, "I must resort to other means to determine the choice I ought to make; and as there is time enough between now and night, I will do it to-day. Go and procure each of you a bow and arrow, and repair to the plain where the horses are exercised. I will soon join you, and will give the Princess Nouronnihar to him who shoots the farthest."

The three princes had nothing to object to the decision of the sultan. When they were dismissed from his presence, they each provided themselves with a bow and arrow, and went to the plain appointed, followed by a great concourse of people.

As soon as the sultan arrived, Prince Houssain, as the eldest, took his bow and arrow, and shot first. Prince Ali shot next, and much beyond him, and Prince Ahmed last of all; but it so happened that nobody saw where his arrow fell; and notwithstanding all the search made by himself and the spectators, it was not to be found. So the sultan determined in favour of Prince Ali, and gave orders for preparations to be made foı the wedding of him and Nouronnihar, which was celebrated a few days after with great magnificence.

Prince Houssain would not honour the feast with his presence. His love for the princess was so sincere and ardent that he could scarcely support with patience the mortification of seeing her marry Prince Ali, who, he said, did not deserve her better nor love her more than himself. In short, his grief was so great that he left the court, and renounced all right of succession to the crown, to turn dervish, and put himself under the discipline of a famous holy man, who had gained great reputation for his holy life.

Prince Ahmed, from the same motive, did not assist at Prince Ali and the Princess Nouronnihar's nuptials any more than his brother Houssain, yet did not renounce the world as he had done. But as he could not imagine what had become of his arrow, he resolved to search for it. With this intent he went to the place where the Princes Houssain's and Ali's were picked up, and proceeding straightforward thence, looked carefully on both sides as he advanced. He went so far that at last he began to think his labour was in vain; yet he felt compelled to proceed, till he came to some steep craggy rocks, which completely prevented any further progress.

At the very foot of these rocks he perceived an arrow, which, to his great astonishment, he found to be the same he had shot. "Certainly," said he to himself, "neither I nor any man living could shoot an arrow so far. There must be some mystery in this; and perhaps fortune, to make amends for depriving me of what I thought the greatest happiness of my life, may have reserved a greater blessing for my comfort."

On looking about, the prince beheld an iron door, which seemed to be locked; but on his pushing against it, it opened, and revealed a staircase, which he walked down with his arrow in his hand. At first he thought he was going into a dark place, but presently he was surrounded by light, and beheld a splendid palace, the admirable structure of which he had not time to consider; for at the same instant a lady of majestic air, and of a beauty heightened by the richness of the jewels which adorned her person, advanced, attended by a troop of ladies, who were scarcely less magnificently dressed than their mistress.

As soon as Ahmed perceived the lady, he hastened to pay his respects; but the lady, addressing him first, said, " Enter, Prince Ahmed, you are welcome."

After these words the lady led Prince Ahmed into a noble hall. She then sat down on a sofa; and when the prince, at her entreaty, had seated himself by her, she continued, " You know that the world is inhabited by genies as well as men; I am Perie Banou, the daughter of one of the most powerful of these genies. I am no stranger to your loves or your travels. The artificial apple which you bought at Samarcand, the carpet which Prince Houssain purchased at Bisnagar, and the tube which Prince Ali brought from Shiraz were of my contrivance. You seemed to me worthy of a better fate than to marry the Princess Nouronnihar; and that you might attain to it, I caused your arrow to fly out of sight, and to strike against the rocks near which you found it. It is in your power to avail yourself of the favourable opportunity which presents itself to make you happy."

As the fairy Perie Banou pronounced the last words with a different tone, and after looking tenderly at the prince, sat with downcast eyes and a modest blush on her cheeks, it was not difficult for him to comprehend what happiness she meant; and he replied, " Could I have the pleasure of making you the partner of my life, I should think myself the happiest of men."

" Then you shall be my husband," answered the fairy, " and I will be your wife. Our fairy marriages are contracted with no other ceremonies than a mutual consent. I will give orders for the preparation of our wedding feast this evening; and in the meanwhile I will show you my palace."

The fairy led Ahmed through the apartments of the palace, where he saw diamonds, rubies, emeralds, and all sorts of fine jewels intermixed with pearls, agate, jasper, and the most precious marbles, together with the richest furniture disposed in the most elegant profusion. At last he entered the hall where the cloth was laid for the feast. It was adorned with an infinite number of wax candles perfumed with amber. A concert accompanied the feast, formed of the most harmonious instruments that were ever heard. After the dessert, which consisted of the choicest fruits and sweetmeats, the fairy Perie Banou and Prince Ahmed rose and repaired to a dais, provided with cushions of fine silk, curiously embroidered. Presently a great number of genies and fairies danced before them, and at last divided themselves into two rows, through which the prince and Perie Banou passed toward their chambers, and after bowing retired.

Every day spent with the fairy Perie was a continued feast, for every day she provided new delicacies, new concerts, new dances, new shows, and new diversions, which were all so gratifying to the senses that Ahmed, if he had lived a thousand years among men, could not have experienced equal enjoyment.

The fairy's intention was not only to give the prince convincing proofs of her love, but to let him see that he could meet with nothing at his father's court comparable to the happiness he enjoyed with her. She hoped by those means to attach Prince Ahmed entirely to herself.

At the end of six months, Prince Ahmed felt a great desire to visit the sultan his father, and know how he was. He mentioned his wish to Perie Banou, who was much alarmed lest this was only an excuse to leave her, and entreated him to forgo his intention.

"My queen," replied the prince, "I did not make the request with any intention of displeasing you, but from a motive of respect towards my father, who, as I have reason to presume, believes that I am dead. But since you do not consent that I should go and comfort him by the assurance of my life, I will deny myself the pleasure, as there is nothing to which I would not submit to please you."

The fairy heard the prince say this with extreme satisfaction.

Meanwhile the Sultan of the Indies, in the midst of the rejoicings on account of the nuptials of Prince Ali and the Princess Nouronnihar, was deeply afflicted at the absence of the other two princes his sons. He was soon informed of the resolution Prince Houssain had taken to forsake the world, and as he knew that he was alive and well, he supported his absence more patiently. He made the most diligent search after Ahmed, and dispatched messengers to all the provinces of his kingdom, with orders to the governors to stop him, and oblige him to return to court; but all the pains he took had not the desired success, and his affliction, instead of diminishing, increased. "Vizier," he one day said, "thou knowest I always loved Ahmed the most of all my sons. My grief is so heavy at his strange absence that I shall sink under it. If thou hast any regard for my life, I beg thee to assist me, and find out where he is."

The grand vizier, anxious to give his king some ease, proposed to send for and consult a sorceress, of whom he had heard many wonders. The sultan consented, and the grand vizier, on her arrival, introduced her into the presence of the ruler.

The sultan said to the sorceress, "Canst thou tell me by thy art and skill what is become of Prince Ahmed my son? If he be alive, where is he? What is he doing? May I hope ever to see him again?"

" Sire," replied the sorceress, " if you will allow me till to-morrow, I will endeavour to satisfy you."

The sultan granted her the time, and promised to recompense her richly.

The sorceress returned the next day and said to the sultan, " Sire, I have not been able to discover anything more than that Prince Ahmed is alive, but as to where he is I cannot tell."

The Sultan of the Indies was obliged to remain satisfied with this answer, which in a small degree relieved his anxiety about the prince.

Prince Ahmed still adhered to his resolution not again to ask permission to leave the fairy Perie Banou, but he frequently talked about his father, and she perceived that he retained his wish to see him. At length, being assured of the sincerity of his affection for herself, she resolved to grant him the permission which he so ardently desired. One day she said to him, " Prince, as I am now fully convinced that I can depend on the fidelity of your love, I grant you leave to visit the sultan your father, on condition that your absence shall not be long. You can go when you please: but first let me give you some advice how you shall conduct yourself. Do not inform your father of our marriage, neither of my quality, nor the place of our residence. Beg of him to be satisfied with knowing that you are happy, and that the sole end of your visit is to make him easy respecting your fate."

After Prince Ahmed had expressed to Perie Banou his sincere gratitude, the fairy summoned twenty horsemen, well mounted and equipped, to attend him. When all was ready, Prince Ahmed took his leave of the fairy. A charger, which was most richly caparisoned, and as beautiful a creature as any in the sultan's stables, was brought to him, and he set forward on his journey.

As it was no great distance, Prince Ahmed soon arrived at his father's capital. The people received him with shouts and followed him in crowds to the palace. The sultan embraced him with great joy, complaining at the same time, with a fatherly tenderness, of the affliction his long absence had occasioned.

"Sire," replied Prince Ahmed, "I could not bear to resign the Princess Nouronnihar to my brother Ali, and I felt that my arrow, though it could not be found, had gone beyond his. The loss of my arrow dwelt continually on my mind, and I resolved to find it. I therefore returned alone to look for it, and I sought all about the plain where Houssain's and Ali's arrows were found, and where I imagined mine must have fallen, but all my labour was in vain. I had gone in the same direction about a league, a distance that the strongest archers could not reach with their arrows, and was about to abandon my search and return home, when I found myself drawn forward against my will. After having gone four leagues, to the end of the plain, where it is bounded by rocks, I perceived an arrow. I ran, took it up, and knew it to be the same which I had shot. Far from blaming your majesty for declaring in favour of my brother Ali, I never doubted but there was a mystery in what had happened to my advantage. But as to the revealing of this mystery, I beg you will not be offended if I remain silent, and that you will be satisfied to know from my own mouth that I am happy and content with my fate. To tell you this, and to relieve your anxiety, was the motive which brought me hither. I must now return, and the only favour I ask is your leave to come occasionally to pay you my duty, and to inquire after your health."

"Son," answered the Sultan of the Indies, "I wish to penetrate no further into your secrets. I can only tell you that your presence has restored to me the joy I have not felt for a long time. You shall always be welcome when you can come to visit me."

Prince Ahmed stayed but three days at his father's

court and on the fourth returned to the fairy Perie Banou, who received him with the greater joy, as she did not expect him so soon. At the end of a month after the prince's return, the fairy, no longer doubting his love for her, proposed herself that he should pay his respects to the sultan. "It is a month," she said, "since you have seen the sultan your father. I think you should not be longer in renewing your visits. Go to him to-morrow, and after that visit him once a month, without speaking to me or waiting for my permission. I readily consent to such an arrangement."

Prince Ahmed went the next morning with the same attendants as before, but much more magnificently mounted, equipped, and dressed, and was received by the sultan with the same joy and satisfaction. For several months he constantly made these visits, and always in a richer and more brilliant equipage.

At last the sultan's counsellors, who judged of Prince Ahmed's power by the splendour of his appearance, sought to make the sultan jealous of his son. They represented that it was but common prudence to discover where the prince had retired, and how he could afford to live so magnificently, since he had no revenue assigned for his expenses; that he seemed to come to court only to insult him, by affecting a more splendid display than himself; and that it was to be feared he might court the people's favour and dethrone him. They represented the danger to be greater, as the prince could not reside far from the capital, for on every visit his attendants were different, their habits new, and their arms clean and bright, as if just come from the maker's hands; and their horses looked as if they had only been walked out. "These are sufficient proofs," they said, "that Prince Ahmed does not travel far, so that we should think ourselves wanting in our duty did we not make our humble remonstrances, in order that, for your own preservation and the good of your people, your majesty may take such measures as you shall think advisable."

When the courtiers had concluded these insinuations, the sultan said, " I do not believe my son Ahmed would act as you would persuade me ; however, I am obliged to you for your advice, and do not doubt that it proceeds from your loyalty to my person."

The Sultan of the Indies said this that his courtiers might not know the impression their words had made on his mind. He was, however, so much alarmed by them, that he resolved to have Prince Ahmed watched. For this end he sent privately for the sorceress, who was introduced by a secret door into his study. " You told me the truth," said he, " when you assured me my son Ahmed was alive. He now comes to my court every month, but I cannot learn from him where he resides. I believe you are capable of discovering his secret. He is at this time with me, and will depart in the morning, without taking leave of me or any of my court. I require you to watch him so as to find out where he retires, and bring me information."

The sorceress left the sultan, and learning by her art the place where Prince Ahmed had found his arrow, went immediately thither, and concealed herself near the rocks so as not to be seen.

The next morning Prince Ahmed set out by daybreak, without taking leave either of the sultan or any of his court, according to custom. The sorceress saw him coming, and watched him and his attendants till she suddenly lost sight of them in the rocks. The steepness of the rocks formed a strong barrier to men, whether on horseback or on foot, so that the sorceress judged that the prince and his retinue had suddenly retired either into some cavern or some underground place, the abode of genies or fairies. When she thought the prince and his attendants must have far advanced into whatever concealment they inhabited, she came out of the place where she had hidden herself, and explored the spot where she had lost sight of them, but could perceive nothing. The sorceress was obliged to be satisfied with the insufficient discovery she had made, and returned to communicate it to the sultan ; but at the same time informed him that she did not despair of obtaining the information he wished.

The sultan was much pleased, and to encourage her presented her with a diamond of great value, telling her it was only a forerunner of the ample recompense she should receive when she had performed the important service which he left to her management. The sorceress, knowing the time when Prince Ahmed would again visit his father, went shortly before that time to the foot of the rock where she had lost sight of him and his attendants, and waited there to execute the project she had formed.

The next morning as Prince Ahmed went out as usual at the iron door, with his attendants, on his journey to the capital, he saw a woman lying with her head on a rock, and complaining as if she was in great pain. He pitied her, turned his horse, and said, "Good woman, I will assist you, and convey you where you shall not only have all possible care taken of you, but where you will find a speedy cure. Rise, and let one of my people take you behind him."

At these words the sorceress made many feigned efforts to rise, pretending that the violence of her illness prevented her. At the same time two of the prince's attendants, alighting, helped her up, and placed her behind one of their companions. They mounted their horses again, and followed the prince, who turned back to the iron gate, which was opened by one of his followers. When he came into the outward court of the fairy's palace, without dismounting himself, he sent to tell her he wanted to speak with her. The fairy came with all imaginable haste, when Prince Ahmed said, "My princess, I desire you would have compassion on this good woman. I recommend her to your care, and am persuaded that you, from inclination, as well as my request, will not abandon her."

The fairy, who had her eyes fixed on the pretended sick woman all the time the prince was speaking, ordered two of her women to take her from the men who supported her, conduct her into an apartment of the palace, and take as much care of her as they would of herself.

Whilst the two women were executing the fairy's commands, she went up to Prince Ahmed, and whispering to him said, "Prince, I commend your compassion, which is worthy of you and your birth; but believe me, this woman is not so sick as she pretends to be. I am much mistaken if she is not sent hither on purpose to occasion you great trouble. But do not be concerned, I will deliver you out of all the snares that shall be laid for you. Go and pursue your journey."

This address of the fairy's did not in the least alarm Prince Ahmed. "My princess," said he, "as I do not remember I ever did, or designed to do, anybody an injury, I cannot believe any one can have a thought of injuring me; but if they have, I shall not forbear doing good whenever I have an opportunity."

So saying, he took leave of the fairy, and set forward again for his father's capital, where he soon arrived, and was received as usual by the sultan, who constrained himself as much as possible to disguise the anxiety arising from the suspicions suggested by his favourites.

In the meantime the two women, to whom Perie Banou had given her orders, conveyed the sorceress into an elegant apartment, richly furnished. When they had put her into bed, the quilt of which was embroidered brocade, and the coverlet cloth of gold, one of the women went out, and returned soon with a china cup in her hand, full of a certain liquor, which she presented to the sorceress, while the other helped her to sit up. "Drink this," said the attendant; "it is the water of the fountain of lions, and a sure remedy. You will feel the effect of it in less than an hour."

The two attendants returned in an hour's time, and found the sorceress seated on the sofa; who, when she saw them open the door of the apartment, cried out, "Oh, the admirable potion! it has wrought its cure; and being thus cured as by a miracle, I would not lose time, but continue my journey."

The two attendants, after they had told the sorceress how glad they were that she was cured so soon, walked before her, and conducted her through several apartments, all more superb than that wherein she had lain, into a large hall, the most richly and magnificently furnished of all the palace.

Perie Banou was seated in this hall, on a throne of massy gold, enriched with diamonds, rubies, and pearls of an extraordinary size, and attended on each hand by a great number of beautiful fairies, all richly dressed. At the sight of so much splendour, the sorceress was not only dazzled, but so struck, that after she had prostrated herself before the throne, she could not open her lips to thank the fairy, as she had proposed. However, Perie Banou saved her the trouble, and said, "Good woman, I am glad I had an opportunity to oblige you, and that you are able to pursue your journey. I will not detain you; but perhaps you may not be displeased to see my palace. Follow my women, and they will show it to you."

The old sorceress, who had not power or courage to say a word, prostrated herself a second time, with her head on the carpet that covered the foot of the throne, and then was conducted by the two fairies through the same apartments which were shown to Prince Ahmed at his first arrival. They at last led her to the iron gate at which Prince Ahmed had brought her in; and after she had taken her leave of them, and thanked them for their trouble, they opened it, and wished her a good journey.

When the sorceress had gone a little way, she turned to observe the door, that she might know it again, but all in vain; for it was invisible to her and all other women. Except in this circumstance, she was very well satisfied with her success, and posted away to the sultan. The sultan, being informed of her arrival, sent for her to come into his apartment.

The sorceress at once related to the sultan the stratagem by which she excited the compassion of Prince Ahmed, her introduction to the Princess Perie Banou, and all the wonders of her fairy abode. Having finished her narrative, she said, "What does your majesty think of these unheard-of riches of the fairy? Perhaps you will rejoice at the good fortune of Prince Ahmed your son. For my part, I shudder when I consider the misfortunes which may happen to you, as the fairy, by her attractions and caresses, may inspire your son with the unnatural design of dethroning his father and of seizing the crown of the Indies."

As the sultan was consulting with his councillors when he was told of the sorceress's arrival, he ordered her to follow him into the council chamber. After having informed his councillors of all he had learnt, and of his fears of the influence of the fairy over his son, one of the councillors said, "The author of this mischief is in your majesty's power. You ought to put him under arrest; I will not say take away his life, but make him a close prisoner."

This advice all the other councillors unanimously applauded.

The sorceress asked of the sultan leave to speak, which being granted, she said, "If you arrest the prince, you must also detain his retinue. But they are all genies. Will they not at once disappear by the power they possess of rendering themselves invisible, and transport themselves instantly to the fairy, and give her an account of the insult offered her husband? And can it be supposed she will let it go unrevenged? Would it not be better to turn the prince's alliance to your advantage by imposing on him some hard task, which, if he performs, will benefit you, and which, if he cannot perform, may give you an honourable pretext for your accusations against him? Request the prince to procure you a tent, which can be carried in a man's hand, and yet be large enough to shelter your whole army."

When the sorceress had finished her speech, the sultan asked his councillors if they had anything better to propose; and finding them all silent, determined to follow her advice.

The next day, when the prince came into his father's presence, the sultan thus addressed him, "My son, I congratulate you on your marriage with a fairy, who I hear is worthy of your love. It is my earnest wish that you would use your influence with your wife to obtain her assistance to do me a great service. You know to what a great expense I am put, every time I engage in war, to provide mules, camels, and other beasts of burden to carry the tents of myself and of my army. Now I am persuaded you could easily procure from the fairy your wife a tent that might be carried in a man's hand, and which would protect my whole army. Pray oblige me in this matter."

Prince Ahmed, hearing this request, was in the greatest trouble what answer to make. At last he replied, "Though I know not how this mystery has been revealed to you, I cannot deny but your information is correct. I have married the fairy you speak of. But I can say nothing as to the influence I have over her. However, I will not fail, though it be with great reluctance, to ask my wife the favour you desire. If I should not come again to pay you my respects, it will be the sign that I have not been able to succeed in my petition; but beforehand, I desire you to forgive me, and consider that you yourself have reduced me to this extremity."

"Son," replied the Sultan of the Indies, "your wife would show that her love to you was very slight if, with the power she possesses as a fairy, she should refuse so trifling a request as that I have begged you to make. Go; only ask her. If she loves you, she will not deny you."

All these reasons of the Sultan of the Indies could not satisfy Prince Ahmed; and so great was his vexation, that he left the court two days sooner than usual.

When he returned, the fairy, to whom he always before had appeared with a gay countenance, at once observed his melancholy, and asked the cause of the change she perceived in him. After much pressing, Ahmed confessed that the sultan had discovered his abode and his marriage with the fairy, though he could not tell by what means. The fairy reminded him of the old woman on whom he had compassion, and said that she was the spy of the sultan, and had told him all she had seen and heard. "But," she said, "the mere knowledge of my abode by the sultan would not so trouble you. There is something else which is the cause of your grief and vexation."

"Perie Banou," said Prince Ahmed at last, "it is even so. My father doubts my fidelity to him, unless I can provide a tent large enough to shelter him, his court, and army when he goes to war, and small enough for a man to carry in his hand."

"Prince," replied the fairy, smiling, "what the sultan your father requests is a trifle. On occasion I can do him more inportant service. Therefore, I shall always take real pleasure in performing whatever you can desire."

Perie Banou then sent for her treasurer, to whom, when she came, she said, " Noor-Jehaun " (which was her name), " bring me the largest tent in my treasury."

Noor-Jehaun returned presently with a small case concealed in the palm of her hand, and presented it to her mistress, who gave it to Prince Ahmed to look at.

When Prince Ahmed saw the small case, which the fairy called the largest tent in her treasury, he fancied she had a mind to banter him. On perceiving this, Perie Banou exclaimed, " What, prince ! do you think I jest with you ? You will see that I am in earnest. Noor-Jehaun," said she to her treasurer, taking the tent out of Prince Ahmed's hands, " go and set it up, that he may judge whether the sultan his father will think it large enough."

The treasurer went out immediately with it from the palace, and carried it to a great distance, and then set it up. The prince found it large enough to shelter two armies as numerous as that of the sultan his father. " You see," said the fairy, " that the tent is larger than your father may have occasion for ; but you must also be informed that it becomes larger or smaller, according to the extent of the army it is to cover, without applying any hands to it."

The treasurer took down the tent, reduced it to its first size, brought it and put it into the prince's hands. He took it, and without staying longer than till the next day mounted his horse, and went with the usual attendants to the sultan his father.

The sultan, persuaded that the tent he had asked for was beyond all possibility, was greatly surprised at the prince's speedy return. He took the tent, and after he had admired its smallness he had it set up in the great plain before mentioned, and found it large enough to cover with ease his whole army. Thereupon his amazement was so intense that he could not recover himself.

The sultan expressed great obligation to the prince for so noble a present, desiring him to return his thanks to the fairy; and to show what a value he set on it, ordered it to be carefully laid up in his treasury. But in his secret bosom he felt greater jealousy than ever of his son, considering that by the fairy's assistance he might effect his dethronement. Therefore, yet more intent on his ruin, he went to consult the sorceress again, who advised him to engage the prince to bring him some of the water of the fountain of lions.

In the evening, when the sultan was surrounded as usual by all his court, and the prince came to pay his respects among the rest, he addressed him in these words: "Son, I have already expressed to you how much I am obliged for the present of the tent you have procured me, which I esteem the most valuable article in my treasury; but you must do one thing more, which will be no less agreeable to me. I am informed that the fairy your spouse makes use of a certain water called the water of the fountain of lions, which cures all sorts of diseases, even the most dangerous; and as I am perfectly well persuaded my health is dear to you, I do not doubt but you will ask her for a bottle of that water, and bring it to me as a sure remedy, which I may use when I have occasion. Do me this important service, and complete the duty of a good son towards a tender father."

Prince Ahmed, who had believed that the sultan his father would be satisfied with so remarkable and useful a tent as the one he had brought, and that he would not impose any new task upon him which might hazard the fairy's displeasure, was thunderstruck at this new request. After a long silence he said, "I beg of your majesty to be assured that there is nothing I would not undertake to procure which may contribute to the prolonging of your life, but I wish it might not be by the means of my wife. For this reason I dare not promise to bring the water. All I can do is, to assure you I will request it of her ; but it will be with as great reluctance as I asked for the tent."

The next morning Prince Ahmed returned to the fairy Perie Banou, and related to her sincerely and faithfully all that had passed at his father's court from the giving of the tent, which he told her he received with the utmost gratitude, to the new request he had charged him to make. He added, " But, my princess, I only tell you this as a plain account of what passed between me and my father. I leave you to your own pleasure, whether you will gratify or reject this new desire. It shall be as you please."

" No, no," replied the fairy, " I will satisfy the sultan, and whatever advice the sorceress may give him (for I see that he hearkens to her counsel) he shall find no fault with you or me. There is much wickedness in this demand, as you will understand by what I am going to tell you. The fountain of lions is situated in the middle of a court of a great castle, the entrance into which is guarded by four fierce lions, two of which sleep while the other two are awake. But let not that frighten you. I will supply you with means to pass by them without danger."

The fairy Perie Banou was at that time at work with her needle ; and as she had by her several balls of thread, she took up one, and presenting it to Prince Ahmed, said, " First take this ball of thread, and I will tell you presently the use of it. In the second place, you must have two horses. One you must ride yourself, and the other you must lead, loaded with a sheep cut into four quarters. In the third place, you must be provided with a bottle, which I will give you, to bring the water in. Set out early to-morrow morning, and when you have passed the iron gate throw before you the ball of thread, which will roll till it reaches the gates of the castle. Follow it, and when it stops, the gates will be open, and you will see the four lions. The two that are awake will, by their roaring, wake the other two. Be not alarmed, but throw each of them a quarter of the sheep, and then clap spurs to your horse and ride to the fountain. Fill your bottle without alighting, and return with the same speed. The lions will be so busy eating they will let you pass unmolested."

Prince Ahmed set out the next morning at the time appointed by the fairy, and followed her directions punctually. When he arrived at the gates of the castle, he distributed the quarters of the sheep among the four lions, and passing through the midst of them with speed, got to the fountain, filled his bottle, and returned safe. When he had proceeded a little distance from the castle gates he turned about; and perceiving two of the lions coming after him, drew his sword, and prepared himself for defence. But as he went forwards, he saw one of them turn out of the road to pass by him, and it showed by its actions that it did not come to do him any harm, but only to go before him. The other stayed behind to follow. He therefore put his sword into its scabbard. Guarded in this manner he arrived at the capital of the Indies; but the lions never left him till they had conducted him to the gates of the sultan's palace; after which they returned the way they had come, though not without alarming the populace, who fled or hid themselves to avoid them, notwithstanding they walked gently and showed no signs of fierceness.

A number of officers came to attend the prince while he dismounted, and conduct him to the apartment of the sultan, who was at that time conversing with his councillors. He approached the throne, laid the bottle at the sultan's feet, kissed the rich carpet which covered the footstool, and rising, said, "I have brought you, sire, the healthful water which your majesty so much wished for; but at the same time I wish you such health as never to have occasion to make use of it."

After the prince had concluded his compliment, the sultan placed him on his right hand, and said, " Son, I am much obliged to you for this valuable present; as also for the great danger you have exposed yourself to on my account; but I have one thing yet to ask of you, after which I shall expect nothing more from your obedience, nor from your interest with your fairy wife. This request is, to bring me a man not above a foot and a half high, whose beard is thirty feet long, and who carries on his shoulders a bar of iron of five hundredweight, which he uses as a quarter-staff."

Next day the prince returned to Perie Banou, to whom he related his father's new demand, " which," he said, " I look on to be a thing more difficult than the two first, for I cannot imagine there is or can be such a man in the world. Without doubt he seeks my ruin; but if there are any means, I beg you will tell me how I may come off with honour this time also."

" Do not alarm yourself, prince," replied the fairy; " you ran a risk in fetching the water of the fountain of lions for your father, but there is no danger in finding this man. He is my brother Schaibar. Though we both had the same parents, he is of so violent a nature that his resentment kindles at the slightest offence; yet, on the other hand, he is so liberal as to oblige any one who shows him a kindness. I will send for him, but prepare yourself not to be alarmed at his extraordinary figure."

" What! my queen," replied Prince Ahmed, " do you say Schaibar is your brother? Let him be ever so ugly or deformed, I shall love and honour him as your nearest relation."

The fairy ordered a gold chafing-dish to be lighted on the porch of her palace. She took some incense and threw it into the fire, when there arose a thick cloud of smoke.

Some moments after the fairy said to Prince Ahmed, "Prince, there comes my brother; do you see him?"

The prince immediately perceived Schaibar, who, as he came forward, looked at the prince with a glance that chilled his soul in his body, and asked Perie Banou, when he first accosted her, who that man was. To which she replied, "His name is Ahmed. He is a son of the Sultan of the Indies, and my husband, brother. I did not invite you to my wedding, because you were engaged in a distant expedition, from which I heard with pleasure you returned victorious; but on my husband's account I have taken the liberty now to call for you."

At these words, Schaibar, gazing at Prince Ahmed with a favourable eye, which, however, diminished neither his fierceness nor savage look, said, "It is enough for me that he is your husband, to engage me to do for him whatever he wishes."

"The sultan his father," replied Perie Banou, "has a curiosity to see you, and I desire he may be your guide to the sultan's court."

"He needs but lead the way; I will follow him," replied Schaibar.

The next morning, Schaibar set out with Prince Ahmed to visit the sultan. When they arrived at the gates of the capital, the people, as soon as they saw Schaibar, either hid themselves in their shops and houses, and shut their doors, or they took to their heels, and communicated their fear to all they met. They stayed not to look behind them; insomuch that Schaibar and Prince Ahmed, as they went along, found all the streets and squares desolate, till they came to the palace, where the guards instead of preventing Schaibar from entering, ran away too. Thus the prince and he advanced without any obstacle to the council-hall, where the sultan was seated on his throne surrounded by his councillors.

Schaibar haughtily approached the throne, and

without waiting for Prince Ahmed to present him, thus addressed the sultan: " Thou hast sent for me. What dost thou wish ? "

The sultan, instead of answering, put his hands before his eyes to exclude so frightful a sight. Schaibar, enraged at this reception, lifted up his bar of iron. " Wilt thou not speak, then ? " he exclaimed, and let it fall directly on the sultan's head, and crushed him to the earth.

He did this before Prince Ahmed had the power to interfere. Then he destroyed all the councillors who were the enemies of Prince Ahmed, and only spared the grand vizier at Prince Ahmed's earnest entreaty. Having completed this dreadful execution, Schaibar left the hall of audience, and went into the middle of the court with the bar of iron on his shoulder. " I know there is a certain sorceress who stirred up the sultan to demand my presence here," he cried, looking at the grand vizier, standing beside Prince Ahmed. " Let her be brought before me."

The grand vizier immediately sent for her, when Schaibar, as he crushed her with his bar of iron, said, " Learn the consequence of giving wicked advice."

" Vizier ! " exclaimed Schaibar, " this is not sufficient. Prince Ahmed, my brother-in-law, must be instantly acknowledged as Sultan of India."

All those who were present cheerfully assented, and made the air resound with cries of " Long live Sultan Ahmed," and in a short time the whole city echoed with the same shouts. Schaibar next ordered the prince to be clothed in the robes of the sultan, and had him instantly installed. And after having paid him homage, and taken the oath of fidelity, he went for his sister, Perie Banou, conducted her to the city in great pomp, and caused her to be acknowledged as Sultana of India.

Prince Ahmed gave to Prince Ali and the Princess Nouronnihar a very considerable province, with its capital, for their establishment. Afterwards he sent an officer to Houssain to acquaint him with the change, and make him an offer of any province he might choose; but that prince thought himself so happy in his solitude, that he desired the officer to return his brother thanks for the kindness he designed him, assuring him of his submission; but that the only favour he desired was, to be indulged with leave to live retired in the place he had chosen for his retreat.

THE STORY OF THE ENCHANTED HORSE

On one of the festival days of spring, just as the Sultan of Shiraz was concluding his public audience, a Hindu appeared at the foot of the throne with an artificial horse richly caparisoned, and so finely modelled that at first sight he was taken for a living animal.

The Hindu prostrated himself before the throne, and pointing to the horse, said to the sultan, " This horse is a great wonder. Whenever I mount him, no matter where I may be, if I wish to transport myself through the air to the most distant part of the world, I can do it in a very short time. This is a wonder which I offer to show your majesty if you command me."

The Emperor of Persia, who was fond of everything that was curious, and who, notwithstanding the many prodigies of art he had seen, had never beheld or heard of anything that equalled this, told the Hindu that he was ready to see him perform as he had promised.

The Hindu instantly put his foot into the stirrup, mounted his horse with admirable agility, and when he had seated himself in the saddle, asked the emperor whither he wished him to go.

" Do you see that mountain ? " said the emperor, pointing to it ; " ride your horse there, and bring me a branch of a palm tree that grows at the bottom of the hill."

The horse carried his rider into the air.

The Emperor of Persia had no sooner declared his will than the Hindu turned a peg, which was in the hollow of the horse's neck, just by the pummel of the saddle; and in an instant the horse rose off the ground and carried his rider into the air with the rapidity of lightning to a great height, rousing the admiration of the emperor and all the spectators. Within less than a quarter of an hour they saw him returning with the palm-branch in his hand; but before he descended, he took two or three turns in the air amid the acclamations of all the people, then alighted on the spot whence he had set off. He dismounted, and going up to the throne, prostrated himself, and laid the branch of the palm tree at the feet of the emperor.

The emperor, who had viewed with admiration and surprise this unheard-of feat which the Hindu had performed, formed a great desire to have the horse, and said to the Hindu, "I will purchase him of you, if he is to be sold."

"Sire," replied the Hindu, "there is only one condition on which I can part with my horse, and that is the gift of the hand of the princess your daughter as my wife. This is the only bargain I can make."

The courtiers about the Emperor of Persia could not forbear laughing aloud at this extravagant proposal of the Hindu; but the Prince Feroze-shah, the eldest son of the emperor and heir to the crown, could not hear it without indignation. "Sire," he said, "I hope you will not hesitate to refuse so insolent a demand, and that you will not allow this juggler to flatter himself for a moment with the idea of being allied to one of the most powerful monarchs in the world. I beg you to consider what you owe to yourself, to your own blood, and the high rank of your ancestors."

"Son," replied the Emperor of Persia, "I will not grant him what he asked—and perhaps he does not seriously make the proposal; and putting my daughter the princess out of the question, I may make another agreement with him. But before I bargain with him, I should be glad to have you examine the horse, try him yourself, and give me your opinion."

On hearing this, the Hindu expressed much joy, and ran before the prince, to help him to mount, and to show him how to guide and manage the horse.

The prince mounted without the Hindu's assistance; and, as soon as he had his feet in the stirrups, without staying for the Hindu's advice, he turned the peg he had seen him use, when instantly the horse darted into the air, quick as an arrow shot out of a bow by the most adroit archer; and in a few moments neither horse nor prince were to be seen. The Hindu, alarmed at what had happened, prostrated himself before the throne, and tried to soften the anger of the sultan. The sultan replied to him and asked, in a passion, why he did not call to the prince the moment he ascended.

"Sire," answered the Hindu, "your majesty saw as well as I with what rapidity the horse flew away. The surprise I was then in deprived me of the use of my speech; but if I could have spoken, the prince had gone too far to hear me. If he had heard me, he knew not the secret to bring the horse back, which, through his impatience, he would not stay to learn. But, sire," added he, "there is room to hope that the prince, when he finds himself at a loss what to do, will perceive another peg, and as soon as he turns that, the horse will cease to rise, and descend toward the ground, and he can turn him to what place he pleases by guiding him with the bridle."

Notwithstanding all these arguments of the Hindu, the Emperor of Persia was much alarmed at the evident danger of his son. "I suppose," replied he, "it is very uncertain whether my son will see the other peg, and make a right use of it. May not the horse, instead of lighting on the ground, fall on some rock, or tumble into the sea with him ?"

"Sire," replied the Hindu, "I can deliver you from this apprehension by assuring you that the horse crosses seas without ever falling into them, and always carries his rider wherever he may wish to go. And your majesty may assure yourself that if the prince does but find the other peg I mentioned, the horse will carry him where he pleases. It is not to be supposed that he will stop anywhere but where he can find assistance and make himself known."

"Your head shall answer for my son's life if he does not return safe," said the sultan.

He then ordered his officers to secure the Hindu, and keep him a close prisoner; after which he retired to his palace, in sorrow that the festival should have ended so unhappily.

Meanwhile the prince was carried through the air with surprising speed. In less than an hour's time he ascended so high that he could not distinguish anything on the earth, but mountains and plains seemed confounded together. He now began to think of returning, and imagined he might do this by turning the same peg the contrary way, and pulling the bridle at the same time. But when he found that the horse still continued to ascend, his alarm was great. He turned the peg several times in different ways, but all in vain. It was then he saw his fault, and apprehended the serious danger he was in from not having learnt the necessary precautions to guide the horse before he mounted. He examined the horse's head and neck with attention, and at last discovered behind the right ear another peg, smaller than the first. He turned that peg, and presently perceived that he descended in the same oblique manner as he had mounted, but not so swiftly.

Night had overshadowed that part of the earth above which the prince was when he found and turned the small peg; and as the horse descended, he by degrees lost sight of the sun, till it grew quite dark; insomuch that, instead of choosing what place he would go to, he was forced to let the bridle lie on the horse's neck, and wait patiently till he alighted, though not without dread lest it should be in the desert, a river, or the sea.

At last the horse stopped on some solid substance about midnight, and the prince dismounted very faint and hungry, having eaten nothing since the morning, when he came out of the palace with his father to assist at the festival. He found himself on the terrace of a splendid palace, surrounded by a balustrade of white marble, breast high; and groping about he reached a staircase, which led down into an apartment, the door of which was half open.

The prince stopped at the door, and listening, heard no other noise than the breathing of some people who were fast asleep. He advanced a little into the room, and by the light of a lamp saw that those persons were black slaves, with naked sabres laid by them; which was enough to inform him that this was the guard-chamber of some sultan or princess. Prince Feroze-shah advanced on tiptoe, without waking the attendants. He drew aside the curtain, went in, and saw a magnificent chamber containing many beds, one alone being on a raised dais, and the others on the floor. A princess slept on the first and her women in the others. He crept softly towards the dais without waking either the princess or her women, and beheld a beauty so extraordinary that he was charmed at the first sight. He fell on his knees, and twitching gently the princess's sleeve, pulled it towards him. The princess opened her eyes, and seeing a handsome young man, was greatly surprised, yet showed no sign of fear.

The prince availed himself of this favourable moment, bowed his head to the ground, and rising said, "Beautiful princess, by the most wonderful adventure you see at your feet a suppliant prince, son of the Emperor of Persia. Pray afford him your assistance and protection."

The personage to whom Prince Feroze-shah so happily addressed himself was the Princess of Bengal, eldest daughter of the ruler of that kingdom, who had built this palace at a short distance from his capital for the sake of the country air. She thus replied: "Prince, you are not in a barbarous country—take courage. Hospitality, humanity, and politeness are to be met with in the kingdom of Bengal, as well as in that of Persia. I grant you the protection you ask—you may depend on what I say."

The Prince of Persia would have thanked the princess, but she would not give him leave to speak. "Notwithstanding I desire," said she, "to know by what miracle you have come hither from the capital of Persia, and by what enchantment you have passed my guards, yet as you must want some refreshment, I will postpone my curiosity, and give orders to my attendants to show you an apartment, that you may rest yourself after your fatigue, and be better able to answer my inquiries."

The princess's attendants were much surprised to see the prince in the princess's chamber, but they at once prepared to obey her commands. They each took a wax candle, of which there were great numbers lighted in the room, and conducted him into a handsome hall, where they brought him a supper; and when he had eaten as much as he wanted they removed the trays, and left him to enjoy the sweets of repose.

The next day the princess prepared to give the prince another interview, and in expectation of seeing him, she took more pains in dressing and adjusting herself at the glass than she ever had before. She tired her women's patience, and made them do and undo the same thing several times. She adorned her head, neck, arms, and waist with the finest and largest diamonds she possessed. The dress she put on was one of the richest stuffs of the Indies, of a most beautiful colour, and made only for royalty. After she had consulted her glass, and asked her women, one after another, if anything was wanting to her attire, she sent to tell the Prince of Persia that she would make him a visit.

The Prince of Persia, who by the night's rest had recovered from the fatigue he had undergone the day before, had just dressed himself when he received notice of the intention of the princess, and expressed himself to be fully sensible of the honour conferred on him. As soon as the princess understood that the Prince of Persia waited for her, she went to pay him a visit. After mutual compliments, the prince related to her the wonders of the magic horse, of his journey through the air, and of the means by which he had found an entrance into her chamber; and then having thanked her for her kind reception, expressed a wish to return and relieve the anxiety of the sultan his father.

When the prince had finished, the princess replied, "I cannot approve, prince, of your going so soon. Grant me at least the favour I ask of a little longer acquaintance; and since I have had the happiness to have you alight in the kingdom of Bengal, I desire you will stay long enough to enable you to give a better account of what you may see here."

The Prince of Persia could not well refuse the princess this favour, after the kindness she had shown him, and therefore politely complied with her request; and the princess's thoughts were directed to render his stay agreeable by all the amusements she could devise.

Nothing went forward for several days but concerts of music, accompanied with feasts in the gardens, or hunting parties in the vicinity of the palace, which abounded with all sorts of deer, and such other beasts peculiar to the kingdom of Bengal as the princess could pursue without danger. After the chase, the prince and princess met in some beautiful spot, where a carpet was spread, and cushions laid for their comfort. There resting themselves, they conversed on various subjects.

Two whole months the Prince of Persia abandoned himself entirely to the will of the Princess of Bengal, yielding to all the amusements she contrived for him, for she did all she could to divert him, as if she thought he had nothing else to do but to pass his whole life with her in this manner. But he now declared seriously he could not stay longer, and begged her to give him leave to return to his father.

"And, princess," observed the Prince of Persia, "that you may not doubt the truth of my affection, I would presume, were I not afraid you would be offended at my request, to ask the favour of taking you along with me."

The princess returned no answer to this address of the Prince of Persia; but her silence and eyes cast down were sufficient to inform him that she had no reluctance to accompany him. The only difficulty she felt was, that the prince knew not well enough how to govern the horse, and she was apprehensive of being involved with him in the same difficulty as when he first made the experiment. The prince soon removed her fear by assuring her she might trust herself with him, for after the experience he had acquired, he defied the Hindu himself to manage the horse better. She thought, therefore, only of concerting measures to get off with him so secretly, that nobody belonging to the palace should have the least suspicion of their design.

The next morning, a little before daybreak, when all the attendants were asleep, they went on the terrace of the palace. The prince turned the horse towards

Persia, and placed him where the princess could easily get up behind him, which she had no sooner done, and was well settled with her arms about his waist for her better security, than he turned the peg. The horse mounted into the air, and making his usual haste, under the guidance of the prince, in two hours' time had carried his riders within sight of the capital of Persia.

The prince would not alight in the city, but directed his course towards his father's summer-palace at a little distance from the capital. He led the princess into a handsome apartment, where he told her, that to do her all the honour that was due to her, he would go and inform his father of their arrival, and return to her soon. He ordered the attendants of the palace, whom he summoned, to provide the princess with whatever she had occasion for.

After the prince had taken his leave of the princess, he ordered a horse to be brought, which he mounted, and set out for the city. As he passed through the streets he was received with shouts by the people, who were overjoyed to see him again. The emperor was holding his divan when his son appeared before him in the midst of his council. He received him with tears of joy and tenderness, and asked him what was become of the Hindu's horse.

This question gave the prince an opportunity of describing the embarrassment and danger he was in when the horse ascended into the air, and how he had arrived at last at the Princess of Bengal's palace, the kind reception he had met with there, and that the motive which had induced him to stay so long with her was the mutual affection they entertained for each other; also, that after promising to marry her, he had persuaded her to accompany him into Persia. "And as I felt assured that you would not refuse your consent," added the prince, "I have brought her with me on the enchanted horse to your summer-palace, and have left her there till I could return and assure her that my promise was not in vain."

After these words the prince prostrated himself before the emperor to obtain his consent. His father raised him up, embraced him a second time, and said to him, "Son, I not only consent to your marriage with the Princess of Bengal, but will go myself and bring her to my palace, and celebrate your wedding this day."

The emperor now ordered that the Hindu should be fetched out of prison and brought before him. When the Hindu was admitted to his presence, he said to him, "I secured thy person, that thy life might answer for that of the prince my son. Thanks be to God, he is returned. Go, take your horse, and never let me see your face more."

The Hindu had learned of those who brought him out of prison that Prince Feroze-shah was returned with a princess, and was also informed of the place where he had alighted and left her, and that the emperor was making preparations to go and bring her to his palace. As soon as he got out of the royal presence, he bethought himself of being revenged on the emperor and the prince. He mounted a horse and, without losing any time, went directly to the summer-palace, and addressing himself to the captain of the guard, told him he came from the Prince of Persia for the Princess of Bengal with orders to carry her behind him through the air to the emperor, who waited in the great square of his palace to gratify the whole court and city of Shiraz with that wonderful sight.

The captain of the guard, who knew the Hindu, and that the emperor had imprisoned him, gave the more credit to what he said because he saw that he was at liberty. He presented him to the Princess of Bengal, who no sooner understood that he came from the Prince of Persia than she consented to what the prince, as she thought, had desired of her.

The Hindu, overjoyed at his success and the ease with which he had accomplished his villainy, mounted his enchanted horse, took the princess behind him with the assistance of the captain of the guard, turned the peg, and instantly the horse rose into the air.

At the same time the Emperor of Persia, attended by his court, was on the road to the summer-palace, where the Princess of Bengal had been left, and the Prince of Persia was advanced before, to prepare the princess to receive his father. The Hindu, to brave them both, and revenge himself for the ill-treatment he had received, appeared over their heads with his prize.

When the Emperor of Persia saw the Hindu, he stopped. His surprise and affliction were the more acute because it was not in his power to punish this affront. He loaded him with a thousand curses, as did also all the courtiers who were witnesses of this insolence and treachery.

The Hindu, little moved with their curses, which just reached his ears, continued his way; while the emperor, extremely mortified at so great an insult, returned to his palace in rage and vexation.

But what was Prince Feroze-shah's grief at beholding the Hindu hurrying away with the Princess of Bengal, whom he loved so passionately! He returned to the summer-palace, where he had last seen the princess, melancholy and broken-hearted.

When he arrived, the captain of the guard, who had learnt his fatal mistake in believing the artful Hindu, threw himself at the prince's feet with tears in his eyes, accused himself of the crime which unintentionally he had committed, and condemned himself to die by his master's hand. "Rise," said the prince to him, "I do not impute the loss of my princess to thee, but to my own want of precaution. In order not to lose time, fetch me a dervish's habit, and take care you do not give the least hint that it is for me."

Not far from the summer-palace there stood a dervish convent, the superior of which was the captain of the guard's particular friend. From him he readily obtained a complete dervish's habit, and carried it to Prince Feroze-shah. The prince immediately pulled off his own dress, put on the dervish garments, and thus disguised, and provided with a box of jewels, which he had brought as a present to the princess, left the palace, uncertain which way to go, but resolved to keep searching till he had found his princess and brought her back, or perished in the attempt.

In the meanwhile the Hindu, mounted on his enchanted horse with the princess behind him, arrived early next morning at the capital of the kingdom of Cashmere. He did not enter the city, but alighted in a wood, and left the princess on a grassy spot, close to a rivulet of fresh water, while he went to seek for food. On his return, after he and the princess had partaken of refreshment, he began to maltreat the princess because she refused to become his wife. As the princess cried out, the Sultan of Cashmere and his court passed through the wood on their return from hunting, and hearing a woman's voice calling for help, went to her rescue.

The sultan, addressing himself to the Hindu, demanded who he was, and wherefore he ill-treated the lady. The Hindu, with great impudence, replied that she was his wife, and asked what had any one to do with his quarrel with her ?

The princess, who neither knew the rank nor quality of the person who came so seasonably to her relief, exclaimed, " My lord, whoever you are whom Heaven has sent to my assistance, have compassion on me. I am a princess. This Hindu is a wicked magician, who has forced me away from the Prince of Persia, to whom I was going to be married, and has brought me hither on the enchanted horse you behold there."

The Princess of Bengal had no occasion to say more.

Her beauty, majestic air, and tears declared that she spoke the truth. Justly enraged at the insolence of the Hindu, the sultan ordered his guards to surround him and strike off his head, which sentence was immediately executed.

The sultan then conducted the princess to his palace, where he lodged her in the most royal apartment, next his own, and commanded a great number of women slaves to attend her.

The Princess of Bengal's joy was boundless at finding herself delivered from the Hindu, of whom she could not think without horror. She flattered herself that the Sultan of Cashmere would complete his generosity by sending her back to the Prince of Persia when she told him her story, and asked that favour of him; but she was much deceived in these hopes, for her deliverer had resolved to marry her himself the next day; and for that end had issued a proclamation, commanding the general rejoicing of the inhabitants of the capital. At the break of day the drums were beaten, the trumpets sounded, and sounds of joy echoed throughout the whole palace.

The Princess of Bengal was awakened by these noisy concerts, but attributed them to a very different cause from the true one. When the Sultan of Cashmere came to wait on her, and had inquired after her health, he told her that all those rejoicings were to render her nuptials the more impressive, and at the same time desired her assent to the union. This declaration put her into such a state of agitation that she fainted away.

The women slaves who were present ran to her assistance, though it was a long time before they succeeded in bringing her to herself. But when she recovered, rather than break the promise she had made to Prince Feroze-shah, by consenting to marry the Sultan of Cashmere, who had proclaimed their wedding before he had asked her consent, she resolved to feign madness. She began to utter the most extravagant expressions before the sultan, and even rose off her seat as if to attack him, insomuch that he was greatly alarmed and afflicted that he had made such a proposal so unseasonably.

When he found that her frenzy rather increased than abated, he left her with her women, charging them never to leave her alone, but to take great care of her. He sent often that day to inquire how she did, but received no other answer than that she was rather worse than better.

The Princess of Bengal continued to talk wildly, and showed other marks of a disordered mind next day and the following, so that the sultan was induced to send for all the physicians belonging to his court to consult them on her disease, and to ask if they could cure her.

When the Sultan of Cashmere saw that his court physicians could not cure her, he called in the most celebrated and experienced of the city, who had no better success. He then sent for the most famous in the kingdom, who prescribed without effect. Afterwards he dispatched to the courts of neighbouring sultans, with promises of munificent rewards to any who should devise a cure for her malady.

Various physicians arrived from all parts and tried their skill, but none could boast of success.

During this interval, Feroze-shah, disguised in the costume of a dervish, travelled through many provinces and towns, involved in grief, and making diligent inquiry after his lost princess at every place he came to. At last, passing through a city of Hindustan, he heard the people talk much of a Princess of Bengal, who had become mad on the day of the intended celebration of her wedding with the Sultan of Cashmere. At the name of the Princess of Bengal, and supposing that there could exist no other Princess of Bengal than her on whose account he had undertaken his travels, he hastened towards the kingdom of Cashmere, and on his arrival at the capital took up his lodging at a khan, where, the same day, he was informed of the story of the princess and the fate of the Hindu magician. The prince was convinced that he had at last found the beloved object he had sought so long.

Being informed of all these particulars, he provided himself with a physician's garments, and his beard having grown long during his travels, he passed the more easily for the character he assumed. He went boldly to the palace, and announced to the chief of the officers his wish to be allowed to undertake the cure of the princess.

Some time had elapsed since any physician had offered himself; and the Sultan of Cashmere with great grief had begun to lose all hope of ever seeing the princess restored to health, though he still wished to marry her. He at once ordered the officer to introduce the physician he had announced. The Prince of Persia being admitted to an audience, the sultan told him the Princess of Bengal could not bear the sight of a physician without falling into most violent transports, which increased her malady; and conducted him into a closet, whence, through a lattice, he might see her without being observed. There Feroze-shah beheld his lovely princess sitting melancholy, with tears in her eyes, and singing an air in which she deplored her unhappy fate, that had deprived her, perhaps for ever, of the object she loved so tenderly. The sight made him more resolute in the hope of effecting her cure. On his leaving the closet, he told the sultan that he had discovered the nature of the princess's complaint, and that she was not incurable; but added withal, that he must speak with her in private and alone, as, notwithstanding her violent agitation at the sight of physicians, he hoped she would hear and receive him favourably.

The sultan ordered the princess's chamber door to be opened, and Feroze-shah went in. As soon as the princess saw him (taking him by his costume to be a physician) she resorted to her old practice of meeting her physicians with threats and indications of attacking them. He made directly towards her, and when he was nigh enough for her to hear him, and no one else, said to her in a low voice, " Princess, I am not a physician, but the Prince of Persia, and am come to procure you your liberty."

The princess, who knew the sound of the voice and recognized his face, notwithstanding he had let his beard grow so long, grew calm at once, and felt a great joy in seeing so unexpectedly the prince she loved. Feroze-shah told her as briefly as possible his travels and adventures, and his determination to find her at all risks. He then desired the princess to tell him of all that had happened to her, from the time she was taken away till that happy moment, telling her it was of the greatest importance to know this, that he might take the most proper measures to deliver her from the tyranny of the Sultan of Cashmere. The princess informed him of all that had occurred, and how she had feigned to be mad so that she might preserve herself for a prince to whom she had given her heart and faith, and not marry the sultan, whom she neither loved nor could ever love.

The Prince of Persia then asked her if she knew what became of the horse, after the death of the Hindu magician. To which she answered, that she knew not what orders the sultan had given; but supposed he would take care of it as a curiosity. As Feroze-shah never doubted but that the sultan had the horse, he communicated to the princess his design of making use of it to convey them both into Persia; and after they had consulted together on the measures they should take, they agreed that the princess should next day receive the sultan. The Sultan of Cashmere was overjoyed when the Prince of Persia stated to him what effect his first visit had had towards the cure of the princess. On the following day, when the princess received him in such a manner as persuaded him her cure was far advanced, he regarded the prince as the greatest physician in the world, and exhorted the princess carefully to follow the directions of so skilful a physician, and then retired. The Prince of Persia, who attended the Sultan of Cashmere on his visit to the princess, inquired of him how the Princess of Bengal came into the dominions of Cashmere thus alone, since her own country was far distant.

The sultan at once informed him of what the princess had related, when he had delivered her from the Hindu magician: adding, that he had ordered the enchanted horse to be kept safe in his treasury as a great curiosity, though he knew not the use of it.

"Sire," replied the pretended physician, "the information which your majesty has given your devoted slave affords me a means of curing the princess. As she was brought hither on this horse, and the horse is enchanted, she hath contracted something of the enchantment, which can be dissipated only by a certain incense which I am acquainted with. If your majesty would entertain yourself, your court, and the people of your capital, with the most surprising sight that ever was beheld, let the horse be brought to-morrow into the great square before the palace, and leave the rest to me. I promise to show you and all that assembly, in a few moments' time, the Princess of Bengal completely restored in body and mind. But the better to effect what I propose, it will be requisite that the princess should be dressed as magnificently as possible, and adorned with the most valuable jewels in your treasury."

The sultan would have undertaken much more difficult things to have secured his marriage with the princess, which he expected soon to accomplish.

The next day the enchanted horse was, by his order, taken out of the treasury, and placed early in the great square before the palace. A report was spread through the town that there was something extraordinary to be seen, and crowds of people flocked thither from all parts, insomuch that the sultan's guards were placed to prevent disorder, and to keep space enough round the horse.

The Sultan of Cashmere, surrounded by all his nobles and ministers of state, was seated in a gallery erected on purpose. The Princess of Bengal, attended by a number of ladies whom the sultan had assigned her, went up to the enchanted horse, and the women helped her to mount. When she was fixed in the saddle, and had the bridle in her hand, the pretended physician placed about the horse at a proper distance many vessels full of lighted charcoal, which he had ordered to be brought, and going round them with a solemn pace cast in handfuls of incense. Then, with downcast eyes, and his hands on his breast, he ran three times about the horse, making as if he pronounced some mystical words. The moment the pots sent forth a dark cloud of smoke—accompanied with a pleasant smell, which so surrounded the princess that neither she nor the horse could be discerned—watching his opportunity, the prince jumped nimbly up behind her, and reaching his hand to the peg, turned it; and just as the horse rose with them into the air, he pronounced these words, which the sultan heard distinctly, "Sultan of Cashmere, when you would marry princesses who implore your protection, learn first to obtain their consent."

Thus the prince delivered the Princess of Bengal, and carried her the same day to the capital of Persia, where he alighted in the square of the palace, before the emperor his father's apartment, who deferred the marriage no longer than till he could make the preparations necessary to render the ceremony pompous and magnificent, and evince the interest he took in it.

After the days appointed for the rejoicings were over, the Emperor of Persia's first care was to name and appoint an ambassador to go to the King of Bengal with an account of what had passed, and to demand his approbation and ratification of the alliance contracted by this marriage ; which the King of Bengal took as an honour, and granted with great pleasure and satisfaction.

THE STORY OF ALADDIN; OR, THE WONDERFUL LAMP

I.—The Idle Boy

In one of the largest and richest cities of China there once lived a poor tailor, named Mustapha. It was only with the greatest difficulty that, by his daily labour, he was able to maintain himself, his wife, and his son.

His son, who was called Aladdin, was a very careless and idle boy. He was accustomed to go out early in the morning and stay out all day, playing in the streets with idle children of his own age.

When he was old enough to learn a trade his father took him into his own shop, and taught him how to use the needle; but no sooner was his back turned than the lad was gone for that day. Mustapha chastised him, but to no purpose, and, to his great grief, was finally forced to abandon him to his idleness. Indeed, he was so much troubled about him that he fell sick and died in a few months.

Aladdin now gave himself entirely over to his idle habits, and was never out of the company of his worthless associates. This course he followed till he was fifteen years old. As he was one day playing in the street, a stranger passing by stood to observe him.

This stranger was a sorcerer, known in the city as the African magician, as he had been but two days arrived from Africa, his native country.

The African magician, seeing in Aladdin's face some-

A sorcerer known as the African magician.

thing which assured him that he was a fit boy for his secret purpose, asked his name and history of some of his companions. When he had learned all that he desired to know, he went up to him, and taking him aside from his comrades said, "Child, was not your father called Mustapha the tailor?" "Yes, sir," answered the boy, "but he has been dead a long time."

At these words the African magician threw his arms about Aladdin's neck, and kissed him several times, with tears in his eyes, saying, "I am your uncle. Your worthy father was my own brother. I knew you at first sight, you resemble him so closely."

Then he gave Aladdin a handful of small money, saying, "Go, my son, to your mother; give my love to her, and tell her that I will visit her to-morrow in order to see the place where my good brother lived so long, and ended his days."

Aladdin ran home. "Mother," said he, "have I an uncle?" "No, child," replied his mother, "you have no uncle." "I am just now come from a man who says he is my uncle and my father's brother," said the boy. "He cried and kissed me when I told him my father was dead, and gave me money, sending his love to you, and promising to come and pay you a visit." "Indeed, child," replied the mother, "your father had no brother, nor have you an uncle on your mother's side."

The next day the magician found Aladdin playing in another part of the town, put two pieces of gold into his hand, and said to him, "Carry this, my child, to your mother. Tell her that I will come and see her to-night, and bid her get us something for supper; but first show me the house where you live."

Aladdin showed the African magician the house, and carried the two pieces of gold to his mother, who went out and bought provisions. She borrowed various pots and pans from her neighbours, and spent the whole day in preparing the supper; and at night when it was ready, she said to her son, "Perhaps the stranger knows not how to find our house; go out and conduct him hither if you meet with him."

II.—The African Magician

Aladdin was just ready to go when the magician came in, loaded with wine and all sorts of fruits. After he had given what he brought into Aladdin's hands, he saluted the boy's mother, and desired her to show him the place where his brother Mustapha used to sit on the sofa; and when she had done so, he fell down and kissed it several times, crying out, with tears in his eyes,—

"My poor brother! How unhappy am I not to have come soon enough to give you one last embrace." Aladdin's mother desired him to sit down in the same place, but he declined. "No," said he, "I will not do that; but give me leave to sit opposite to it, that, although I see not the master of a family so dear to me, I may at least behold the place where he used to sit."

The magician then made choice of a place, and sat down. "My good sister," said he, "do not be surprised because you have never seen me before. I have been forty years absent from this country, and during that time have travelled into the Indies, Persia, Arabia, Syria, and Egypt, and afterwards into Africa, where I took up my permanent abode.

"At last I was desirous to see my native country again, and to embrace my dear brother, so I made the necessary preparations, and set out. Nothing ever afflicted me so much as the sad news of my brother's death. But it is a comfort for me to find, as it were, my brother in his son."

The magician, perceiving that the widow wept, changed the conversation, and turning towards Aladdin, asked him, "What business do you follow, my boy?"

At this question the youth hung down his head, and was not a little abashed when his mother answered, "Aladdin is an idle fellow. His father strove to teach him his trade, but could not succeed; and since his death the boy does nothing but idle away his time in the streets, as you saw him, and I despair of his ever coming to any good. For my own part, I am now resolved to turn him out of doors."

After these words Aladdin's mother burst into tears, and the magician said, "This is not well, nephew; you must think of helping yourself. There are many sorts of trades; perhaps you do not like your father's, and would prefer another. I will try to help you. I will take a shop for you, and furnish it with all sorts of fine stuffs and linens; then with the money you make by selling them you can lay in fresh goods, and live in an honourable way. Tell me freely what you think; you shall always find me ready to keep my word."

This plan just suited Aladdin. He told the magician that he was much obliged for his kind offer. "Well, then," said the magician, "I will take you with me to-morrow, clothe you handsomely, and afterwards we will open a shop."

III.—The Ring in the Stone

The widow no longer doubted that the magician was her husband's brother. She thanked him for his good intentions, and after supper the man took his leave.

He came again the next day, and took Aladdin with him to a clothier. There he bade his nephew choose what garments he liked.

When the lad found himself handsomely dressed, he returned thanks to his uncle, who said, "As you are soon to be a merchant, it is proper you should frequent these shops." He then showed him the largest and finest mosques, took him to the khans, or inns, where the merchants and travellers lodged, and afterwards to the Sultan's palace; and at last he brought him to his own khan, where, meeting with some merchants he knew, he gave them a banquet in order to bring them and his nephew together.

This entertainment lasted till night, when Aladdin would have taken leave of his uncle to go home. The magician, however, would not let him go by himself, but conducted him to his mother, who was transported with joy, and bestowed a thousand blessings on her brother-in-law.

Early the next morning the magician called again for Aladdin. He then led him out at one of the gates of the city to some magnificent palaces, which were surrounded by beautiful gardens. At each building he came to he asked Aladdin if he did not think it splendid; and the youth was always ready to answer, "This is a finer house, uncle, than any we have yet seen."

By this plan the cunning magician led Aladdin some way into the country; and as he meant to carry him still further, he took an opportunity to sit down in one of the gardens, on the brink of a fountain of clear water, pretending to be very tired. "Come, nephew," said he, "you must be weary; let us rest ourselves."

The magician next pulled from his girdle a handkerchief filled with cakes and fruit; and while they were eating these dainties he begged his nephew to forsake bad company. "For," said he, "you will soon be at man's estate."

When they had eaten as much as they desired, they pursued their walk through gardens and beyond. At last they arrived between two mountains divided by a narrow valley. "We will go no further now," said the magician to Aladdin; "I will show you here some extraordinary things. While I strike a light gather up all the loose dry sticks you can see, and we shall use them to kindle a fire."

Aladdin soon collected a great heap of sticks. The magician presently set them on fire, and threw some incense amongst them, pronouncing several magical words, the meaning of which Aladdin did not understand.

The magician had scarcely done so when the earth opened just before him, and discovered a stone with a brass ring fixed in it. Aladdin was so frightened that he would have run away; but the magician caught hold of him, and gave him such a box on the ear that he knocked him down.

Aladdin got up trembling, and said to the magician, "What have I done, uncle, to be treated in this severe manner?" "I occupy the place of your father," answered the magician, "and you ought to make no reply to my chastisement. But, child," added he, softening, "do not be afraid; for I shall not ask anything of you but that you obey me implicitly, if you would reap the advantages which I intend you to obtain.

"Know, then, that under this stone there is hidden a treasure which is destined to be yours, and which will make you richer than the greatest monarch in the world. No person but yourself is permitted to lift this stone, or enter the cave; so you must do what I command."

IV.—The Underground Palace

Aladdin was amazed at all he saw and heard, and rising, said, "Well, uncle, what is to be done? I am ready to obey you in all things." "Take hold of the ring," said the other, "and lift up that stone."

The magician presently set the sticks on fire.

"Indeed, uncle," replied Aladdin, "I am not strong enough." "If I help you, we shall not be able to do anything," answered the magician. "Take hold of the ring and lift up the stone." Aladdin did as the magician bade him, raised the stone with ease, and laid it on one side.

When the stone was pulled up there appeared a short staircase leading downwards to a door. "Descend those steps, my son," said the magician, "and open that door. It will lead you into a palace, divided into three great halls. In each of these halls you will see four large brass cisterns placed on each side, full of gold and silver; but take care you do not meddle with the contents of any of them.

"Before you enter the first hall be sure to tuck up your robe, and then pass through it and the second into the third. Above all things, do not touch the walls, nor even allow your clothes to do so; for if you do, you will die instantly. At the end of the third hall you will find a door which opens into a garden planted with fine fruit trees. Walk across the garden to a terrace, where you will see a niche before you, and in that niche a lighted lamp.

"Take down the lamp and put out the light. When you have thrown away the wick and poured out the liquid, put the lamp in your waistband and bring it to me. Do not be afraid that the liquid will spoil your clothes, for it is not oil, and the lamp will be quite dry as soon as the liquid is thrown out."

The magician then drew a ring from his finger, and put it on one of Aladdin's, saying, "It is a talisman against all evil, so long as you obey me. Go therefore boldly, and we shall both be rich all our lives."

Aladdin descended the steps and found the three halls. He went through them with care, took down the lamp from the niche, and having thrown away the wick and poured out the liquid, put it into his waistband.

"You will see a niche before you, and in that niche a lighted lamp."

But as he came down from the terrace he stopped to observe the trees, which were loaded with extraordinary fruit of various colours. The white were pearls; the clear and transparent, diamonds; the red, rubies; the green, emeralds; the blue, turquoises; the purple, amethysts; and the yellow, opals.

Aladdin, ignorant of their value, would have preferred figs or grapes or pomegranates; but he resolved to gather some of every sort. So he thrust into the bosom of his robe as many jewels as it would hold.

The youth now returned to the mouth of the cave, where the magician awaited him. As soon as Aladdin saw him he cried, "Pray, uncle, help me out." "Give me the lamp first," replied the magician. "Indeed, uncle," answered Aladdin, "I cannot now, but I will as soon as I get out of this."

The African magician was determined that he would have the lamp before he would help him up; but Aladdin refused to give it to him till he was out of the cave.

The man flew into a passion, threw a little of his incense into the fire, and pronounced two magical words. Then the stone which had closed the hole moved once more into its place, shutting Aladdin into the cave.

V.—The Jinn

Aladdin now knew that the magician was no uncle of his, but one who designed him evil. The truth was that the man had learned from his magic books the secret and the value of the wonderful lamp, and because of this had made his journey to China. His art had also told him that he must receive it as a gift from the hands of another person. Hence he had employed young Aladdin for his own purpose. When he now found that his attempt had failed, he set out on his return to Africa.

Meanwhile Aladdin called out lustily to the magician to tell him he was ready to give him the lamp, but all in vain. He descended to the bottom of the steps, to return to the palace, but found that the door was now shut.

He then sat down on the steps without any hope of ever seeing the light again. In this great emergency he clasped his hands together in agony of mind, and in doing so he happened to rub the ring which the magician had put on his finger. Immediately a jinn of frightful aspect appeared and said,—

"What dost thou wish? I am ready to obey thee. I serve him who possesses the ring—I, and the other slaves of that ring."

At another time Aladdin would have been frightened at the sight of the jinn, but the danger he was now in gave him courage to answer, "Whoever thou art, deliver me from this place."

He had no sooner spoken these words than he found himself on the very spot where the magician had last left him, and no sign of cave or opening or disturbance of the earth was to be seen. With a heart full of thankfulness he made the best of his way home.

When he got within his mother's door, the joy of seeing her and his weakness for want of food made him so faint that he remained for a long time as if he were dead. As soon as he recovered, he told his mother all that had happened to him, and they were both very loud in their complaints against the cruel magician.

Aladdin slept very soundly till late the next morning. As soon as he awoke he arose, dressed himself, and then asked his mother for his breakfast. "Alas, child," she said in a sad tone, "I have not a bit of bread to give you. But I have a little cotton which I have spun; I will go and sell it, and buy bread."

"Mother," replied Aladdin, "keep your cotton for another time, and give me the lamp I brought home with me yesterday. I will go and sell it, and the money I shall get for it will serve both for breakfast and dinner, and perhaps supper too."

Aladdin's mother took down the lamp from a shelf and said to her son, "Here it is, but it is very dirty; if it were a little cleaner, I believe it would bring something more." She took some sand and water to clean it, but had no sooner begun to rub it than in an instant a hideous jinn appeared before her, and said to her in a voice of thunder,—

"What dost thou wish? I am ready to obey thee as thy slave, and the slave of all those who have that lamp in their hands—I, and the other slaves of the lamp."

Aladdin's mother swooned away with fear; but Aladdin snatched the lamp out of her hand, and said boldly, "I am hungry; bring me something to eat."

The jinn vanished, and soon returned with a tray holding twelve silver dishes full of the most delicious viands, six large cakes, two flagons of wine, and two silver cups. All these he placed upon a carpet and disappeared.

Meanwhile Aladdin had fetched some water and sprinkled it on his mother's face, and it was not long before she came to herself. "Mother," said Aladdin, "be not afraid; get up and eat."

VI.—The Slave of the Lamp

"Child," said Aladdin's mother, "to whom are we obliged for this?" "It is no matter, mother," said Aladdin; "let us sit down and eat. When we have finished our meal, I will tell you."

The mother and son sat at breakfast till it was dinner-time, and then they thought it would be best to take the two meals together; yet after this they found they should have enough left for supper, and two meals for the next day.

Then Aladdin's mother went and sat down by her son on the sofa, saying, "I hope now that you will tell me what passed between the jinn and you." This he did without more delay.

She was now in great amazement, and said, "But, son, what have we to do with jinns? How came that vile jinn to speak to me and not to you?" "Mother," answered Aladdin, "the jinn you saw is not the one who appeared to me, for he called himself the slave of the ring; and the one you saw called himself the slave of the lamp."

"What! " cried the mother, "was your lamp, then, the cause of the trouble? Ah, my son, take it out of my sight. I had rather you would sell it than touch it again; and you must part also with the ring, nor have anything more to do with jinns."

"With your leave, mother," replied Aladdin, "I shall now take care how I sell a lamp which may be so useful. That false magician would not have come so far to secure it if he had not known its value. Let us make use of it without exciting the jealousy of our neighbours.

"But I will take it out of your sight, and put it where I can find it when I want it. The ring I cannot part with, for without that you had never seen me again; therefore I hope you will give me leave to wear it always on my finger." Aladdin's mother replied that he might do as he pleased in that matter.

By the next night the two had eaten all the provisions the jinn had brought; and the following day Aladdin, putting one of the silver dishes under his vest, went out early to sell it. Meeting a dealer, he asked him if he would buy it. The cunning dealer examined it, and as soon as he found that it was good silver, asked Aladdin how much he desired for it.

Aladdin told him he would trust to his judgment and honour. The dealer at once took a piece of gold out of his purse and gave it to him, though it was only the sixtieth part of the real value of the plate.

With this money mother and son purchased provisions enough to last them some time. After this manner they lived, till Aladdin had sold the twelve dishes singly to the dealer for the same sum of money; for this man, after the first time, dared not offer him less, for fear of losing so good a bargain. For the tray the dealer laid down ten pieces of gold, with which Aladdin was very well satisfied.

When all the money was spent, Aladdin had recourse again to the lamp. He took it in his hands, rubbed it, and the jinn immediately appeared, and said, "What dost thou wish? I am ready to obey thee as thy slave, and the slave of all those who have that lamp in their hands—I, and the other slaves of the lamp." "Bring me something to eat," Aladdin said. The jinn disappeared, and presently returned with a tray and dishes as before, set them down, and vanished.

When the food was eaten, Aladdin took one of the dishes and went to look for his dealer; but a goldsmith called to him, and said, "My lad, I imagine that you have something to sell to the dealer whom I often see you visit; but perhaps you do not know that he is a great rogue. I will give you the full worth of what you have to sell."

Aladdin at once pulled his plate from under his vest and showed it to the goldsmith, who at a single glance saw that it was made of the finest silver, and asked him if he had sold such as that to the dealer. Then Aladdin told him that he had sold him twelve of the same kind for a piece of gold each.

"What a villain!" cried the goldsmith. Then he took a pair of scales, weighed the dish, and offered to pay down immediately sixty pieces of gold for it.

Aladdin thanked him for his fair dealing, and never afterwards went to any other merchant.

VII.—The Sultan's Daughter

Though Aladdin and his mother had an inexhaustible treasure in their lamp, yet they lived with the same frugality as before. Aladdin frequented the shops of the principal merchants, and oftentimes joining in their conversation, acquired a knowledge of the world, and a desire to improve himself. He also came to know that the fruits which he had gathered when he took the lamp were stones of great value; but he had the prudence not to mention this to any one.

One day, as he was walking about the town, he heard an order proclaimed commanding the people to keep within doors while the Sultan's daughter went to the bazaar and returned. This filled Aladdin with eager desire to see the Princess's face, and he placed himself behind the door of one of the booths.

Soon the Princess came. She was attended by a great crowd of ladies and slaves, who walked on each side and behind her. When she came within three or four paces of the door behind which Aladdin was hidden, she took off her veil. The youth had then a full view of her face.

The Princess was a noted beauty. Her eyes were large, lively, and sparkling; her smile bewitching; her nose faultless; her mouth small; her lips as red as rubies. It is not therefore surprising that Aladdin was quite dazzled and enchanted at the sight of her.

After the Princess had passed by, Aladdin went home. His mother perceived him to be more thoughtful than usual, and asked if he was ill. He at once told his mother all his adventure, and said, "I love the Princess more than I can express, and will ask her in marriage of the Sultan."

Aladdin's mother laughed aloud. "Alas, child," said she, "what are you thinking of? You must be mad to talk thus."

"I assure you, mother," replied Aladdin, "that I am not mad. I foresaw that you would mock me, but I am resolved to demand the Princess in marriage of the Sultan, her father; nor do I despair of success. I have the slaves of the lamp and of the ring to help me.

"And I have another secret to tell you. Those fruits which I got from the trees in the garden are jewels fit for the greatest monarch; and I am sure that the offer of them will secure the favour of the Sultan. You have a fine large porcelain dish to hold them. Fetch it, and let us see how they will look when placed in it."

Aladdin's mother brought the china dish, and he took out the jewels and placed them in order. Then their brightness so dazzled the eyes of both mother and son, that they were astonished beyond measure.

The good woman, emboldened by the sight of these rich jewels, promised to go early on the next morning to the palace of the Sultan. Aladdin rose before day-break, and having eagerly awakened his mother, pressed her to go to the Sultan's palace before the Grand Vizier and the great officers of state went in to take their seats in the Sultan's divan.

Aladdin's mother then took the china dish, wrapped it in two fine damask kerchiefs, and set out for the Sultan's palace. When she came to the gates she found that the Grand Vizier and the lords of the court had just gone in; but although the crowd of people was great, she got into the divan—a spacious hall, the entrance to which was very magnificent. She placed herself just before the Sultan, Grand Vizier, and the great lords, who sat in council on his right and left hand. Several causes were called, according to their order, pleaded, and adjudged. Then the Sultan returned to his own apartment.

Aladdin's mother, seeing the Sultan retire, and all the people depart, resolved to go home; and on her arrival she said to Aladdin,—

"Son, I have seen the Sultan, and am very well persuaded he has seen me too, for I placed myself just before him; but he was so much taken up with those who attended on all sides of him that I pitied him, and

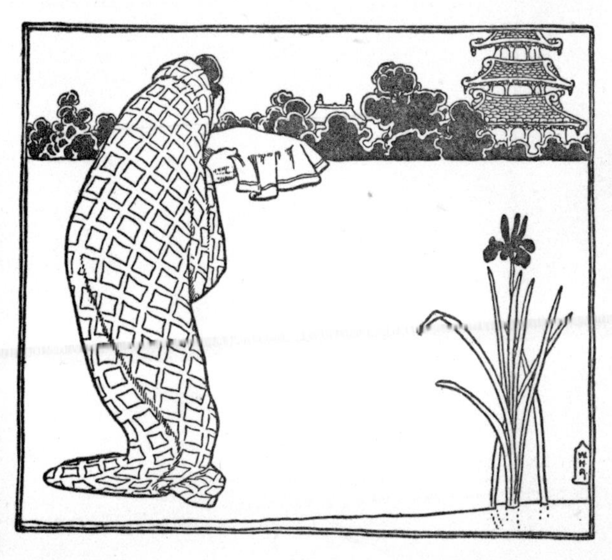

wondered at his patience. At last he rose up suddenly and went away; at which I was well pleased, for indeed I began to lose all patience myself. But there is no harm done. I will go again to-morrow; perhaps the Sultan may not be so busy."

The next morning she went to the palace as early as on the day before, but when she came there she found the gates of the divan shut. She went six times afterwards, and though she always placed herself directly before the Sultan, she had as little success as on the first morning.

On the sixth day, however, after the Sultan had returned to his apartment, he said to his Grand Vizier, " I have for some time observed a certain woman, who attends every day that I give audience, with something wrapped up in a cloth. She always stands before me. If this woman comes to our next audience, do not fail to call her."

The Grand Vizier made answer by lowering his hand and then lifting it up above his head, to show his willingness to lose the latter if he failed to obey his master's command.

VIII.—The Rival Suitors

On the next day of audience Aladdin's mother came before the Sultan, bowed her head down to the carpet which covered the platform of the throne, and remained in that posture until he bade her rise. Then

he said to her, " Good woman, what business brings you here ? "

Aladdin's mother prostrated herself a second time, and when she arose, said, " Monarch of monarchs, I beg of you to assure me of your forgiveness."

" Well," replied the Sultan, " I will forgive you, be

your fault what it may, and no hurt shall come to you ; speak boldly." So she told him her story, concluding with the expression of her son's wish to marry the beautiful Princess.

The Sultan listened without showing the least anger ; but before he gave her any answer, he asked her what she had brought tied up in the linen cloth. She took the china dish, which she had set down at the foot of the throne, untied the cloth which covered it, and presented it to the Sultan.

The Sultan's amazement was very great when he saw so many beautiful jewels collected in the dish. He remained for a long time lost in admiration. Then he received the present, saying, "How rich ! how beautiful ! " After he had admired and handled all the jewels, he turned to his Grand Vizier and said, "Behold, admire, wonder ! and confess that your eyes never before beheld jewels so rich and beautiful."

The Vizier was charmed. "Well," continued the Sultan, "ought I not to bestow my dear daughter on one who values her at so great a price ? "

"I cannot but own," replied the Grand Vizier, "that the present is worthy of the Princess; but I beg of your Majesty to grant me three months before you come to a final decision. I hope that, before that time, my son, whom you have regarded with favour, will be able to make a still nobler present."

The Sultan granted his request, and then said to the woman, "Good woman, go home and tell your son that I cannot marry the Princess, my daughter, to any one for at least three months ; at the end of that time come again."

Aladdin thought himself the most happy of all men upon hearing his mother's news, and thanked her warmly for the pains she had taken in the affair. When two of the three months were passed, his mother one evening went out to buy some oil, and found in the streets of the city signs of general rejoicing—the houses dressed with foliage, silks, and carpeting, and all the people full of joy.

The streets were crowded with officers mounted on fine horses, each attended by a great many footmen. Aladdin's mother asked the oil merchant what was the meaning of all this festivity. " Whence come you, good woman," said he, " that you do not know that the Grand Vizier's son is to marry the Sultan's daughter to-night ? She will presently return from the bazaar, and these officers are to conduct her to the palace."

Aladdin's mother, on hearing this news, ran home very quickly. " Child," she cried, " you are undone ! This night the Grand Vizier's son is to marry the Princess."

At this account Aladdin was thunderstruck. But he determined, if possible, to prevent the marriage.

Making his way into his chamber, he took the lamp and rubbed it, when immediately the jinn appeared. " Hear me," said Aladdin. " I am about to impose on thee a hard task. The Sultan's daughter, who was promised me as my bride, is this night to be married to the son of the Grand Vizier. Bring them both hither to me as soon as the festivities of the marriage are over."

" Master," replied the jinn, " I obey you."

Aladdin supped with his mother as was their custom, and then went to his own apartment, where he sat up to await the return of the jinn.

In the meantime the marriage feast took place in the Sultan's palace. But no sooner had the guests departed than the jinn, by an invisible agency, transported the bride and bridegroom in an instant into the house of Aladdin's mother.

" Remove the bridegroom," said Aladdin to the jinn. " Keep him a prisoner till to-morrow morning, and then return with him here." On Aladdin being left alone with the Princess, he explained to her the trick practised upon him by the Sultan, her father. He then begged her to rest, while he kept guard at the door of the room with a drawn sword in his hand.

At break of day the jinn appeared at the appointed hour, bringing back the Vizier's son. Then at Aladdin's command he transported the bride and bridegroom into the palace of the Sultan.

At the instant that the jinn had set down the bride and bridegroom in the palace, the Sultan came to offer his good wishes to his daughter. He kissed the Princess on the forehead, but was surprised to see her look so sad. He thereupon went immediately to his wife's apartment, and told her in what state he had found the Princess. "Sire," said the Sultan's wife, "I will go and see her. She will not receive me in the same manner."

The Princess received her mother with sighs and tears. At last, after having been reminded of the duty of telling her mother all her thoughts, she gave an account of all that had happened to her; on which her mother told her to keep silence, as no one would believe so strange a tale. In the evening the same thing happened again. And on the third day the Princess told her father of the strange events. He therefore declared that her marriage with the Grand Vizier's son was cancelled.

This sudden change in the mind of the Sultan caused great astonishment. Nobody but Aladdin knew the secret, and he kept it carefully; and neither the Sultan nor the Grand Vizier had the least idea that Aladdin had any hand in the strange adventures that had befallen the bride and bridegroom.

IX.—Forty Trays of Gold

On the very day that the three months expired, the mother of Aladdin again went to the palace, and stood in the same place in the divan.

After having prostrated herself, she said to the Sultan, " Sire, I come to ask of you the fulfilment of the promise you made to my son." The Sultan little thought that he would hear any more of the matter. But after a few words with the Vizier, he replied, " Good woman, I am ready to keep my word, and to make your son happy. But as he must be able to support the Princess in royal state, you may tell him I will fulfil my promise as soon as he shall send me forty trays of gold full of the same kind of jewels you have already brought to me, and carried by the like number of black slaves, who shall be led by as many young and handsome white slaves, all magnificently dressed."

Aladdin's mother retired. On her way home she laughed within herself at her son's foolish imagination. " Where," said she, " can he get so many large gold trays, and such precious stones to fill them ? " When she came home, full of these thoughts, she told Aladdin what the Sultan had said, and added, " The Sultan expects your answer immediately, but I believe he may wait long enough ! "

" Not so long, mother, as you imagine," replied Aladdin. " This demand will prove no bar to my marriage with the Princess."

Aladdin retired to his own apartment, and called the jinn of the lamp to his aid. Within a very short time a train of forty black slaves, led by the same number of white slaves, appeared in the street. Each black slave carried on his head a tray of gold, full of precious stones—diamonds, rubies, and emeralds.

Aladdin then addressed his mother: "Madame, pray lose no time; return to the palace with this present."

As soon as the procession had set out, with Aladdin's mother at its head, the whole city was thronged with crowds of people. The spectators were filled with the greatest wonder at the graceful bearing, elegant form, and wonderful likeness of the slaves, their grave walk at an equal distance from each other, the lustre of their jewelled girdles, and the brilliancy of the precious stones in their turbans.

They went into the Sultan's divan in regular order, one part turning to the right, and the other to the left. After they had formed a semicircle before the Sultan's throne, the black slaves laid the golden trays on the carpet and prostrated themselves, and at the same time the white slaves also made their obeisance. When they rose the black slaves uncovered the trays, and then all stood still with their arms crossed over their breasts.

In the meantime Aladdin's mother, having prostrated herself, said to the Sultan, "Sire, my son knows that this present is unworthy of the notice of your daughter, the Princess, but hopes that your Majesty will accept of it, and make it agreeable to her."

The Sultan, overpowered at the sight, replied without hesitation, "Go and tell your son that I wait with open arms to embrace him." As soon as Aladdin's mother had retired, the Sultan ordered that the Princess's attendants should come and carry the trays into the apartment of their mistress.

In the meantime Aladdin's mother had reached her own home. "My son," said she, "the Sultan has declared that you shall now marry the Princess. He waits for you."

Aladdin retired to his chamber. There he rubbed his lamp, and the jinn appeared. "Jinn," said Aladdin, " convey me at once to a bath, and supply me with the richest robe ever worn by a monarch."

No sooner were the words out of his mouth than the jinn transported him into a bath of the finest marble. He was then well rubbed and washed with various scented waters. After he had passed through several degrees of heat, he came out quite a different man from what he was before. His skin was as clear as that of a child, his body light and free ; and when he returned into the hall, he found, instead of his own poor raiment, a splendid robe, the magnificence of which greatly astonished him.

The jinn helped him to dress, and transported him back to his own chamber, where he asked him if he had any other commands. " Yes," answered Aladdin : " bring me a charger that surpasses in beauty and goodness the best in the Sultan's stables. Furnish also twenty slaves to walk by my side and follow me, and twenty more to go before me in two ranks. Besides these, bring my mother six women slaves to attend her, as richly dressed as any of the Princess's, and each carrying a complete dress fit for any Sultan's wife. I want also ten thousand pieces of gold in each of ten purses ; go, and make haste."

The jinn at once disappeared, but presently returned with the horse, the forty slaves, ten of whom carried each a purse containing ten thousand pieces of gold, and six women slaves, each carrying on her head a complete dress for Aladdin's mother.

He presented the slaves and the dresses to his mother. Of the ten purses Aladdin took four, which he gave to his mother ; the other six he left in the hands of the slaves, with an order to throw the money by handfuls among the people. The six slaves who carried the purses he likewise ordered to march before him.

When Aladdin had thus prepared himself he began his march ; and though he had never ridden on horseback before, he bore himself with a grace the best horseman might envy. The people among whom he passed made the air echo with their shouts, especially when the gold fell among them.

On Aladdin's arrival at the palace the Sultan embraced him with joy; and when the young man would have fallen at his feet, he held him by the hand, and made him sit down near his throne. He shortly afterwards led him, amidst the sounds of sweetest music, to an entertainment, at which the Sultan and Aladdin ate by themselves, and the great lords of the court sat at different tables.

After the feast the Sultan asked Aladdin if he would complete the ceremonies of the marriage that day. "Sire," said Aladdin, "I beg you to permit me first to build a palace worthy to receive the Princess, your daughter. I pray you to grant me a piece of ground near your own palace, and I will have the new building completed with the utmost expedition." The Sultan granted this request, and again embraced him; after which Aladdin took his leave.

Aladdin at once returned home. He retired to his own chamber, took the lamp, and summoned the jinn to him. "Jinn," said Aladdin, "build me a palace fit to receive the Princess. Let its materials be porphyry, jasper, agate, and the finest marble. Let its walls be of massive gold and silver bricks. Let each side contain six windows, and let the lattices of these (except one, which must be left unfinished) be enriched with precious stones. Let there be an inner and an outer court, and a spacious garden; and provide a safe treasure-house, filled with gold and silver. Let there be also kitchens and storehouses, stables full of the finest horses, and hunting equipage, officers, attendants, and slaves, both men and women."

The Sultan granted this request.

(*See p.* 119.)

X.—The Unfinished Window

When Aladdin gave these commands, the sun had set. The next morning at daybreak the jinn presented himself, and transported him in a moment to the palace he had built and equipped. The jinn led him through all the apartments, where he found officers and slaves, habited according to their rank. In the treasury Aladdin saw large vases of different sizes, piled up to the top with money, ranged all round the chamber. In the stables were some of the finest horses in the world. The storehouses were filled with all things necessary, both for food and for ornament.

When Aladdin had examined every portion of the palace, he said, " Jinn, there is one thing wanting—namely, a fine carpet for the Princess to walk upon from the Sultan's palace to mine." This was at once supplied.

Aladdin next requested his mother to go to the Princess, and tell her that the palace would be ready for her in the evening. She went, attended by her women slaves, in the same order as on the preceding day. The Sultan himself came to meet her, and was surprised to find that she was now more richly attired than his own daughter. This gave him a higher opinion of Aladdin, who took such care of his mother, and made her share his wealth and honours.

Shortly after her departure, Aladdin, mounting his horse, left his paternal home for ever. Nor did he forget to take with him the wonderful lamp, to which he owed all his good fortune, nor yet to wear the magic ring. The Sultan entertained him with the utmost magnificence ; and at night, on the conclusion of the marriage ceremonies, the Princess took a tender leave of the Sultan, her father.

On her arrival at the new palace, Aladdin was ready

to receive her at the entrance, and led her into a large hall, where a noble feast was served. The dishes were of solid gold, and contained the most delicate foods. The vases, basins, and goblets were of gold also, and of exquisite workmanship. The Princess, dazzled to see so much wealth collected in one place, said to Aladdin, "I thought, Prince, that nothing in the world was so beautiful as the palace of my father, the Sultan; but the sight of this hall alone is sufficient to show I have been deceived."

Next morning the attendants of Aladdin presented themselves to dress him, and brought him another habit, as rich and magnificent as that worn the day before. He then ordered one of the horses to be got ready, mounted him, and went, in the midst of a numerous retinue of slaves, to the Sultan's palace to entreat him to take a repast in the new palace.

The nearer the Sultan approached the wonderful palace the more he was struck with its beauty; but when he entered it, came into the hall, and saw the windows, enriched with diamonds, rubies, and emeralds, all large perfect stones, he was completely surprised, and said to his son-in-law, "This palace is one of the wonders of the world. But what most surprises me is, that the hall should be left with one of its windows unfinished." "Sire," answered Aladdin, "I wished that *you* should have the glory of finishing this hall." "I take your intention kindly," said the Sultan, "and will give orders about it immediately."

After the repast the Sultan was informed that the jewellers and goldsmiths of the city were already in waiting. "I sent for you," said he, "to fit up this window in as great perfection as the others. Examine them well, and make all the dispatch you can."

The jewellers and goldsmiths examined the three-and-twenty windows with great attention. Then the principal jeweller, speaking for the rest, said, "Sire, we are all willing to obey you, but among us all we cannot furnish jewels enough for so great a work." "I have more than are necessary," said the Sultan; "come to my palace, and you shall choose as many as may answer your purpose."

When the Sultan returned to his palace, he ordered his jewels to be brought out, and the jewellers took a great quantity, which they soon used up, without having made any great advance in their work. They came again several times for more, but in a month's time they had not finished half their work. In short, they used all the jewels the Sultan had, and then borrowed some from the Vizier; but still the work was far from being finished.

Aladdin, who knew that all the Sultan's endeavours to make this window like the rest would be in vain, then ordered them to undo what they had done, and to carry all the jewels back to the Sultan and to the Vizier. They undid the work in a few hours and retired, leaving Aladdin alone in the hall.

He then took the lamp, which he always carried about him, rubbed it, and presently the jinn appeared. "Jinn," said Aladdin, "make this window like the rest." Aladdin went out of the hall, and returning soon after found the window like the others.

Meanwhile the jewellers had gone to the palace and presented the precious stones to the Sultan. He ordered a horse to be brought, and rode to his son-in-law's palace, to inquire why he had ordered the making of the window to be stopped. Aladdin conducted him to the grand saloon, where the Sultan, to his great surprise, found that the window which had been left imperfect was now as perfectly finished as the others.

He fancied at first that he was mistaken; but when he was convinced that the window had been finished in so short a time, he embraced Aladdin and kissed him between the eyes. "My son," said he, "what a man you are to do such surprising things, and always in the twinkling of an eye! The more I know you, the more I admire you."

After this Aladdin often went in great state, sometimes to one mosque, and sometimes to another, and at other times to visit the Grand Vizier or the principal lords of the court. Every time he went out his two slaves threw handfuls of money among the people as he passed by. This gained him the love and blessings of the populace. At the same time, he took care to pay all due respect to the Sultan.

XI.—New Lamps for Old

Aladdin had lived in this manner for several years, when the African magician determined to find out whether he had perished in the subterranean cave or not. So by means of magic he learned that Aladdin, instead of dying in the cave, had made his escape, and was living in royal splendour by the aid of the jinn of the wonderful lamp.

On the very next day the magician set out for the capital of China, where he took up his lodgings in a large knan.

He then quickly learned about the wealth, charities, happiness, and splendid palace of Prince Aladdin. Directly he saw the wonderful fabric, he knew that none but the jinns, the slaves of the lamp, could have performed such wonders.

On his return to the khan he found out by magic that the lamp was in the palace. "Well," said he, rubbing his hands in great glee, "I shall have the lamp, and then I will make Aladdin return to his poverty."

The next day the magician learned that Aladdin had gone on a hunting tour, which was to last for eight days, of which only three had expired.

He went to a coppersmith and asked for a dozen

Children collected, who hooted at him.

copper lamps. The master of the shop told him he had not so many by him, but if he would have patience till the next day they should be made ready. The magician desired him to take care that they should be handsome and well polished.

The next day the magician called for the lamps, and having paid the man his full price, put them into a basket, and went to the gateway of Aladdin's palace. Then he began crying, "Who will give me old lamps for new?" As he went along a crowd of children collected, who hooted at him; and all who chanced to be passing by thought him a madman, to offer to change new lamps for old.

But the magician still continued crying, "Who will give me old lamps for new?" He repeated this so often that the Princess, hearing a man cry something, and seeing a great mob crowding about him, sent one of her women slaves to learn what he was selling.

The slave returned, laughing so heartily that the Princess rebuked her. "Madam," answered the slave, "who can forbear laughing, to see an old man with a basket on his arm full of fine new lamps, asking to change them for old ones?"

Another female slave, hearing this, said, "Now you speak of lamps, there is an old one upon a shelf in Prince Aladdin's robing-room, and whoever owns it will not be sorry to find a new one in its stead. Let the Princess try if this old man will really give a new lamp for an old one."

The Princess, who knew not the true value of Aladdin's lamp, at once commanded a slave to take it and make the exchange. The slave obeyed, went out of the hall, and no sooner got to the palace gates than he saw the African magician. He called to him, and said, "Give me a new lamp for this old one."

The magician never doubted that this old lamp was the one he wanted. He snatched it eagerly out of the slave's hand, and offering him the basket, bade him choose which he liked best. The slave picked out one, and carried it to the Princess.

The magician now made the best of his way to his khan. His purpose was accomplished, and by his silence he got rid of the children and the mob.

As soon as he was out of sight of the two palaces he hastened down the least-frequented streets. Then having pursued his way through the suburbs, which were very extensive, he at length reached a lonely spot, where he stopped till the darkness of the night should fall.

When it became quite dark, he pulled the lamp out of his breast and rubbed it. At that summons the jinn appeared, and said, "What wouldst thou have? I am ready to obey thee as thy slave, and the slave of all those who have that lamp in their hands—both I and the other slaves of the lamp."

"I command thee," replied the magician, "to transport me and the palace of Aladdin, with all the people in it, to Africa."

The jinn made no reply, but with the assistance of the other jinns obeyed the order immediately.

XII.—The Slave of the Ring

Early the next morning, when the Sultan went to admire Aladdin's palace, it could nowhere be seen. He could not comprehend how so large a palace should vanish so soon and not leave the least trace behind, so he ordered the Grand Vizier to be sent for.

The Grand Vizier intimated his suspicion that the palace had been built by magic, and had been removed by the same power. He induced the Sultan to send his guards, and to have Aladdin seized as a prisoner of state. The Prince was surrounded just as he was returning from the hunt.

On his son-in-law being brought before him, the

"You ought to know where your palace stood."

Sultan would not hear a word from him, but ordered him to be put to death. The decree, however, caused so much discontent among the people that the Sultan, fearing a rebellion, was obliged to grant him his life.

When Aladdin found himself at liberty, he again addressed the Sultan: "Sire, I pray you to let me know my crime." "Your crime!" answered the Sultan; "follow me, and I will show you." The Sultan then took Aladdin into the apartment from whence he was wont to look at the palace of his daughter, and said, "You ought to know where your palace stood; tell me what has become of it."

Aladdin was speechless. At last he said, "It is true I do not see the palace. It has vanished; but I had no concern in its removal. I beg you to give me forty days; and if in that time I cannot restore it, I will offer my life to be disposed of at your pleasure." The Sultan agreed to this.

For three days Aladdin wandered about the city, exciting the wonder and compassion of the multitude by asking everybody he met if they had seen his palace. On the third day he wandered into the country, and as he was approaching a river he fell down the bank with so much violence that he rubbed the ring which the magician had given him; and immediately the same jinn appeared whom he had seen in the cave where the magician had left him.

"What wouldst thou have?" said the jinn. "I am ready to obey thee as thy slave—both I and the other slaves of the ring."

Aladdin replied, "Jinn, show me where the palace now stands, or transport it back." "Your command," answered the jinn, "is not wholly in my power. I am only the slave of the ring, and not of the lamp."

"I command thee, then," replied Aladdin, "to transport me to the spot where my palace stands." These words were no sooner out of his mouth than the jinn transported him into Africa, where his palace stood at no great distance from a large city; and placing him exactly under the window of the Princess's apartment, left him.

Now one of the attendants of the Princess saw him, and told her mistress. The Princess immediately opened the window. Aladdin, perceiving his wife, saluted her with joy. Then she said, "I have ordered the private door to be opened for you; enter the palace, and come up to me without delay."

Soon he found his way to the chamber of the Princess. After embracing, and shedding tears of joy, the Prince and Princess sat down, and Aladdin said, "I beg of you, Princess, to tell me what is become of an old lamp which stood upon a shelf in my robing-chamber."

"Alas!" answered the Princess, "I was foolish enough to change the old lamp for a new one, and the next morning I found myself in this country, which I am told is Africa."

"Princess," said Aladdin, "you have explained all by telling me that we are in Africa. Tell me where the old lamp is now." "The African magician carries it wrapped up in his bosom," said the Princess; "for he pulled it out before me and showed it to me in triumph."

"Princess," said Aladdin, "I think I have found the means of delivering you and of regaining possession of the lamp. I will go to the town and disguise myself. I will return by noon, and I beg that the private door may be opened at the first knock."

When Aladdin had left the palace he saw a peasant going into the country, and hastened after him. Then he made a proposal to him to change clothes, which the man agreed to do. Aladdin next entered the neighbouring city and sought out the shops. He went into that of the druggist, and asked if he had a certain powder which he named.

The druggist, judging Aladdin to be very poor, told

him he had it, but that it was very costly; upon which Aladdin pulled out his purse, and showing him some gold, asked for half a drachm of the powder. Thereupon the druggist weighed the powder and gave it to him, telling him the price was a piece of gold. Aladdin put the money into his hand, and hastened to the palace.

When he came into the Princess's apartment, he said to her, "Princess, you must take your part in my scheme. You must assume a most friendly manner towards the magician, and ask him to partake of an entertainment in your apartment. Ask him to exchange cups with you, and then give him the cup containing this powder. On drinking it he will instantly fall asleep, and we will obtain the lamp."

The Princess on the next visit of the magician gave him an invitation to an entertainment, which he most willingly accepted. At the close of the evening she asked him to exchange cups with her. He drank from the drugged cup out of compliment to the Princess, and at once fell backward lifeless on the sofa.

No sooner had the African magician fallen backward than the door opened, and Aladdin was admitted to the hall. The Princess rose from her seat and ran to embrace him, but he stopped her, and said, "Princess, retire to your apartment, and let me be left alone."

When the Princess had gone out of the hall, Aladdin shut the door and took the lamp from the magician's bosom. Then he rubbed it, and the jinn immediately appeared.

"Jinn," said Aladdin, "transport this palace instantly to the place from whence it was brought hither." At once the palace was transported back to China.

Next morning after the restoration of Aladdin's palace the Sultan was looking out of his window, and mourning over the fate of his daughter, when he saw his son-in-law's palace in the old place. Joy and gladness filled his heart. He at once ordered a horse to be saddled, thinking he could not make haste enough to reach the place.

Aladdin rose that morning at daybreak, and went up into the hall of twenty-four windows, from whence he perceived the Sultan approaching. He received him at the foot of the great staircase, and helped him to dismount.

He then led the Sultan into the Princess's apartment. The happy father embraced her with tears of joy; and the Princess, on her part, showed her extreme pleasure. After a short interval, devoted to explanations of all that had happened, the Sultan said to Aladdin, "My son, be not displeased at my proceedings; they arose from the strength of my paternal love, and therefore you ought to forgive the excesses to which it hurried me." "Sire," replied Aladdin, "I have not the least reason to complain of your conduct, since you did nothing but what your duty seemed to require."

XIII.—The Magician's Brother

Now the African magician had a younger brother, who was as skilful and wicked a magician as himself. Not hearing from his elder brother as usual, this man used magic to discover what had become of him. He found that his brother was dead; also, that the person who had punished him was of mean birth, though married to a Princess, a Sultan's daughter.

The magician departed for China without delay, and after crossing plains, rivers, mountains, deserts, and a long tract of rugged country, he arrived there after great exertion.

When he came to the capital of China he took lodgings in a khan. His magic art soon revealed to him that Aladdin was the person who had been the cause of his brother's death. He heard, too, all the people in the city talking of a holy woman called Fatima, who was retired from the world, and of the miracles she wrought. He made some inquiries about this holy woman, and what sort of miracles she performed.

"What!" said the person whom he addressed, "have you never seen or heard of her? She is the admiration of the whole town for her fasting and her good life. Except on Mondays and Fridays, she never stirs out of her little cell; and on those days on which she comes into the town she does an infinite deal of good, for whenever she meets with sick people she puts her hand on them and cures them."

Having found out the place where the holy woman lived, the magician went at night and killed her. In the morning he dyed his face of the same hue as hers, and having arrayed himself in her garb, took her stick and went straight to the palace of Aladdin.

As soon as the people saw the holy woman, as they imagined the man to be, they gathered about him in a crowd. Some begged his blessing, others kissed his hand, and others the hem of his garment; while others, suffering from disease, stooped for him to lay his hands upon them.

He came at last to the square before Aladdin's palace. The crowd and the noise were so great that the Princess, who was in the hall of four-and-twenty windows, heard it, and asked one of her maidens to see what was the matter. The girl soon told her it was a great crowd of people collected about the holy woman to be cured of their diseases.

The Princess, who had long heard of this woman, but had never seen her, was very desirous to speak with her, and the chief officer told her it was an easy matter to bring her in if she desired it; so the Princess immediately sent four slaves for the pretended holy woman.

As soon as the crowd saw the attendants from the palace they made way, and the magician advanced to meet them. "Holy woman," said one of the slaves, "the Princess has sent for you." "The Princess does me too great an honour," replied the false Fatima; and then he followed the slaves into the palace.

When the pretended Fatima had made her bow, the Princess said, "My good mother, I have one thing to request of you: stay with me that I may learn from your good example."

"Princess," said the false Fatima, "I beg of you not to ask what I cannot consent to do without neglecting my prayers." "That shall be no hindrance," answered the Princess. "I have a great many apartments; you shall choose which you like best, and have as much liberty as if you were in your own cell."

The magician, who really desired nothing more than to introduce himself into the palace, did not excuse himself further. "Princess," said he, "I dare not presume to oppose the will of so good and great a lady."

Upon this the Princess, rising up, said, "Come with me, and choose a room for yourself." The magician followed the Princess, and out of all the apartments chose that which was the worst.

Afterwards the Princess would have brought him back to dine with her; but he, considering that he should then be obliged to show his face, begged of her to excuse him, telling her that he never ate anything but bread and dried fruits. The Princess said, "You may be as free here, good mother, as if you were in your own cell. I will order you a dinner, which shall be served in your own room; but remember I expect to see you as soon as you have finished."

After the Princess had dined, the false Fatima again waited upon her. "My good mother," said the Princess, "I am overjoyed to see so holy a woman as yourself in this palace. Pray, how do you like it? And before I show it all to you, tell me first what you think of this hall."

Fatima surveyed the hall from one end to the other, and then said to the Princess, "This hall is truly admirable, and wants but one thing." "What is that, good mother?" demanded the Princess.

"Princess," said the false Fatima, "forgive me the liberty I have taken, but my opinion is that if a roc's egg were hung up in the middle of the dome, your palace would be the wonder of the universe."

XIV.—The End of the Tale

"My good mother," said the Princess, "what is a roc, and where may one get such an egg?"

"Princess," replied Fatima, "it is a bird of prodigious size which inhabits the summit of Mount Caucasus; the architect who built your palace can get you an egg of this bird."

After the Princess had thanked the false Fatima, she conversed with her upon other matters, but could not forget the roc's egg, which she resolved to request of Aladdin when next he should visit her apartments. She did so, and he said, "Princess, it is enough that you think it wants such an ornament; you shall see that there is nothing which I would not do for your sake."

Aladdin then went up into the hall of four-and-twenty windows, where, pulling the lamp out of his bosom, he rubbed it, upon which the jinn appeared. "Jinn," said Aladdin, "bring a roc's egg, to be hung up in the middle of the dome of the palace hall."

Aladdin had no sooner said these words than the hall shook as if ready to fall, and the jinn said, in a loud and terrible voice, "Is it not enough that I and the other slaves of the lamp have done everything for you, but you must command me to bring my master and hang him up in the midst of this dome? This request deserves that you, the Princess, and the palace should be reduced to ashes; and you are only spared because the prayer does not come from yourself.

"Its true author is the brother of the African magician, your enemy. He is now in your palace, disguised in the habit of the holy woman Fatima. His design is to kill you, therefore take care of yourself." After these words the jinn disappeared.

Aladdin at once resolved what to do. He returned to the Princess's apartment, sat down, and complained of a great pain in his head which had suddenly seized him. On hearing this, the Princess told him how she had invited the holy Fatima to stay with her, and that the woman was now in the palace; and at the request of the Prince, she ordered her to be summoned.

When the pretended Fatima came, Aladdin said, "Come hither, good mother. I am tormented with a violent pain in my head, and request your assistance." So saying, he arose, but held down his head. The counterfeit Fatima advanced towards him, with his hand all the time on a dagger concealed in his girdle. But Aladdin, observing this, snatched the weapon from his hand and pierced him to the heart with it.

"My dear Prince, what have you done?" cried the Princess in surprise. "You have killed the holy woman!"

"No, my Princess," answered Aladdin, "I have not killed Fatima. This wicked man," added he, uncovering his face, "is the brother of the African magician. He has killed Fatima, and disguised himself in her clothes with intent to murder me."

Thus was Aladdin delivered from the two brothers who were magicians. Within a few years afterwards the Sultan died in a good old age. And as he left no son the Princess succeeded him, and she and Aladdin reigned together for many years in great happiness.

THE HISTORY OF ALI BABA AND THE FORTY ROBBERS

THERE once lived in a town of Persia two brothers, one named Cassim and the other Ali Baba. Their father divided a small inheritance equally between them. Cassim married a very rich wife and became a wealthy merchant. Ali Baba married a woman as poor as himself and lived by cutting wood and bringing it on three asses into the town to sell.

One day when Ali Baba was in the forest, and had just cut wood enough to load his asses, he saw at a distance a great cloud of dust which seemed to approach him. He observed it with attention and soon distinguished a body of horsemen, whom he suspected might be robbers. To save himself he determined to leave his asses, and after driving them into a thicket out of sight he climbed a large tree growing on a high rock. Its branches were thick enough to conceal him and yet enabled him to see all that passed.

The horsemen numbered forty, and were all well mounted and armed. They came to the foot of the rock on which the tree stood and there dismounted. Every man unbridled his horse, tied it to a shrub, and gave it a feed of corn from a bag he had brought behind him. Then each of them removed his saddle-bag, which seemed to Ali Baba to be full of gold and silver from its weight. One, whom he took to be the captain, came under the tree in which Ali Baba was

He climbed a large tree.

hidden, and making his way through some bushes, pronounced these words, " Open, Sesame ! "

As soon as the captain of the robbers had thus spoken, a door opened in the rock ; and after he had made all his troop enter before him, he followed them, when the door shut of itself.

The robbers stayed some time within the rock, during which time Ali Baba, fearful of being caught, remained in the tree.

At last the door opened again, and the captain came out first and stood to see the troop all pass by him, when Ali Baba heard him make the door close by pronouncing these words, " Shut, Sesame ! "

Every man at once went and bridled his horse and mounted. When the captain saw them all ready, he put himself at their head, and they returned the way they had come.

Ali Baba followed them with his eyes as far as he could see them, and afterwards stayed a considerable time before he descended. Remembering the words the captain of the robbers used to cause the door to open and shut, he had the curiosity to try if his pronouncing them would have the same effect. Accordingly he went among the bushes, and perceiving the door concealed behind them, stood before it and said, " Open, Sesame ! "

The door instantly flew wide open. Ali Baba, who expected a dark, dismal cavern, was surprised to see a well-lighted and spacious chamber, which received the light from an opening at the top of the rock. In the chamber were all sorts of provisions, rich bales of silk, brocade, and valuable carpeting piled on one another, gold and silver ingots in great heaps, and money in bags. The sight of all these riches made him suppose that this cave must have been occupied for ages by robbers who had succeeded one another.

Ali Baba went boldly into the cave and collected as much of the gold coin as he thought his three asses could carry. The gold was in bags, and when he had loaded the asses, he laid wood over the bags in such a manner that they could not be seen. When he had passed in and out as often as he wished, he stood before the door, and pronouncing the words, "Shut, Sesame!" the door closed of itself. He then made the best of his way to town.

When Ali Baba got home, he drove his asses into his little yard, shut the gates very carefully, threw off the wood that covered the panniers, carried the bags into his house, and ranged them in order before his wife. He then emptied the bags, which raised such a great heap of gold as dazzled his wife's eyes, and he told her the whole adventure from beginning to end, and, above all, recommended her to keep it secret.

The wife rejoiced greatly at their good fortune and wanted to count all the gold, piece by piece. " Wife," said Ali Baba, " you do not know what you undertake when you speak of counting the money. You will never get done. I will dig a hole and bury it. There is no time to be lost."

" You are in the right, husband," replied she ; " but let us know, as nigh as possible, how much we have. I will borrow a measure and measure it while you dig the hole."

Away the wife ran to the house of her brother-in-law, Cassim, who lived just by, and addressing herself to his wife, desired the loan of a measure for a little while. Her sister-in-law asked her whether she would have a great or a small one, and she asked for a small one.

The sister-in-law fetched it, but as she knew Ali Baba's poverty, she was curious to learn what his wife wanted to measure, and artfully putting some suet at the bottom of the measure, brought it to her, with an excuse that she was sorry she had made her stay so long, but that she could not find it sooner.

Ali Baba's wife went home, set the measure on the

Ali Baba bringing out the bags of gold.

heap of gold, filled it, and emptied it, till she had done.

She was very well satisfied to find the number of measures amounted to so many as they did, as was also her husband, who had now finished digging the hole. While Ali Baba was burying the gold, his wife, to show her exactness and diligence to her sister-in-law, carried the measure back, but without taking notice that a piece of gold had stuck to the bottom. " Sister," said she, giving it to her, " you see that I have not kept your measure long. I am obliged to you for it and return it with thanks."

As soon as Ali Baba's wife was gone, Cassim's wife looked at the bottom of the measure and was surprised to find a piece of gold sticking to it. Envy immediately possessed her breast. " What ! " said she, " has Ali Baba gold so plentiful as to measure it ? Whence has he all this wealth ? "

Cassim her husband was at his counting-house. When he came home, his wife said to him : " Cassim, I know you think yourself rich, but Ali Baba is infinitely richer than you. He does not count his money, but measures it."

Cassim desired her to explain the riddle, which she did by telling him the stratagem she had used to make the discovery, and showed him the piece of money, which was so old that they could not tell in what ruler's reign it was coined.

Cassim, after he had married the rich widow, had never treated Ali Baba as a brother, but neglected him ; and now, instead of being pleased, he conceived a base envy at this brother's prosperity. He could not sleep all that night and went to him in the morning before sunrise. " Ali Baba," said he, " I am surprised at you ; you pretend to be miserably poor, and yet you measure gold. My wife found this at the bottom of the measure you borrowed yesterday."

By this discourse, Ali Baba perceived that Cassim

and his wife knew what he had so much reason to conceal; but what was done, could not be undone. Therefore, without showing the least surprise or trouble, he confessed all, and offered his brother part of the treasure to keep the secret.

"I must know exactly where this treasure is," replied Cassim, haughtily; "and how I may visit it myself when I choose. Otherwise I will go and inform against you, and then you will not only get no more, but will lose all you have, and I shall receive a share for my information."

Ali Baba told him all he desired to know, even to the very words he was to use to gain admission into the cave.

Cassim rose the next morning long before the sun and set out for the forest with ten mules bearing great chests, which he designed to fill with gold. He followed the road Ali Baba had pointed out to him, and it was not long before he reached the rock and found the place by the tree and other marks of which his brother had told him. When he reached the entrance of the cavern, he pronounced the words, "Open, Sesame!"

The door immediately opened, and when he was in, closed on him. In examining the cave, he was greatly astonished to find much more riches than he had expected from Ali Baba's relation. He quickly laid at the door of the cavern as many bags of gold as his ten mules could carry; but his thoughts were now so full of the great riches he should possess, that he could not think of the necessary word to make the door open. Instead of "Open, Sesame," he said "Open, Barley!" and was much amazed to find that the door remained fast shut. He named several sorts of grain, but still the door would not open.

Cassim had never expected such an incident, and was so alarmed at the danger he was in that the more he endeavoured to remember the word "Sesame" the more his memory was confounded, and he had as much forgotten it as if he had never heard it mentioned. He threw down the bags he had loaded himself with and walked distractedly up and down the cave, without having the least regard to the riches that were around him.

About noon the robbers visited their cave. As they approached they saw Cassim's mules straggling near the rock, with great chests on their backs. Alarmed at this, they galloped at full speed to the cave. They drove away the mules, who strayed through the forest so far that they were soon out of sight. Then the robbers, with their naked sabres in their hands, went directly to the door, which, when their captain pronounced the proper words, immediately opened.

Cassim, who heard the noise of the horses' feet, at once guessed the arrival of the robbers and resolved to make one effort for his life. He rushed to the door, and no sooner saw it open than he ran out and threw the robber captain down, but could not escape the other robbers, who, with their scimitars, cut off his head.

The first care of the robbers after this was to examine the cave. They found all the bags which Cassim had brought to the door, ready to load on his mules, and carried them to their places, but they did not miss what Ali Baba had taken away before. Then holding a council, and deliberating on the occurrence, they guessed that Cassim, when he was in, had not been able to get out, but could not imagine how he had learned the secret words by which alone he could enter. They could not deny the fact of his being there; and to terrify any person or accomplice who should attempt the same thing, they agreed to cut Cassim's body into four quarters and hang two on one side and two on the other, within the door of the cave. They had no sooner taken this resolution than they put it in execution; and when they had nothing more to detain them, left the place of their hoards well closed. They mounted their horses, and went to beat the roads again and attack the caravans they might meet.

In the meantime Cassim's wife was very uneasy when night came and her husband had not returned. She ran to Ali Baba in great alarm and said: "I believe, brother-in-law, that you know Cassim has gone to the forest and on what account. It is now night, and he has not come back. I am afraid some misfortune has happened to him."

Ali Baba told her that she need not frighten herself, for Cassim would certainly not think it proper to come into the town till the night was pretty far advanced.

Cassim's wife, considering how much it concerned her husband to keep the business secret, was easily persuaded to believe her brother-in-law. She went home and waited patiently till midnight. Then her fear redoubled, and her grief was the more marked because she was forced to keep it to herself. She repented her foolish curiosity and cursed her desire to pry into the affairs of other people. She spent all the night in weeping; and as soon as it was day, went to her brother and sister-in-law, telling them by her tears the cause of her coming.

Ali Baba did not wait for his sister-in-law to ask him to go to see what was become of Cassim, but begging her to moderate her affliction, departed immediately with his three asses. He went to the forest, and when he came to the rock, having seen neither his brother nor the mules on the way, was seriously alarmed at finding some blood near the door. He took this for an ill omen; but when he had pronounced the proper words, and the door had opened, he was struck with horror at the dismal sight of his brother's body. He was not long in determining how he should pay the last dues to his brother, and having loaded one of his asses with the body, covered it over with wood. The other two asses he loaded with bags of gold, covering them with wood also as before. Then he bid the door shut and came away; but was so cautious as to stop some time at the end of the forest, that he might not go into the town before night. When he reached home he drove the two asses loaded with gold into his little yard and left the care of unloading them to his wife, while he led the other to his sister-in-law's house.

Ali Baba knocked at the door, which was opened by Morgiana, a clever intelligent slave, who was fruitful in inventions to meet the most difficult circumstances. When he came into the court, he unloaded the ass, and taking Morgiana aside said to her: "You must observe close secrecy. I have brought your master's body. We must bury him as if he had died a natural death. Go now and tell your mistress. I leave the matter to your wit and skilful devices."

Ali Baba helped to place the body in Cassim's house and then returned with his ass.

Morgiana went out early the next morning to a druggist, and asked for a sort of lozenge which was considered efficacious in the most dangerous disorders. The apothecary inquired who was ill. She replied with a sigh, "My good master Cassim himself, and he can neither eat nor speak."

In the evening Morgiana went to the same druggist again, and with tears in her eyes asked for an essence which they used to give to sick people only when at the last extremity. "Alas!" said she, taking it from the apothecary, "I am afraid that this remedy will have no better effect than the lozenges, and that I shall lose my good master."

Moreover, as Ali Baba and his wife were often seen going between Cassim's and their own house all that day, and seemed melancholy, nobody was surprised in the evening to hear the lamentable shrieks and cries of Cassim's wife and of Morgiana, who gave out everywhere that Cassim was dead. The next morning at daybreak, Morgiana went to an old cobbler whom she knew to be always early at his stall, and bidding him good morrow, put a piece of gold into his hand, saying, "Baba Mustapha, bring with you your sewing tackle and come with me; but I must tell you, I shall blindfold you when you come to a certain place."

Baba Mustapha hesitated a little at these words. "Oh! oh!" replied he, "you would have me do something against my conscience or against my honour?"

"God forbid that I should ask anything contrary to your honour!" said Morgiana, putting another piece of gold into his hand. "Only come along with me and fear nothing."

Baba Mustapha went with Morgiana, who, after she had bound his eyes with a handkerchief at the place she had mentioned, guided him to her deceased master's house, and never unloosed his eyes till he had entered the room where she had the body. "Baba Mustapha," said she, "you must make haste and sew the parts of this body together; and when you have done, I will give you another piece of gold."

When Baba Mustapha had finished his task, she blindfolded him again, gave him the third piece of gold as she had promised, and recommending secrecy to him, led him back to the place where she first bound his eyes. There she pulled off the bandage, and let him go home, but watched him till he was quite out of sight to make sure that he returned towards his stall. The next day four neighbours carried the corpse to the burying-ground, following the priest, who recited some prayers. Ali Baba came after with some neighbours. Morgiana, who had been a slave to the deceased, came last in the procession, weeping, beating her breast, and tearing her hair. Cassim's wife stayed at home mourning, uttering woeful cries with the women of the neighbourhood, who came, according to custom, during the funeral, and joining their wailings with hers, filled the quarter far and near with sounds of sorrow.

The manner of Cassim's melancholy death was concealed and hushed up between his widow, Morgiana, and Ali Baba, with so much contrivance that nobody in the city had the least knowledge or suspicion of the cause of it. Three or four days after the funeral, Ali Baba removed his few goods openly to his sister-in-law's house, where it was agreed that he should in future live; but the money he had taken from the robbers he conveyed thither by night. Lastly, he entrusted his eldest son with the entire management of Cassim's warehouse.

While these things were being done, the forty robbers again visited their retreat in the forest. Great, then, was their surprise to find Cassim's body taken away, with some of their bags of gold. "We are certainly discovered," said the captain. "The removal of the body and the loss of more of our money plainly shows that the man whom we killed had an accomplice; and for our own lives' sake, we must try to find him. What say you, my lads?"

All the robbers approved of the captain's proposal.

"Well," said the captain, "one of the boldest and most skilful among you must go into the town, disguised as a traveller and a stranger, to try if he can hear any talk of the man whom we have killed, and endeavour to find out who he was and where he lived. This is a matter of the first importance, and for fear of treachery, I propose that whoever undertakes this business without success, even though the failure arises only from an error of judgment, shall suffer death."

Without waiting for the sentiments of his companions, one of the robbers started up and said, "I submit to this condition and think it an honour to expose my life to serve the troop."

After this robber had received great commendations from the captain and his comrades, he disguised himself; and taking his leave of the troop that night, went into the town just at daybreak, and walked up and down, till accidentally he came to Baba Mustapha's stall, which was always open before any of the shops.

Baba Mustapha was seated with an awl in his hand, just going to begin work. The robber saluted him, bidding him good morrow; and perceiving that he was old, said: "Honest man, you begin to work very early. Is it possible that one of your age can see so well? I question, even if it were somewhat lighter, whether you could see to stitch."

"You do not know me," replied Baba Mustapha; "for old as I am I have extraordinary good eyes; and you will not doubt it when I tell you that I sewed the body of a dead man together in a place where I had not so much light as I have now."

"Where was that?" asked the robber.

"You shall know no more," answered Baba Mustapha.

The robber felt sure that he had discovered what he sought. He pulled out a piece of gold, and putting it into Baba Mustapha's hand, said to him: "I do not want to learn your secret, though I can assure you that you might safely trust me with it. The only thing I desire of you is to show me the house where you did this work."

"If I were disposed to do you that favour," replied Baba Mustapha, "I assure you I cannot. I was taken to a certain place, whence I was led blindfold to the house, and afterwards brought back in the same manner. You see, therefore, the impossibility of my doing what you desire."

"Well," replied the robber, "you may, however, have some remembrance of the way that you were led blindfold. Come, let me blind your eyes at the same place. We will walk together; perhaps you may be able to go where you did before, and as everybody ought to be paid for their trouble, there is another piece of gold for you. Gratify me in what I ask you."

So saying, he put another piece of gold into the shoemaker's hand.

The two pieces of gold were great temptations to Baba Mustapha. He looked at them a long time in his hand, without saying a word, but at last he pulled out his purse and put them in it. "I am not sure that I can remember the way exactly," said he to the robber; "but since you desire, I will try what I can do."

At these words Baba Mustapha rose, to the great joy of the robber, and led him to the place where Morgiana had bound his eyes. "It was here that I was blindfolded," said Baba Mustapha; "and afterwards I turned this way."

The robber tied his handkerchief over the shoemaker's eyes and walked by him till he stopped directly before Cassim's house, where Ali Baba then lived. The thief marked the door with a piece of chalk, which he had ready in his hand, and then he pulled off the bandage from Baba Mustapha's eyes and asked him if he knew whose house that was. Baba Mustapha replied he did not live in the neighbourhood, and he could not tell.

The robber, finding he could discover no more from Baba Mustapha, thanked him for the trouble he had taken and left him to go back to his stall, while he returned to the forest, persuaded that he should be very well received.

A little after the robber and Baba Mustapha had parted, Morgiana went out of Ali Baba's house on some errand, and on her return, seeing the mark the robber had made, stopped to observe it. "What can be the meaning of this mark?" said she to herself. "Somebody intends my master no good. However, with whatever intention it was done, it is advisable to guard against the worst."

Accordingly, she fetched a piece of chalk and marked two or three doors on each side, in the same manner, without saying a word to her master or mistress.

By this time the robber had rejoined his troop in the forest. He told the others of his success, rejoicing over his good fortune in meeting so soon with the only person who could inform him of what he wanted to know. The robbers listened to him with the utmost satisfaction; and the captain, after commending his diligence, addressed himself to them all, and said: "Comrades, we have no time to lose. Let us set off well armed; but that we may not excite any suspicion, let only one or two go into the town together and we will meet at the great square. In the meantime our comrade who brought us the good news and I will go and find the house he has marked, that we may consult what had best be done."

This speech and plan were approved by all. They were soon ready, and filed off in parties of two each, and got into the town without being in the least suspected. The captain and he who had visited the town in the morning as a spy came in last. The spy led the captain into the street where he had marked Ali Baba's residence; and when they came to the first of the houses which Morgiana had marked, he pointed it out. But the captain observed that the next door was chalked in the same manner and in the same place; and showing it to his guide, asked him which house it was, that or the first. The guide was so confounded that he knew not what answer to make, and he was still more puzzled when he and the captain saw five or six houses similarly marked. He assured the captain, with an oath, that he had marked but one, and could not tell who had chalked the rest, so that he could not distinguish the house which the cobbler had stopped at.

The captain, finding that their design had proved abortive, went directly to the great square where the robbers were to meet and told his troop that they had lost their labour and must return to their cave. He himself set them the example, and they separated in parties of two and returned as they had come.

When the troop was all got together, the captain told them the reason of their returning; and presently the robber who had acted as spy was declared deserving of death and was killed.

But as the safety of the troop required the discovery of the second intruder into the cave, another of the gang offered to go and seek out the intruder's dwelling. He promised himself that he should succeed better than his unlucky predecessor, and his offer being accepted, he went and corrupted Baba Mustapha, as the other had done; and being shown the house, marked it in a place more remote from sight with red chalk.

Not long afterward, Morgiana, whose eyes nothing could escape, went out, and seeing the red chalk mark, and arguing that some evil was planned against her master, marked the neighbouring houses in the same place and manner.

The robber, at his return to his company, prided himself much on the care he had taken. He believed he had adopted a sure way of distinguishing Ali Baba's house from the others, and the captain and all of them thought that now they must succeed. They conveyed themselves into the town with the same caution as before; but when the robber spy and his captain came to the street where Ali Baba lived they found several doors marked instead of one, at which the captain was enraged, and the spy was in as great confusion as the former guide.

Thus the captain and his troop were forced to retire a second time, and much more dissatisfied; and the robber who had been the author of the mistake underwent the same punishment as the other spy.

The captain, having lost two brave fellows of his troop, was afraid of diminishing it too much by pursuing this plan to get information of the residence of their plunderer. It was evident that their heads were not so good as their hands on such occasions, and he therefore resolved to take on himself the important commission.

Accordingly, he went and addressed himself to Baba Mustapha, who did him the same service he had done the other robbers. The captain did not set any particular mark on the house, but examined and observed it so carefully, that it was impossible for him to mistake it. Well satisfied with his attempt, and informed of what he wanted to know, he returned to the forest; and when he came into the cave, where the troop waited for him, said, "Now, comrades, nothing can prevent our full revenge, as I am certain of the house; and on my way hither I have thought how to put the revenge into execution; but if any one can form a better plan, let him communicate it."

He then told his plan, and as they approved of it, ordered them to go into the villages about and buy nineteen mules, with thirty-eight large leather jars, one full of oil and the others empty.

In two or three days' time the robbers had purchased the mules and jars, and the captain, after having put one of his men into each jar with the weapons which he thought fit, leaving open the seam which had been undone to allow them a chance to breathe, rubbed the jars on the outside with oil from the full vessel.

Things being thus prepared, the nineteen mules were loaded with thirty-seven robbers in jars and the jar of oil. Then the captain, as their driver, set out with them, and reached the town by the dusk of the evening, as he had intended. He led them through the streets till he came to Ali Baba's, at whose door he designed to knock; but Ali Baba was sitting in the doorway after supper to take a little fresh air. The robber stopped his mules, addressed Ali Baba, and said: "I have brought some oil a great way to sell at to-morrow's market, and it is now so late that I do not know where to lodge. If I should not be troublesome to you, do me the favour to let me pass the night with you, and I shall be very much obliged by your hospitality."

Though Ali Baba had seen the captain of the robbers in the forest and had heard him speak, it was impossible to know him in the disguise of an oil merchant. He told him he was welcome, and immediately opened his gates for the mules to go into the yard. At the same time he called to a slave and ordered him, when the mules were unloaded, to put them into the stable and feed them; and then went to Morgiana to bid her get a good supper for his guest. After they had finished supper, Ali Baba charged Morgiana afresh to take care of his guest.

In the meantime the captain of the robbers went into the yard, and took off the lid of each jar, and gave his comrades orders what to do. Beginning at the first jar and so on to the last, he said to each man, "As soon as I throw some pebbles from the chamber window where I lie, do not fail to come out, and I will immediately join you."

After this he returned into the house, and Morgiana taking up a light conducted him to his chamber. There she left him; and he, to avoid any suspicion, put the light out soon after and lay down in his clothes, that he might be the more ready to rise.

Morgiana began preparations for the morrow's breakfast; but while she was doing this, the oil burned out of the lamp she was using, and there was no more oil in the house, nor any candles. What to do she did not know. Abdalla, a fellow-servant, seeing her very uneasy, said, "Do not fret yourself, but go into the yard and take some oil out of one of the jars."

Morgiana thanked Abdalla for his advice, took the oil-pot, and went into the yard; when as she came nigh the first jar, the robber within said softly, "Is it time?"

Though naturally much surprised at finding a man in the jar instead of the oil she wanted, she immediately felt the importance of keeping silence, as Ali Baba, his family, and herself might be in great danger; and collecting herself, without showing the least emotion, she answered, "Not yet, but presently."

She went quietly in this manner to all the jars, giving the same answer till she came to the jar of oil.

By this means Morgiana found that her master Ali Baba had admitted thirty-eight robbers into his house, and that this pretended oil merchant was their captain. She made what haste she could to fill her oil-pot and returned to her kitchen, where, as soon as she had lighted her lamp, she took a great kettle, went again to the oil-jar, filled the kettle, set it on a large wood fire, and as soon as it boiled, went and poured enough into every jar to stifle and destroy the robber within.

When this action was executed without any noise, as she had intended, she returned to the kitchen with the empty kettle; and having put out the fire she had made to boil the oil, and the lamp also, she remained silent, resolving not to go to rest till she had observed through a window of the kitchen, which opened into the yard, what might follow.

She had not waited long before the captain of the robbers got up, opened the window, and finding no light and hearing no noise, or any one stirring in the house, gave the appointed signal by throwing little stones, several of which hit the jars, as he doubted not by the sound they gave. He then listened, but not hearing or perceiving anything whereby he could judge that his companions stirred, he began to grow very uneasy, and threw stones a second and also a third time. He could not comprehend the reason that none of his men should answer his signal. Much alarmed, he went softly down into the yard, and going to the first jar, asked the robber, whom he thought alive, if he was in readiness. Then he smelt the hot boiled oil, and suspected that his plot to murder Ali Baba and plunder his house was discovered. Examining all the jars, one after another, he found that all his gang were dead; and, enraged to despair at having failed in his design, he forced the lock of a door that led from the yard to the garden, and climbing over the garden wall made his escape.

When Morgiana saw him depart, she went to bed, satisfied and pleased to have succeeded so well in saving her master and family.

Ali Baba rose before day, and, followed by a slave, went to the baths, entirely ignorant of the important events which had happened at home.

When he returned, he was very much surprised to see the oil-jars, and wondered that the merchant was not gone with them and the mules. He asked Morgiana, who opened the door, the reason. "My good master," answered she, "God preserve you and all your family. You will be better informed of what you wish to know when you have seen what I have to show you."

As soon as Morgiana had shut the door, Ali Baba followed her, and she requested him to look into the first jar and see if there was any oil. Ali Baba did so, and seeing a man started back in alarm and cried out. "Do not be afraid," said Morgiana, "the man you see there is dead."

"Ah, Morgiana," said Ali Baba, "explain yourself."

"I will," replied Morgiana. "Moderate your astonishment and do not excite the curiosity of your neighbours, for it is of great importance to keep this affair secret. Look into the other jars."

Ali Baba examined all the other jars, one after another; and when he came to that which contained oil, found the oil nearly gone. He stood for some time motionless, looking at the jars, without saying a word, so great was his surprise. At last, when he had recovered himself, he asked, "And what is become of the merchant?"

"Merchant!" answered Morgiana; "he is as much a merchant as I am. I will tell you who he is and what is become of him; but you had better hear the story in your own room, for it is time that you had your broth after your bathing."

They went indoors and Morgiana told all she had done, from first observing the mark on the house to the destruction of the robbers and the flight of their captain.

On hearing of these brave deeds from the lips of Morgiana, Ali Baba said to her: "God, by your means, has delivered me from the snares these robbers laid for my destruction. I therefore owe my life to you; and, for a token of my acknowledgment, I give you your liberty from this moment. I will complete your recompense later."

Ali Baba's garden was very long and shaded at the farther end by a great number of large trees. Near these he and the slave Abdalla dug a trench, long and wide enough to hold the bodies of the robbers; and as the earth was light, they were not long in doing it. When the burial was finished, Ali Baba hid the jars and weapons; and as he had no occasion for the mules, he sent them at different times to be sold in the market by his slave.

While Ali Baba took these measures, the captain of the forty robbers returned to the forest with inconceivable mortification. He did not stay long. The loneliness of the gloomy cavern became frightful to him. He determined, however, to avenge the fate of his companions and to accomplish the death of Ali Baba.

For this purpose he returned to the town and took a lodging in a khan, and disguised himself as a merchant selling silks. Under this assumed character he gradually conveyed a great many sorts of rich stuffs and fine linen from the cavern to his lodging, but with all the necessary precautions to conceal the place whence he brought them. In order to dispose of the merchandise, he rented a warehouse, and it happened to be opposite Cassim's, which Ali Baba's son had occupied since the death of his uncle.

The robber took the name of Cogia Houssain. Ali Baba's son was, from his vicinity, one of the first to converse with Cogia Houssain, and the robber strove to cultivate his friendship. Two or three days after Cogia Houssain was settled, Ali Baba came to see his son, and the captain of the robbers recognized him at once. After this he became more attentive than ever to Ali Baba's son, made him some small presents, and often asked him to dine and sup with him, when he treated him very handsomely.

Ali Baba's son did not choose to continue under such obligation to Cogia Houssain, but was so much straitened for want of room in his house that he could not entertain him. He therefore acquainted his father, Ali Baba, with his wish to invite Cogia Houssain in return.

Ali Baba with great pleasure took the treat on himself. "Son," said he, "to-morrow get Cogia Houssain to accompany you, and as you pass by my door, call in. I will go and order Morgiana to provide a supper."

The next day Ali Baba's son and Cogia Houssain met by appointment, took their walk, and as they returned, Ali Baba's son led Cogia Houssain through the street where his father lived, and when they came to the house, stopped and knocked at the door. "This, sir," said he, "is the home of my father. From the account I have given him of your friendship, he has charged me to procure him the honour of your acquaintance; and I desire you to add this pleasure to those for which I am already indebted to you."

Ali Baba received Cogia Houssain with a smiling countenance and in the most obliging manner one could wish. He thanked him for all the favours he had done his son; adding withal, the obligation was the greater as his son was a young man, not much acquainted with the world, and that he might contribute to his information.

Cogia Houssain returned the compliment by assuring Ali Baba that though his son might not have acquired the experience of older men, he had good sense equal to the experience of many others. After a little more conversation on different subjects, he offered to take his leave, when Ali Baba, stopping him, said: "Where are you going, sir, in so much haste? I beg you would do me the honour to sup with me. Though my entertainment may not be worthy your acceptance, such as it is, I heartily offer it."

"Sir," replied Cogia Houssain, "I am thoroughly persuaded of your good-will; but the truth is, I can eat no victuals that have any salt in them. Therefore judge how I should feel at your table."

"If that is the only reason," said Ali Baba, "it ought not to deprive me of the honour of your company; for, in the first place, there is no salt ever put into my bread, and as to the meat we shall have to-night, I promise you there shall be none in that. Therefore you must do me the favour to stay."

Ali Baba went into the kitchen and ordered Morgiana to put no salt to the meat which was to be served that night.

Morgiana, who was always ready to obey her master, could not help being surprised at his strange order. "Who is this man," said she, "who eats no salt with his meat? Your supper will be spoiled."

" Do not be angry, Morgiana," replied Ali Baba. " He is an honest man. Therefore do as I bid you."

Morgiana obeyed, though with no little reluctance, and had a curiosity to see this man who ate no salt. To this end, when she had finished what she had to do in the kitchen, she helped Abdalla to carry up the dishes ; and looking at Cogia Houssain, knew him at first sight, notwithstanding his disguise, to be the captain of the robbers, and examining him very carefully perceived that he had a dagger under his garment.

When Abdalla came for the dessert of fruit and had put it with the wine and glasses before Ali Baba, Morgiana retired, dressed herself neatly, girded her waist with a silver-gilt girdle, to which there hung a poniard with a hilt of the same metal, and put a handsome mask on her face. When she had thus arrayed herself, she said to Abdalla, " Take your tambourine, and let us go and divert our master and his son's friend."

Abdalla took his tambourine and played all the way into the hall before Morgiana, who, when she came to the door, made a low obeisance by way of asking leave to exhibit her skill, while Abdalla left off playing. " Come in, Morgiana," said Ali Baba, " and let Cogia Houssain see what you can do, that he may tell us what he thinks of your performance."

Cogia Houssain, who did not expect this diversion after supper, began to fear he should not be able to take advantage of the opportunity he thought he had found ; but hoped if he now missed his purpose, to secure it another time, by keeping up a friendly intercourse with the father and son. Therefore, though he could have wished Ali Baba would have declined the dance, he pretended to be obliged to him for it, and expressed his satisfaction at what he saw.

As soon as Ali Baba and Cogia Houssain had done talking, Abdalla commenced to play on the tambourine and at the same time sung an air, to which Morgiana, who was an excellent performer, danced in such a manner as would have created admiration in any company.

After she had danced several dances with much grace, she drew the poniard, and holding it in her hand, began a dance, in which she outdid herself by the many different figures, light movements, and the surprising leaps and wonderful exertions with which she accompanied it. At last she snatched the tambourine from Abdalla with her left hand, and holding the dagger in her right, presented the other side of the tambourine, after the manner of those who get a livelihood by dancing and solicit the liberality of the spectators.

Ali Baba put a piece of gold into the tambourine, as did also his son; and Cogia Houssain, seeing that she was coming to him, had pulled his purse out of his bosom to make her a present. But while he was putting his hand in the purse, Morgiana plunged the poniard into his heart.

Ali Baba and his son, shocked at this action, cried out aloud. "Unhappy woman!" exclaimed Ali Baba, "what have you done to ruin me and my family?"

"It was to preserve, not to ruin, you," answered Morgiana; "for see here," continued she, opening the pretended Cogia Houssain's garment and showing the dagger, "what an enemy you had entertained! Look well at him and you will find him to be both the false oil merchant and the captain of the gang of forty robbers. Before I saw him, I suspected him as soon as you told me you had such a guest. You now find that my suspicion was not groundless."

Ali Baba, who immediately felt the new obligation he had to Morgiana for saving his life a second time, embraced her. "Morgiana," said he, "I gave you your liberty and then promised you that my gratitude should not stop there, but that I would soon give you higher proofs of its sincerity, which I now do by making you my daughter-in-law."

Then addressing himself to his son, he said: "I believe you, son, to be so dutiful a child that you will not refuse Morgiana for your wife. You see that Cogia Houssain sought your friendship with a design to take away my life; and if he had succeeded, there is no doubt but he would have sacrificed you also to his revenge. Consider that by marrying Morgiana you marry the preserver of my family and your own."

The son, far from showing any dislike, readily consented to the marriage, not only because he would not disobey his father, but also because it was agreeable to his inclination. After this they buried the captain of the robbers with his comrades. A few days later, Ali Baba celebrated the wedding of his son and Morgiana with a great feast and the usual dancing, and had the satisfaction to see that his friends and neighbours whom he invited had no knowledge of the true motives of the marriage.

Ali Baba did not visit the robbers' cave for a whole year, as he supposed the other two members of the troop, whom he could get no account of, might be alive. At the year's end, when he found they had not made any attempt to disturb him, he had the curiosity to make another journey to the place where the treasure was concealed in the forest. He mounted his horse, and when he came to the cave he alighted and tied his horse to a tree. Then approaching the entrance he pronounced the words, "Open, Sesame!" and the door opened.

He entered the cavern, and by the condition he found things in judged that nobody had been there since the captain had fetched the goods for his shop. It was quite evident that all the robbers who knew of the cave were dead, and Ali Baba believed he was the only person in the world who had the secret of opening it, and that all the treasure was at his sole disposal. He put as much gold into his saddle-bags as his horse could carry, and returned to town. Some years later he carried his son to the cave and taught him the secret of opening and shutting the door. The son handed the secret down to his posterity, who, using their good fortune with moderation, lived in great honour and splendour.

THE STORY OF SINDBAD THE SAILOR

In the reign of the Caliph Haroun al-Raschid there lived at Bagdad a poor porter called Hindbad. One day, when the weather was very hot, he was employed to carry a heavy burden from one end of the town to the other. Being much fatigued, he took off his load and sat on it to rest near a large mansion.

He was much pleased that he stopped at this place; for an agreeable smell of wood of aloes, mixed with the scent of rose-water, came from the house, and completely perfumed and embalmed the air. Besides, he heard a concert of instrumental music, accompanied with the harmonious notes of nightingales and other birds. This charming melody and the smell of several sorts of savoury dishes made the porter conclude there was a feast, and great rejoicings within. His business seldom led him that way, and he knew not to whom the mansion belonged; but he went to some of the servants, whom he saw standing at the gate in magnificent apparel, and asked the name of the proprietor.

"How," replied one of them, "do you live in Bagdad, and know not that this is the house of Sindbad the Sailor, that famous voyager, who has sailed around the world?"

The porter lifted up his eyes to heaven and said: "Almighty Creator of all things, consider the differences between Sindbad and me! I am every day ex-

He was employed to carry a heavy burden.

posed to fatigues and calamities, and can scarcely get coarse barley-bread for myself and my family, whilst happy Sindbad expends immense riches and leads a life of continual pleasure. What has he done to obtain from Thee a lot so agreeable ? And what have I done to deserve one so wretched ? "

Whilst the porter was thus indulging his melancholy, a servant came out of the house and, taking him by the arm, bade him follow him, for Sindbad his master wanted to speak to him.

The servant brought him into a great hall, where a number of people were gathered around a table. At the upper end sat a comely, venerable gentleman, with a long white beard, and behind him stood a number of officers and domestics, all ready to attend him. This person was Sindbad. Hindbad, whose fear was increased at the sight of so many people and of a banquet so rich, saluted the company trembling. Sindbad told him to draw near, seated him at his right hand, and served him.

The porter's complaint had been heard by Sindbad himself through the window, and this it was that induced him to have Hindbad brought in. When the repast was over, Sindbad addressed his conversation to Hindbad and inquired his name and employment, and said, " I wish you to repeat here what you lately said in the streets."

At this request, Hindbad hung down his head in confusion and replied, " My lord, I confess that my fatigue put me out of humour, and occasioned me to utter some indiscreet words which I beg you to pardon."

" Do not think I am so unjust," resumed Sindbad, " as to resent such a complaint. But I must rectify your error concerning myself. You think, no doubt, that I have acquired without labour and trouble the ease and indulgence which I now enjoy. But do not mistake. I did not attain to this happy condition without enduring for several years more trouble of body and mind than can well be imagined. Yes, gentlemen," he added, speaking to the whole company, "I assure you that my sufferings have been of a nature so extraordinary as would deprive the greatest miser of his love of riches; and as an opportunity now offers, I will, with your leave, relate the dangers I have encountered, which I think will not be uninteresting to you."

The First Voyage

I squandered the greater part of my paternal inheritance in youthful dissipation; but at length I saw my folly, and became convinced that riches were not of much use when applied to such purposes as those to which I had devoted them; and I reflected that the time I spent in dissipation was of still greater value than gold, and that nothing could be more truly deplorable than poverty in old age. Feeling the truth of this reflection, I resolved to collect the small remains of my patrimony and to sell my goods by auction. In short, I determined to employ to some profit the small sum I had rcmaining; and no sooner was this resolution formed than I put it into execution. I repaired to Balsora, where I embarked with several merchants in a vessel which had been equipped at our united expense.

We set sail, and steered towards the East Indies by the Persian Gulf. I was at first troubled with the sickness that attacks voyagers by sea; but I soon recovered my health. In the course of our voyage we touched at several islands, and sold or exchanged our merchandise. One day, when our vessel was in full sail, we were unexpectedly becalmed before a small island which appeared just above the water, and in its verdure resembled a beautiful meadow. The captain ordered the sails to be lowered, and gave permission to those passengers who wished it to go ashore, and of this number I formed one. But while we were enjoying ourselves the island suddenly trembled and we felt a severe shock.

The people who had remained in the ship perceived the earthquake in the island, and immediately called to us to re-embark, or we should all perish ; but what we supposed to be an island was nothing but the back of a whale. The most active of the party jumped into the boat, whilst others threw themselves into the water, to swim to the ship ; as for me, I was still on the island, or, more properly speaking, on the whale, when it dived below the surface ; and I had only time to seize a piece of wood which had been brought to make a fire with, when the monster disappeared beneath the waves. Meantime the captain, willing to avail himself of a fair breeze which had sprung up, set sail with those who had reached his vessel, and left me to the mercy of the waves. I remained in this deplorable situation the whole of that day and the following night. On the return of morning, I had neither strength nor hope left ; but a breaker happily threw me on an island.

Though extremely enfeebled by the fatigues I had undergone, nevertheless I tried to creep about in search of some herb or fruit that might satisfy my hunger. I found some, and had also the good luck to meet with a stream of excellent water. Having in a great measure regained my strength, I began to explore the island, and entered a beautiful plain, where I perceived a horse grazing. I bent my steps towards it, trembling between fear and joy, for I could not ascertain whether I was advancing to safety or to perdition. I remarked, as I approached, that the creature was a mare, tied to a stake ; her beauty attracted my attention, but whilst I was admiring her I heard from underground the voice of a man, who shortly after appeared, and, coming to me, asked me who I was. I related my adventure to him; whereupon he took me by the hand, and led me into a cave, where I found some other persons, who were not less astonished to see me than I was to meet them there.

I ate some food which they offered me; and upon my asking them what they did in a place which appeared so barren, they replied that they were grooms to King Mihragè, who was the sovereign of that isle; and that they came hither every year, about this season, with some mares belonging to the king.

The following day they returned, with the mares, to the capital of the island, whither I accompanied them. On our arrival, King Mihragè, to whom I was presented, asked me who I was, and by what chance I had reached his dominions; and when I had satisfied his curiosity, he expressed pity at my misfortunes. At the same time, he gave orders that I should be taken care of, and be supplied with everything I might want.

As I was a merchant, I associated with persons of my own profession. I sought, in particular, such as were foreigners, partly to hear some intelligence of Bagdad, and partly in the hope of meeting some one with whom I could return; for the capital of King Mihragè is situated on the seacoast, and has a beautiful port, where vessels from all parts of the world daily arrive.

As I was standing one day near the port, I saw a ship come towards the land. When the crew had cast anchor, they began to unload its goods, and the merchants to whom the cargo belonged took it away to their warehouses. Happening to cast my eyes on some of the packages, I saw my name written thereon, and having attentively examined them, I recognized them as the same which I had embarked in the ship in which I left Balsora. I also recollected the captain; but as I felt assured that he thought me dead, I went

A breaker happily threw me on an island.

up to him, and asked him to whom those parcels belonged.

"I had on board with me," replied he, "a merchant of Bagdad, named Sindbad. One day when we were near an island, or at least what appeared to be one, he went ashore with some other passengers, on this supposed island, which was nothing but an enormous whale that had fallen asleep on the surface of the water. The fish no sooner felt the heat of a fire they lighted on its back to cook their provisions, than it began to move and flounce about in the sea.

"Most of the persons who were on it were drowned, and the unfortunate Sindbad was one of the number. These parcels belonged to him; and I have resolved to sell them, that if I meet with any of his family I may be able to pay over to them the profit I shall have made on the principal." "Captain," said I then, "I am that Sindbad, whom you supposed dead, but who is still alive; and these parcels are my property and merchandise."

When the captain heard me speak thus he exclaimed: "Great Heaven! whom shall I trust? There is no longer truth in man! With my own eyes I saw Sindbad perish; the passengers I had on board were also witnesses of his death; and you have the assurance to say that you are that same Sindbad! At first sight you appeared a man of probity and honour; yet you assert an impious falsity, to possess yourself of some merchandise which does not belong to you." "Have patience," replied I, "and do me the favour to listen to what I have to say." I then related in what manner I had been saved, and by what accident I had met with King Mihragè's grooms, who had brought me to his court.

The captain was rather staggered at my discourse, but was soon convinced that I was not an impostor; for some people who arrived from his ship knew me, and began to congratulate me on my fortunate escape.

At last he recollected me himself, and embracing me, exclaimed: "Heaven be praised that you have happily escaped from that great peril! Here are your goods; take them, for they are yours." I thanked him, and praised his honourable conduct.

I selected the most precious and valuable things in my bales as presents for King Mihragè. As this prince had been informed of my misfortunes, he asked me where I had obtained such rare curiosities. I related to him the manner in which I had recovered my property, and he had the condescension to express his joy at my good fortune. He accepted my presents, and gave me others of far greater value. Hereupon I took my leave, and re-embarked in the same vessel in which I had come; having first exchanged what merchandise remained for products of the country consisting of aloes and sandal wood, camphor, nutmegs, cloves, pepper, and ginger.

We touched at several islands, and at last landed at Balsora, from whence I came here, having realized about a hundred thousand sequins. I returned to my family, and was received by them with the joy of true and sincere friendship. I purchased slaves of both sexes, and bought a magnificent house and grounds. Thus I established myself, determined to forget the hardships I had endured, and to enjoy the pleasures of life.

The Second Voyage

I HAD resolved, after my first voyage, to pass the rest of my days in tranquillity at Bagdad. But the desire of seeing foreign countries, and carrying on some traffic by sea, returned. I bought merchandise and set off a second time with some merchants whose probity I could rely on. We embarked in a good vessel, and recommending ourselves to the care of Allah, we began our voyage.

We went from island to island, and bartered our goods very profitably. One day we landed on an island that was covered with a variety of fruit trees, but so deserted that we could not discover any habitation, or the trace of a human being. We walked in the meadows and along the brooks that watered them; and whilst some of my companions were amusing themselves with gathering fruits and flowers, I took out some of the wine and provisions I had brought with me, and seated myself by a little stream under some trees which afforded a delightful shade.

When I had satisfied my hunger, sleep gradually stole over my senses. I cannot say how long I slept, but when I awoke the ship was no longer in view. I was much surprised at this circumstance, and rose to look for my companions; but they were all gone, and I could only just descry the vessel in full sail, at such a distance that I soon lost sight of it.

You may imagine what were my reflections when I found myself in this dismal state. I thought I should have died with grief. I reproached myself a thousand times for my folly in not being contented with my first voyage, which ought to have satisfied my craving for adventure; but all my regrets were of no avail, and my repentance came too late. At length I resigned myself to the will of Heaven; and not knowing what would become of me, I ascended a high tree, from whence I looked on all sides, to try if I could discover some object to inspire me with hope. Casting my eyes towards the sea, I could discern only water and sky; but perceiving on the land side a white spot, I descended from the tree, and taking up the remainder of my provisions, I walked towards the object. As I approached, I perceived it to be a ball of prodigious size, and when I got near enough to touch it, I found it was soft. I walked round it to see if there was an opening, but could find none; and the ball appeared so smooth that any attempt to climb it would have been fruitless. Its circumference might be about fifty paces.

The sun was then near setting. The air grew suddenly dark, as if obscured by a thick cloud. I was surprised at this change, but how much did my amazement increase when I perceived it to be occasioned by a bird of most extraordinary size, which was flying towards me. I recollected having heard sailors speak of a bird called a roc; and I concluded that the great white ball which had drawn my attention must be the egg of this bird. I was not mistaken; for shortly afterwards it lighted on the white ball, and placed itself as if to sit upon it.

When I saw this huge fowl coming I drew near to the egg, so that I had one of the claws of the bird just before me. This claw was as big as the trunk of a large tree. I tied myself to the claw with the linen of my turban, in hopes that the roc, when it took its flight the next morning, would carry me with it out of that desert island.

My project succeeded; for at break of day the roc flew away, and bore me to such a height that I could no longer distinguish the earth; then it descended with such rapidity that I almost lost my senses. When the roc had alighted, I quickly untied the knot that bound me to its foot, and had scarcely released myself when it darted on a serpent of immeasurable length, and seizing the snake in its beak, flew away.

The place in which the roc left me was a very deep valley, surrounded on all sides by mountains of such height that their summits were lost in the clouds, and so steep that there was no possibility of climbing them. This was a fresh embarrassment; for I had no reason to rejoice at my change of situation, when I compared it with the island I had left.

As I walked along this valley, I remarked that it was strewn with diamonds, some of which were of astonishing size. I amused myself for some time by examining them, but soon perceived from afar some objects which destroyed my pleasure, and created in me great fear. These were a great number of serpents, so long and large that the smallest of them could have swallowed an elephant with ease. During the daytime they hid themselves in caves from the roc, their mortal enemy, and only came out when it was dark.

I passed the day in walking about the valley, resting myself occasionally when an opportunity offered; and when the sun set I retired into a small cave, where I thought I should be in safety. I closed the entrance, which was low and narrow, with a stone large enough to protect me from the serpents, but which yet allowed a little light to pass into the cave. I supped on part of my provisions, and could plainly hear the serpents, which began to make their appearance. Their tremendous hissings caused me great fear, and, as you may suppose, I did not pass a very restful night.

When the day appeared the serpents retired. I left my cave with trembling, and may truly say that I walked a long time on diamonds without feeling the least desire to possess them. At last I sat down, and notwithstanding my agitation, after making another meal off my provisions I fell asleep, for I had not once closed my eyes during all the previous night. I had scarcely begun to doze, when something falling near me, with a great noise, awoke me. It was a large piece of fresh meat, and at the same moment I saw a number of other pieces rolling down the rocks from above.

I had always supposed the account to be fictitious which I had heard related by seamen and others, of the Valley of Diamonds, and of the means by which merchants procured these precious gems. I now knew it to be true. The method of proceeding is this: The merchants go to the mountains which surround the

The roc flew away, and bore me to such a height that I could no longer distinguish the earth.

valley about the time that the eagles hatch their young.

They cut large pieces of meat, and throw them into the valley; and the diamonds on which the lumps of meat fall stick to them. The eagles, which are larger and stronger in that country than in any other, seize these pieces of meat, to carry to their young at the top of the rocks. The merchants then run to the eagles' nests, and by various noises oblige the birds to retreat, and then take the diamonds that have stuck to the pieces of meat. I had supposed it impossible ever to leave this valley, and began to look on it as my tomb; but now I changed my opinion, and turned my thoughts to the preservation of my life.

I began by collecting the largest diamonds I could find, and with these I filled my leather bag in which I had carried my provisions. I then took one of the largest pieces of meat, and tied it tightly round me with the linen of my turban; in this state I laid myself on the ground, tightly securing my leather bag round me.

I had not been long in this position before the eagles began to descend, and each seized a piece of meat, with which it flew away. One of the strongest darted on the piece to which I was attached, and carried me up with it to its nest. The merchants then began their cries to frighten away the eagles; and when they had obliged the birds to quit their prey, one of them approached, but was much surprised and alarmed on seeing me.

He soon, however, recovered from his fear; and instead of inquiring by what means I came there, began to quarrel with me for trespassing on what he called his property. "You will speak to me with pity instead of anger," said I, "when you learn by what means I reached this place. Console yourself; for I have diamonds for you as well as for myself, and my diamonds are more valuable than those of all the other merchants added together. I have myself chosen some of the finest at the bottom of the valley, and have them in this bag." Saying this, I showed him my store. I had scarcely finished speaking, when the other merchants, perceiving me, flocked round me with great astonishment, and their wonder was still greater when I related my history.

They conducted me to the place where they lived together, and on seeing my diamonds they all expressed their admiration, and declared they had never seen any to equal them in size or in quality. The nest into which I had been transported belonged to one of these merchants, for each merchant has his own. I entreated him, therefore, to choose for himself from my stock as many as he pleased. He contented himself with taking only one, and that too the smallest I had; and as I pressed him to take more, without fear of wronging me, he refused. "No," said he, "I am very well satisfied with this, which is sufficiently valuable to spare me the trouble of making any more voyages to complete my little fortune."

The merchants had been for some days in that spot, and as they now appeared to be contented with the diamonds they had collected, we set off all together on the following day, and travelled over high mountains, which were infested by prodigious serpents; but we had the good fortune to escape them. We reached the nearest port in safety, and from thence embarked for the Isle of Roha, where I exchanged some of my diamonds for valuable merchandise. We set sail for other islands; and at last, after having touched at several ports, we reached Balsora, from which place I returned to Bagdad. The first thing I did was to distribute a great deal of money amongst the poor; and I enjoyed with credit and honour the remainder of my immense riches, which I had acquired with such labour and fatigue.

The Third Voyage

The agreeable life I led in my prosperity soon obliterated the remembrance of the dangers I had encountered in my two voyages; but as I was in the prime of life, I grew tired of passing my days in slothful repose; and banishing all thoughts of the perils I might have to face, I set off from Bagdad with some rich merchandise of the country, which I carried with me to Balsora. There I again embarked with other merchants. We made a long voyage, and touched at several ports, and by these means carried on a very profitable commerce.

One day, as we were sailing in the open sea, we were overtaken by a violent tempest, which made us lose our reckoning. The storm continued for several days, and drove us near an island, which the captain would gladly have avoided approaching, but we were under the necessity of casting anchor there. When the sails were furled, the captain told us that this region and some of the neighbouring isles were inhabited by hairy savages, who would come to attack us. He further declared that although they were only dwarfs, we must not attempt to make any resistance; for as their number was inconceivable, if we should happen to kill one they would pour upon us like locusts, and destroy us.

This account put the whole crew in a terrible consternation, and we were too soon convinced that the captain had spoken the truth. We saw coming towards us an innumerable multitude of hideous savages, entirely covered with red hair, and about two feet high. They threw themselves into the sea, and swam to the ship, which they soon completely surrounded. They began to climb the sides and ropes of the vessel with so much swiftness and agility that their feet scarcely seemed to touch them, and soon came swarming upon the deck.

You may imagine the situation we were in, not daring to defend ourselves, nor even to speak to these intruders, to endeavour to avert the impending danger. They unfurled the sails, cut the cable from the anchor, and after dragging the ship ashore, obliged us to disembark. Then they conveyed us to another island, from whence they had come. All voyagers carefully avoided this island, for the dismal reason you are going to hear; but our misfortune had led us there, and we were obliged to submit to our fate.

We left the shore, and penetrating further into the island, we found some fruits and herbs, which we ate to prolong our lives as much as possible; for we all expected to be sacrificed. As we walked on we perceived at some distance a large building, towards which we bent our steps. It was a large and lofty palace, with folding gates of ebony, which opened as we pushed them. We entered the courtyard, and saw facing us a vast apartment, with a vestibule, on one side of which was a large heap of human bones, while on the opposite side appeared a number of spits for roasting. We trembled at this spectacle, and fell on the earth, where we remained a considerable time, paralysed with fear and unable to move.

The sun was setting; and while we were in the piteous state I have described, the door of the apartment suddenly opened with a loud noise, and there entered a black man of frightful aspect, and as tall as a large palm-tree. In the middle of his forehead gleamed a single eye, red and fiery as a burning coal; his front teeth were long and sharp, and projected from his mouth, which was as wide as that of a horse, with the under lip hanging on his breast; his ears resembled those of an elephant, and covered his shoulders, and his long and curved nails were like the talons of an immense bird. At the sight of this hideous giant we all fainted, and remained a long time like dead men.

At last our senses returned, and we saw him seated under the vestibule, glaring at us with his piercing eye. When he had scanned us well, he advanced towards us, and stretching forth his hand to seize me, took me up by the poll, and turned me round every way, as a butcher would handle the head of a sheep.

After having well examined me, finding me meagre, and little more than skin and bone, he released me. He took up each of my companions in their turn, and examined them in the same manner, and as the captain was the fattest, ate him up. When he had finished his repast, he returned to the vestibule, where he lay down to sleep, and snored louder than thunder. He did not wake till the next morning; but we passed the night in the most agonizing suspense. When daylight returned the giant awoke, and went abroad, leaving us in the palace.

When we supposed him at some distance, we began to give vent to our lamentations; for the fear of disturbing the giant had kept us silent during the night. The palace resounded with our groans. Although there were many of us, and we had but one common enemy, the idea of delivering ourselves by his death never occurred to any one of us. But however difficult of accomplishment such an enterprise might have been, we ought to have made the attempt at once.

We deliberated on various methods of action, but could not determine on any; and submitting ourselves to the will of Allah, we passed the day in walking over the island, and eating what plants and fruit we could meet with, as we had done the preceding day. Towards evening we sought for some shelter in which to pass the night, but finding none we were obliged to return to the palace.

The giant duly returned to sup on one of our com-

Stretching forth his hand to seize me.

panions. After his hideous meal he fell asleep and snored till daybreak, when he arose and went out as before. Our situation appeared to be so hopeless that some of my comrades were on the point of throwing themselves into the sea, rather than be sacrificed by the horrible monster; and they advised the rest to follow their example; but one of the company thus addressed them: "We are forbidden to kill ourselves; and even were such an act permitted, would it not be more rational to endeavour to destroy the barbarous giant, who has destined us to such a cruel death?"

As I had already formed a project of that nature, I now communicated it to my fellow-sufferers, who approved of my design. "My friends," said I then, "you know that there is a great deal of wood on the seashore. If you will take my advice, we can make some rafts, and when they are finished we will leave them in a proper place till we can find an opportunity to make use of them. In the meantime we can put in execution the design I propose to you to rid ourselves of the giant. If my stratagem succeeds, we may wait here with patience till some vessel passes, by means of which we may quit this fatal isle; if, on the contrary, we fail, we shall have recourse to our rafts, and put to sea." My advice was approved by all; and we immediately built some rafts, each large enough to support three persons.

We returned to the palace towards evening, and the giant arrived a short time after us. Again one of our party was sacrificed to his inhuman appetite. But we were soon revenged on him for his cruelty. After he had finished his horrible meal, he laid himself down as usual to sleep. As soon as we heard him snore, nine of the most courageous amongst us, and myself, took each a spit, and heating the points red hot, thrust them into his eye, and blinded him.

The pain which the giant suffered made him groan hideously. He suddenly raised himself, and threw his arms about on all sides, to seize some one, and sacrifice him to his rage; but fortunately we had time to throw ourselves on the ground in places where he could not set his feet on us. After having sought us in vain, he at last found the door, and went out, bellowing with pain.

We quitted the palace immediately after the giant, and repaired to that part of the shore where our rafts lay. We set them afloat, and waited till daybreak before embarking on them, in case we should see the giant approach, with some guide to lead him to us; but we hoped that if he did not make his appearance by that time, and if his cries and groans, which now resounded through the air, ceased, we might suppose him dead; and in that case we proposed remaining in the island till we could obtain some safer mode of transport. But the sun had scarcely risen when we perceived our cruel enemy, accompanied by two giants nearly as huge as himself, who led him, and a great number of others, who walked very rapidly before him.

At this sight we immediately ran to our rafts and rowed away as fast as possible. The giants seeing this, provided themselves with large stones, hastened to the shore, and even ventured to their waists into the sea to hurl the stones at us, which they did so adroitly that they sank all the rafts excepting that I was upon. Thus I and two companions were the only men who escaped, the others being all drowned.

As we rowed with all our strength, we were soon beyond reach of the stones.

When we had gained the open sea, we were tossed about at the mercy of the winds and waves, and we passed that day and night in the most cruel suspense; but on the morrow we had the good fortune to be thrown on an island, where we landed with great joy.

We found some excellent fruit, which soon recruited our exhausted strength.

When night came on we went to sleep on the sea-shore; but were soon awakened by the noise made on the ground by the scales of an immense serpent, long as a palm-tree. It was so near to us that it devoured one of my companions, notwithstanding the efforts he made to extricate himself from its deadly grasp.

My other comrade and myself immediately took to flight. "O Allah!" I exclaimed, "what a horrible fate will be ours! Yesterday we were rejoicing at our escape from the cruelty of a giant and the fury of the waves, and to-day we are again terrified by a peril not less dreadful."

As we walked along, we remarked a large high tree, on which we proposed to pass the night, hoping we might there be in safety. We ate some fruit as we had done on the preceding day, and at the approach of night we climbed the tree. We soon heard the serpent, which came hissing to the foot of the tree; it raised itself against the trunk, and meeting with my companion, who had not climbed so high as I, it swallowed him and retired.

I remained on the tree till daybreak, when I came down, more dead than alive; indeed I could only anticipate the same fate.

I collected a great quantity of small wood and furze; and tying it in faggots, put it round the tree in a large circle, and tied some across to cover my head. I enclosed myself within this circle when the evening came on, and sat down with the dismal consolation that I had done all in my power to preserve my life. The serpent returned with the intention of devouring me, but he could not succeed, being prevented by the rampart I had formed. The whole night he was watching me; at last day returned, and the serpent retired, but I did not venture out of my fortress till the sun shone.

I was so fatigued with watching, as well as with the exertion of forming my retreat, and had suffered so much from the serpent's pestilential breath, that death appeared preferable to a repetition of such horror. I ran towards the sea with the intention of putting an end to my existence : but Allah pitied my condition ; and at the moment that I was going to throw myself into the sea, I descried a vessel at a great distance. I cried out with all my strength, and unfolded and waved my turban, to attract the attention of those on board. This had the desired effect ; all the crew saw me, and the captain sent a boat to bring me off.

As soon as I was on board, the merchants and seamen were eager to learn by what chance I had reached that desert island ; and after I had related to them all that had happened, they expressed their joy at my fortunate escape from so many perils. Then, as they supposed I must be in want of something to eat, they pressed upon me the best they had ; and the captain, observing that my clothes were torn, had the generosity to give me some of his.

We remained a considerable time at sea, and touched at several islands ; at length we landed on the Island of Salahat, where the merchants began to unload their goods to sell or exchange them. One day the captain called me to him, and said, "Brother, I have in my possession some goods which belonged to a merchant who was for some time on board my ship. As this merchant is dead, I am going to have them valued, that I may render an account of them to his heirs, should I ever meet them." The bales of which he spoke were already upon deck. He showed them to me, saying, "These are the goods. I wish you to take charge of them and traffic with them, and you shall receive for your trouble what is usually given in such cases." I consented, and thanked him for the opportunity he afforded me of employing myself.

The clerk of the ship registered all the bales with the names of the merchants to whom they belonged; when he asked the captain in what name he should register those destined for my charge, the captain replied, "In the name of Sindbad the Sailor." I could not hear my own name without emotion; and looking at the captain, I recognized in him the very same person who in my second voyage had left me on the island where I had fallen asleep by the side of a brook, and who had put to sea without waiting for me. I did not at first recollect him, so much was he changed in appearance since the time when I last saw him. As he thought me dead, it is not to be wondered at that he did not recognize me. "Captain," said I to him, "was the merchant to whom these things belonged called Sindbad?" "Yes," returned he, "that was his name; he was from Bagdad, and embarked on board my vessel at Balsora. One day, when we went ashore on an island for fresh water, he was left behind—I know not through what mistake. None of the crew noted his absence till four hours after, when the wind blew so fresh against us that it was impossible to return." "You believe him to be dead?" said I. "Most assuredly," replied the captain. "Then open your eyes," cried I, "and convince yourself that the same Sindbad whom you left on the desert island is now before you."

At these words the captain fixed his eyes on me, and after scrutinizing me very attentively, at last recollected me. "God be praised!" cried he, embracing me; "I am delighted that fortune has given me an opportunity of repairing my fault. Here are your goods, which I have preserved with care, and always had valued at every port I stopped at. I return them to you with the profit I have made on them."

From the Island of Salahat we went to another, where I provided myself with cloves, cinnamon, and other spices. At length, after a long voyage, we arrived at Balsora, from whence I came to Bagdad with so much wealth that I did not know the amount of it. I gave a great deal to the poor, and bought a considerable quantity of land.

The Fourth Voyage

THE pleasures and amusements in which I indulged, after my third voyage, had not charms sufficiently powerful to deter me from venturing on the sea again. I gave way to my love for traffic and adventure. I settled my affairs, and furnished myself with the merchandise suited to the places I intended to visit, and travelled towards Persia, some of the provinces of which I traversed, till at last I reached a port, where I embarked. We set sail, and touched at several points of the mainland, and at some of the Oriental islands; but one day we were surprised by a sudden squall of wind. Our sails were torn in a thousand pieces; and the vessel, becoming ungovernable, was driven on a sandbank and went to pieces. A great number of the crew perished, and the cargo was swallowed up by the waves.

With some other merchants and seamen I had the good fortune to get hold of a plank; we were all drawn by the strength of the current to an island that lay before us. We found some fruits and fresh water, which recruited our strength, and we lay down to sleep in the spot where the waves had thrown us. The next morning, when the sun was risen, we left the shore, and advancing into the island, perceived some habitations, towards which we bent our steps. When we drew near, a great number of blacks came forward, and, surrounding us, made us prisoners. They seemed to divide us among themselves, and then led us away to their houses.

Five of my comrades and myself were taken into the same place. Our captors made us sit down, and then offered us a certain herb, inviting us by signs to eat of it. My companions, without considering that the people did not eat of it themselves, only consulted their hunger and devoured it greedily. I had a sort of presentiment that this herb was given us for no good purpose, and refused even to taste it; and it was well I did so, for a short time after I perceived that my companions soon lost all sense of their position, and did not know what they said. The blacks then served us with some rice dressed with the oil of the cocoanut; and my comrades, not being sensible of what they did, ate ravenously of this mess. I likewise partook of it, but fed sparingly.

The blacks had given us the herb first to turn our brains, and thus banish the sorrow which our miserable condition would create, and the rice was given to fatten us. As these men were anthropophagi, they designed to feast on us when we were in good condition. My poor companions fell victims to the barbarous custom of these wretches, because they had lost their senses, and could not foresee their destiny. As for me, instead of fattening as the others had done, I grew thinner every day. The fear of death, which constantly haunted me, poisoned the food I took, and I fell into a state of languor, which was in the end very beneficial to me; for when the blacks had devoured my comrades, they were content to let me remain till I should be worth eating.

In the meantime I was allowed a great deal of liberty, and my actions were scarcely observed. This afforded me the opportunity one day of quitting the habitation of the blacks, and escaping. I walked for seven days, taking care to avoid those places continually which appeared inhabited, and living on cocoanuts, which afforded me both drink and food.

On the eighth day I came to the seashore; here I

saw some white people employed in gathering pepper, which grew very plentifully in that place. They came towards me as soon as they perceived me, and asked me in Arabic from whence I came.

Delighted to hear my native language once more, I readily satisfied their curiosity.

I remained with them until they had collected as much pepper as they chose to gather. They made me embark with them in the vessel which had conveyed them, and we soon reached another island, from whence they had come. My deliverers presented me to their king, who was a good prince. He had the patience to listen to the recital of my adventures, which astonished him ; and he ordered me some new clothes, and desired I might be taken care of. This island was very populous, and abounded in all sorts of articles for commerce. The pleasantness of my new quarters began to console me for my misfortunes, and the kindness of this generous prince made me completely happy. Indeed, I appeared to be his greatest favourite.

I remarked one thing which appeared to me very singular ; every one, the king not excepted, rode on horseback without saddle, bridle, or stirrups. I one day took the liberty to ask his majesty why such things were not used in his city ; he replied that he had never heard of the things of which I spoke.

I immediately went to a workman, and gave him a model from which to make the tree of a saddle. When he had executed his task, I myself covered the saddle-tree with leather richly embroidered in gold, and stuffed it with hair. I then applied to a locksmith, who made me a bit and some stirrups also, according to the patterns I gave him.

When these articles were completed, I presented them to the king, and tried them on one of his horses. The prince then mounted his steed, and was so pleased with its accoutrements, that he testified his approbation by making me considerable presents. I was then obliged to make several saddles for his ministers and the principal officers of his household, who all rewarded me with very rich and handsome gifts. I also made some for the wealthiest inhabitants of the town, by which I gained great reputation and credit.

As I constantly attended at court, the king said to me one day, " Sindbad, I love you ; and I know that all my subjects who have any knowledge of you entertain a high regard for you. I have one request to make, which you must not deny me." " O king," replied I, " there is nothing your majesty can command which I will not perform, to prove my obedience to your orders. Your power over me is absolute." " I wish you to marry," resumed the prince, " that you may have a tender tie to attach you to my dominions, and prevent your returning to your native country." As I did not dare to refuse the king's offer, he bestowed on me in marriage a lady of his court who was noble, beautiful, rich, and accomplished. After the ceremony of the nuptials I took up my abode in the house of my wife, and lived with her for some time in perfect harmony. Nevertheless I was discontented with my situation, and designed to make my escape at the first convenient opportunity, and return to Bagdad.

While I was thus meditating an escape, the wife of one of my neighbours, with whom I was very intimate, fell sick and died. I went to console the widower, and finding him in the deepest affliction, I said to him, " May God preserve you, and grant you a long life ! " " Alas ! " replied he, " I have only one hour to live." " Oh," resumed I, " do not suffer such dismal ideas to take possession of your mind ; I hope that I shall enjoy your friendship for many years." " I wish with all my heart," said he, " that your life may be of long duration. As for me, the die is cast, and this day I shall be buried with my wife : such is the custom which our ancestors have established in this island, and which is still inviolably observed; the husband is interred alive with his dead wife, and the living wife with the dead husband. Nothing can save me, and every one submits to this law."

Whilst he was relating to me this singularly barbarous custom, the bare idea of which filled me with horror, his relations, friends, and neighbours came to make arrangements for the funeral. They dressed the corpse of the woman in the richest attire, as on the day of her nuptials, and decorated her with all her jewels. They then placed her on an open bier, and the procession set out. The husband, dressed in mourning, went immediately after the body of his wife, and the relations followed. They bent their course towards a high mountain, and when they had reached the summit, a large stone was raised which covered a deep pit, and the body was let down into the pit in all its sumptuous apparel and ornaments. Thereupon the husband took his leave of his relations and friends, and without making any resistance suffered himself to be placed on a bier, with a jug of water and seven small loaves by his side; he was then let down into the pit as his wife had been. This mountain extended to a great distance, reaching even to the seashore, and the pit was very deep. When the ceremony was ended the stone was replaced, and the company retired. I need scarcely tell you that I was particularly affected by this ceremony. I could not avoid telling the king my sentiments on this subject. "O king," said I, "I cannot express my astonishment at the strange custom which exists in your dominions, of interring the living with the dead; in the whole course of my travels I never heard of so cruel a decree." "What can I do, Sindbad?" replied the king; "it is a law common to all ranks, and even I submit to it. I shall be interred alive with the queen, my consort, if she happens to die first." "Will your majesty allow me to ask," resumed I, "if strangers are obliged to conform to this custom?" "Certainly," said the king, "they are not exempt when they marry on the island."

I returned home thoughtful and sad. The fear that my wife might die before me, and that I must be interred with her, distressed me beyond measure. I soon had good reason to fear: she was taken dangerously ill, and died in a few days.

Thereupon I made my escape to the seashore. At the end of two or three days I perceived a vessel just sailing out of the harbour, and passing by the spot where I was. I made signals with my turban, and cried aloud with all my strength. They heard me on board, and dispatched the boat to fetch me. When the sailors inquired by what misfortune I had got in that place, I replied that I had been wrecked two days since on that shore, with all my merchandise. Fortunately for me these people did not stop to consider whether my story was probable, but, satisfied with my answer, they took me into the boat with my bales. When we had reached the vessel the captain never thought of doubting the tale of the wreck.

At length I arrived happily at Bagdad, with immense riches. To show my gratitude to Heaven for the mercies shown me, I spent a great deal in charity, giving money for the support of the mosques and for the relief of the poor.

The Fifth Voyage

THE pleasures I now enjoyed soon made me forget the perils I had endured; yet these delights were not sufficiently attractive to prevent my forming the resolution of venturing a fifth time on the sea. I again provided myself with merchandise and sent it overland to the nearest seaport. Unwilling to trust again to a captain, and wishing to have a vessel of my own, I built and equipped one at my own expense. As soon as it was ready I loaded it and embarked; and as I had not sufficient cargo of my own to fill it, I received on board several merchants of different nations, with their goods.

We hoisted our sails to the first fair wind, and put to sea. After sailing for a considerable time, the first place we stopped at was a desert island, where we found the egg of a roc, as large as that of which I spoke on a former occasion. It contained a small roc, almost hatched; for its beak had begun to pierce through the shell. The merchants who were with me broke the egg with hatchets, cut out the young roc piece by piece, and roasted it. I had seriously advised them not to touch the egg, but they would not attend to me.

They had scarcely finished their meal, when two immense clouds appeared in the air at a considerable distance from us. The captain knew by experience what it was, and cried out that the father and mother of the young roc were coming. He warned us to re-embark as quickly as possible, to escape the danger which threatened us. We took his advice, and set sail immediately.

The two rocs approached, uttering the most terrible screams, which they redoubled on finding their egg broken and their young one destroyed. Designing to revenge themselves they flew away towards the mountains from whence they came, and disappeared for some time, while we used all diligence to sail away, and prevent what nevertheless befell us.

They soon returned, and we perceived that each had an enormous piece of rock in its claws. When they were exactly over our ship they stopped, and, suspending themselves in the air, one of them let fall the piece of rock it held. The skill of the pilot, who suddenly turned the vessel, prevented our being crushed by its fall; but the stone fell close to us into the sea, in which it made such a chasm that we could almost see the bottom. The other bird, unfortunately for us, let its piece of rock fall so directly on the ship that it broke and split our vessel into a thousand pieces. The sailors and passengers were all crushed to death or drowned. I myself was under water for some time; but rising again to the surface, I had the good fortune to seize a piece of the wreck. Swimming sometimes with one hand and sometimes with the other, still clutching the plank I had seized, I at length reached an island where the shore was very steep. But I contrived to clamber up the beach, and got on land.

I seated myself on the grass to recover from my fatigue. When I had rested I rose, and advanced into the island to reconnoitre the ground. This region seemed to me like a delicious garden. Wherever I turned my eyes I saw beautiful trees, some loaded with green, others with ripe fruits, and transparent streams meandering between them. I ate of the fruits, which I found excellent, and quenched my thirst at the inviting brooks.

When night came, I lay down on the grass in a convenient spot. But I did not sleep an hour at a time; and I passed the greater part of the night in lamenting my fate, and reproaching myself for the imprudence of venturing from home, where I had possessed everything that could make me comfortable. These reflections led me so far, that I meditated the idea of taking my own life; but day returned with its cheerful light, and dissipated my gloomy thoughts. I rose, and walked amongst the trees, though not without some degree of trepidation.

When I had advanced a little way into the island, I perceived an old man, who appeared very decrepit. He was seated on the bank of a little rivulet. I approached and saluted him: he replied only by a slight inclination of the head. I asked him what he was doing, but instead of answering, he made signs to me to take him on my shoulders, and cross the brook, making me understand that he wanted to gather some fruit.

I supposed he wished me to render him this piece of service; and taking him on my back, I waded through the stream. When I had reached the other side, I stooped, and desired him to alight; instead of complying, this old man, who appeared to me so decrepit, nimbly threw his legs, which I now saw were covered with a skin like a cow's, over my neck, and seated himself fast on my shoulders, at the same time squeezing my throat so violently that I expected to be strangled; this alarmed me so much that I fainted away.

Notwithstanding my condition, the old man kept his place on my neck, and only loosened his hold sufficiently to allow me to breathe. When I had somewhat recovered, he pushed one of his feet against my stomach, and kicking my side with the other, obliged me to get up. He then made me walk under some trees, and forced me to gather and eat the fruit we found. He never quitted his hold during the day; and when I wished to rest at night, he laid himself on the ground with me, always clinging to my neck. He never failed to awaken me in the morning, and then he made me get up and walk, kicking me all the time. Imagine how miserable it was to me to bear this burden, without the possibility of getting rid of it.

One day I chanced to find on the ground several dried gourds, which had fallen from the tree that bore them. I took a large one, and after having cleared it well, I squeezed into it the juice of several bunches of grapes, which the island produced in great abundance. When I had filled the gourd, I placed it in a particular spot, and some days after returned with the old man. On tasting the contents I found the

Taking him on my back, I waded through the stream.

juice converted into excellent wine, which for a little time made me forget the ills that weighed upon me. The drink gave me new vigour, and raised my spirits so high that I began to sing and dance as I went along.

Perceiving the effect this beverage had taken on my spirits, the old man made signs to me to let him taste it. I gave him the gourd, and the liquor pleased his taste so well that he drank it to the last drop. There was enough to inebriate him, and the fumes of the wine very soon rose into his head ; he then began to sing after his own manner, and to sway to and fro on my shoulders. Finding he no longer held me tight, I threw him on the ground, where he lay motionless. I then took a large stone and crushed him to death.

I was much rejoiced at having got rid of this old man ; and I walked towards the seashore, where I met some people who belonged to a vessel which had anchored there to get fresh water. They were very much astonished at seeing me and hearing the account of my adventure. "You had fallen," said they, "into the hands of the Old Man of the Sea, and you are the first of his captives whom he has not strangled. This island is famous for the number of persons he has killed. The sailors and merchants who land here never dare approach except in a strong body."

After giving me this information, they took me to their ship, whose captain received me with the greatest politeness, when he heard what had befallen me. He set sail, and in a few days we anchored in the harbour of a large city, where the houses were built of stone.

One of the merchants of the ship had contracted a friendship for me. He entreated me to accompany him, and conducted me to the quarters set apart for foreign merchants. He gave me a large sack, and then introduced me to some people belonging to the city, who were also furnished with sacks. He requested them to take me with them to gather cocoanuts, and said to me: "Go, follow them, and do as they do; and do not stray from them, for your life will be in danger if you leave them." He gave me provisions for the day, and I set off with my new friends.

We arrived at a large forest of tall straight trees, the trunks of which were so smooth that it was impossible to climb up to the branches where the fruit grew. These were all cocoanut trees; and we proposed to knock down the fruit and fill our sacks. On entering the forest, we saw a great number of monkeys of all sizes, who fled at our approach, and ran up the trees with surprising agility. The merchants who were with me collected stones, and threw them with great force at the monkeys, who had reached some of the highest branches. I did the same, and soon perceived that these animals were aware of our proceedings. They gathered the cocoanuts, and threw them down at us with gestures which plainly showed their anger and spite. By this contrivance we obtained nuts enough to fill our sacks—a thing utterly impracticable by any other method.

When we had collected a sufficient quantity, we returned to the city, where the merchant who had sent me to the forest gave me the value of the cocoanuts I had brought. At last I had collected such a quantity of cocoanuts, that I sold them for a considerable sum.

The vessel in which I came had sailed with the merchants, who had loaded it with the cocoanuts they had purchased. I waited for the arrival of another, which shortly after came into harbour to take in a cargo of the same description. I sent on board all the cocoanuts which belonged to me; and when the ship was ready to sail I took leave of the merchant to whom I was under so much obligation.

We set sail, and steered towards the Island of Comari. In this island I exchanged all my cocoanuts for aloe-wood; and I then, like the other merchants, engaged on my own account in a pearl fishery, in which I employed many divers. I had soon collected by these means a great number of very large and perfect gems, with which I joyfully put to sea, and arrived safely at Balsora, from whence I returned to Bagdad. Here I sold for a large sum the aloes and pearls which I had brought with me. I bestowed a tenth part of my profit in charity, as I had done on my return from every former voyage, and endeavoured by all kinds of relaxation to recover from my fatigues.

The Sixth Voyage

I feel convinced, my friends, that you all wonder how I could be tempted again to expose myself to the caprice of fortune, after I had undergone so many perils in my other voyages. I am astonished myself when I think of it. It was fate alone that impelled me, at the expiration of a year, to venture a sixth time on the changeful sea.

Instead of taking the route of the Persian Gulf, I passed through some of the provinces of Persia and the Indies, and arrived at a seaport, where I embarked in a good ship, with a captain who was determined to make a long voyage. Long indeed it proved, but at the same time unfortunate; for the captain and pilot lost their way, and did not know how to steer. They at length found out where we were; but we had no reason to rejoice at the discovery, for the captain astonished us all by suddenly quitting his post, and uttering the most lamentable cries. He threw his turban on the deck, tore his beard and beat his head, like a man distraught. We asked the reason of this violent grief, and he replied: "I am obliged to announce to you that we are in the greatest peril. A rapid current is hurrying the ship along, and we shall all perish in less than a quarter of an hour. Pray

Allah to deliver us from this dreadful danger, for nothing can save us unless He takes pity on us." He then gave orders for setting the sails; but the ropes broke in the attempt, and the ship became entirely unmanageable, and was dashed by the current against a rock, where it split and went to pieces. Nevertheless we had time to disembark our provisions, as well as the most valuable part of the cargo.

When we were assembled on the shore the captain said: "God's will be done! Here we may dig our graves, and bid each other an eternal farewell; for we are in a place so desolate that no one who ever was cast on this shore returned to his own home." This speech increased our distress.

The mountain, at the foot of which we were, formed one side of a large and long island. The coast was covered with the remains of vessels which had been wrecked on it; and the scattered heaps of bones, which lay strewn about in every direction, convinced us of the dreadful fact that many lives had been lost in this spot. Almost incredible quantities of merchandise of every sort were heaped up on the shore.

In every other region it is common for a number of small rivers to discharge themselves into the sea; but here a large river of fresh water takes its course from the sea, and runs along the coast to a dark cave, the entrance to which is extremely high and wide. The most remarkable feature in this place is, that the mountain is composed of rubies, crystals, and other precious stones. Here, too, a kind of pitch, or bitumen, distils from the rock into the sea, and the fishes which eat it return it in the form of ambergris, which the waves leave on the shore.

To complete the description of this place, I have only to mention that it is impossible for a ship to avoid being dragged thither, if it comes within a certain distance. If a sea breeze blows, the wind assists the current, and there is no remedy; and if the wind comes from land, the high mountain impedes its effect, and causes a calm, which allows the current full force, and then it whirls the ship against the coast, and dashes it to pieces as it shattered ours. In addition to this, the mountain is so steep that it is impossible to reach the summit or indeed to escape by any means.

We remained on the shore, quite heartbroken, expecting to die. We had divided our provisions equally, so that each person lived a longer or a shorter time according to the manner in which he husbanded his portion.

Those who died first were interred by the others. I had the dismal office of burying my last companion; for, besides managing my share of provisions with more care than the rest had shown in the consumption of theirs, I had also a store which I kept concealed from my comrades. Nevertheless, when I buried the last of them, I had so little food left that I imagined I must soon follow him.

But Allah still had pity on me, and inspired me with the thought of going to the river which lost itself in the recesses of the cave. I examined the stream with great attention; and it occurred to me that, as the river ran under ground, it must in its course come out to daylight again. I therefore conjectured that if I constructed a raft, and placed myself on it, the current of the water might perhaps bring me to some inhabited country. If I perished, it was but altering the manner of my death; but if, on the contrary, I got safely out of this fatal place, I should not only escape the cruel death by which my companions perished, but might also meet with some fresh opportunity of enriching myself.

These reflections made me work at my raft with fresh vigour. I made it of thick pieces of wood and great cables, of which there was abundance on the coast. I tied them closely together, and formed a strong framework. When it was completed, I placed on it a cargo of rubies, emeralds, ambergris, crystal, and also some gold and silver stuffs. When I had stowed all these things so as to balance the raft, I embarked on my vessel, guiding it with two little oars which I had provided; and driving along with the current, I resigned myself to the will of God.

As soon as I was under the vault of the cavern I lost the light of day; the current carried me on, but I was unable to discern its course. I rowed for some days in this obscurity without ever perceiving the least ray of light. During this time I consumed no more of my provisions than was absolutely necessary to sustain nature; but, frugal as I was, they came to an end. I then fell into a sweet sleep. I cannot tell whether I slept long; but when I awoke I was surprised to find myself in an open country, near a bank of the river, to which my raft was fastened, and in the midst of a large concourse of blacks. I rose and saluted them; they spoke to me, but I could not understand them.

At this moment I felt so transported with joy that I could scarcely believe myself awake. Being at length convinced that my deliverance was not a dream, I pronounced aloud these Arabic words: "Invoke the Almighty, and He will come to thy assistance. Close thine eyes, and while thou sleepest Allah will change thy fortune from evil to good."

One of the blacks, who understood Arabic, hearing me speak thus, advanced towards me, and spoke as follows: "Brother, be not surprised at seeing us; we live in this country, and we come hither to-day to this river, which flows from the neighbouring mountain, to water our fields by cutting canals to admit the water. We observed that the current bore something along, and we immediately ran to the bank to see what it was, and perceived this raft; one of us instantly swam to it, and guided it to shore. We fastened it as you see, and were waiting for you to wake. We entreat you to relate to us your history, which must be very extraordinary; tell us from whence you came." I requested him first to give me some food, and promised to satisfy their curiosity when I had eaten.

They produced several kinds of meat, and when I had satisfied my hunger I related to them all that had happened to me. They appeared to listen to my story with great admiration. As soon as I had finished my history, their interpreter told me that I had astonished them with my relation, and I must go myself to the king, to recount my adventures; for they were of too extraordinary a nature to be repeated by any one but by the person himself to whom they had happened. I replied that I was ready to do anything they wished. The blacks then sent for a horse, which arrived shortly after; they placed me on it, and while some walked by my side to show me the way, certain stalwart fellows hauled the raft out of the water, and followed me, carrying it on their shoulders, with the bales of rubies.

We went together to the city in Serendid, for this was the name of the island; and the blacks presented me to their king. I approached the throne on which he was seated, and saluted him in the manner adopted towards sovereigns in India, namely, by prostrating myself at his feet and kissing the earth. The king bade me rise; and receiving me with an affable air, he seated me by his side. He first asked me my name. I replied that I was called Sindbad, surnamed the Sailor, from having made several voyages; and ended, that I was a citizen of Bagdad. "How then," said the monarch, "came you into my dominions, and from whence have you arrived?"

I concealed nothing from the king, but related to him all you have heard me tell; he was so pleased with it that he ordered the history of my adventures to be written in letters of gold, that it might be preserved amongst the archives of his kingdom. The raft was then produced, and the bales were opened in his presence. He admired the aloe-wood and ambergris, but above all the rubies and emeralds, as he had none in his treasury equal to them in value.

Perceiving that he examined my valuables with pleasure, I prostrated myself before him, and took the liberty of saying: "O king, not only am I your servant, but the cargo of my raft also is at your disposal, if your majesty will do me the honour of accepting it." The king smiled, and replied that he did not desire to possess anything which belonged to me; that instead of diminishing my riches, he should add to them, and that when I left his dominions I should carry with me proofs of his liberality. I could only reply to this by praying for his prosperity and by praising his generosity.

He ordered one of his officers to attend me, and placed some of his own servants at my disposal. The officers faithfully fulfilled the charge with which they were entrusted, and conveyed all the bales to the place appointed for my lodging. I went every day at certain hours to pay my court to the king, and employed the rest of my time in seeing the city.

The Island of Serendid is situated exactly under the equinoctial line, so that the days and nights are of equal length. The principal town is situated at the extremity of a beautiful valley, formed by a mountain which is in the middle of the island, and which is by far the highest in the world; it is discernible at sea at a distance of three days' sail. I made a devotional journey up the mountain, to the spot where Adam was placed on his banishment from Paradise; and I had the curiosity to ascend the summit.

When I came back to the city I entreated the king to grant me permission to return to my native country, and he acceded to my request in the most obliging and honourable manner. He commanded me to receive a rich present from his treasury ; and when I went to take my leave, he placed in my hands another gift, still more considerable than the first, and at the same time gave me a letter for the Commander of the Believers, our sovereign lord, saying : " I request you to deliver for me this letter and this present to the Caliph Haroun al-Raschid, and to assure him of my friendship." I took the present and the letter with the greatest respect, and promised his majesty that I would most punctually execute the orders with which he was pleased to honour me. Before I embarked the king sent for the captain and the merchants with whom I was to sail, and charged them to pay me all possible attention.

The letter of the King of Serendid was written on the skin of a certain animal highly prized in that country on account of its rareness ; it is of a yellowish colour. The letter itself was in characters of azure, and it contained the following words in the Indian language :—

" THE KING OF THE INDIES, WHO IS PRECEDED BY A THOUSAND ELEPHANTS, WHO LIVES IN A PALACE THE ROOF OF WHICH GLITTERS WITH THE LUSTRE OF A HUNDRED THOUSAND RUBIES, AND WHO POSSESSES IN HIS TREASURY TWENTY THOUSAND CROWNS ENRICHED WITH DIAMONDS, TO THE CALIPH HAROUN AL-RASCHID.

" Although the present that we send you be inconsiderable, yet receive it as a brother and a friend, in consideration of the friendship we bear you in our heart. We feel happy in having an opportunity of testifying this friendship to you. We ask the same share in your affections, as we hope we deserve it, being of a rank equal to that you hold. We salute you as a brother. Farewell."

The present comprised, firstly, a vase made of one single ruby, pierced and worked into a cup of half a foot in height and an inch thick, filled with fine round pearls, all weighing half a drachm each ; secondly, the skin of a serpent, which had scales as large as an ordinary coin, and which possessed the peculiar virtue of preserving those who lay on it from all disease ; thirdly, fifty thousand drachms of the most exquisite aloe-wood, together with thirty pieces of camphor as large as pistachio-nuts ; and lastly, a female slave of the most enchanting beauty, whose clothes were covered with jewels.

The ship set sail, and after a long but fortunate voyage, we landed at Balsora, from whence I returned to Bagdad. The first thing I did after my arrival was to execute the commission I had been entrusted with. I took the letter of the King of Serendid and presented myself at the gate of the Commander of the Faithful, followed by the beautiful slave and some of my family, who carried the presents which had been committed to my care. I mentioned the reason of my appearance there, and was immediately conducted to the throne of the caliph. I prostrated myself at his feet, explained my errand, and gave him the letter and the present. When he read the contents, he inquired of me whether it was true that the King of Serendid was as rich and powerful as he reported himself to be in his letter.

I prostrated myself a second time, and when I arose, replied, " Commander of the Faithful, I can assure your majesty that the King of Serendid does not exaggerate his riches and grandeur ; I have seen his wealth and magnificence. The splendour of his palace cannot fail to excite admiration. When this prince wishes to appear in public, a throne is prepared for him on the back of an elephant ; on this he sits, and proceeds between two rows, composed of his ministers, favourites, and others belonging to the court. Before him, on the same elephant, sits an officer with a golden lance in his hand; and behind the throne another stands with a pillar of gold, on the top of which is placed an emerald about half a foot long and an inch thick. The king is preceded by a guard of a thousand men habited in silk and gold stuffs, and mounted on elephants richly caparisoned.

"While the king is on his march, the officer who sits before him on the elephant proclaims from time to time with a loud voice: 'This is the great monarch, the powerful Sultan of the Indies, whose palace is covered with a hundred thousand rubies, and who possesses twenty thousand diamond crowns. This is the crowned monarch, greater than ever was Solima, or the great Mihragè.'

"After he has pronounced these words, the officer who stands behind the throne cries, in his turn: 'This monarch, who is so great and powerful, must die, must die, must die!' The first officer then resumes: 'Glory be to Him who lives and dies not.'"

The caliph was satisfied with my discourse, and dismissed me with a rich present.

The Seventh and Last Voyage

On my return from my sixth voyage, I absolutely relinquished all thoughts of ever venturing again on the seas. I was past the prime of life, and at an age which required rest; and besides this, I had sworn never more to expose myself to the perils I had so often experienced. I prepared therefore to enjoy my life in quiet and repose.

One day one of my servants came to tell me that an officer of the caliph wanted to speak to me. I left the table, and went to him. "The caliph," said he, "has ordered me to acquaint you that he wishes to see you." I followed the officer to the palace, and he presented me to the prince, whom I saluted by prostrating myself at his feet. "Sindbad," said the caliph, "I want you to do me a service. You must go once more to the King of Serendid with my answer and presents; it is but right that I should make him a proper return for the civility he has shown me."

This order of the caliph's was a thunderbolt to me. "Commander of the Faithful," replied I, "I am ready to execute anything with which your majesty may desire to entrust me; but I humbly entreat you to consider that I am worn down with the unspeakable fatigues I have undergone. I have even made a vow never to leave Bagdad." I then took occasion to relate the long history of my adventures, which he had the patience to listen to attentively. When I had done speaking, the caliph said: "I confess that these are extraordinary adventures; nevertheless they must not prevent your making the voyage I propose, for my sake: it is only to the Island of Serendid. Execute the commission I entrust you with, and then you will be at liberty to return. But you must go; for you must be sensible that it would be highly derogatory to my dignity if I remained under obligation to the king of that island."

As I plainly saw that the caliph had resolved on my going, I signified to him that I was ready to obey his commands. He seemed much pleased, and ordered me a thousand sequins to pay the expenses of the voyage.

In a few days I was prepared for my departure; and as soon as I had received the presents from the caliph, together with a letter written with his own hand, I set off and took the route of Balsora, from whence I embarked. After a pleasant voyage, I arrived at the Island of Serendid. I immediately acquainted the ministers with the commission I had come to execute, and begged them to procure me an audience as soon as possible.

The monarch immediately recollected me, and evinced great joy at my visit. " Welcome, Sindbad," said he. " I assure you I have often thought of you since your departure. Blessed be this day in which I see you again ! " After thanking the king for his kindness, I delivered the letter and the presents of the caliph, which he received with every mark of satisfaction and pleasure.

The caliph sent him a complete bed of gold tissue, estimated at a thousand sequins, fifty robes of a very rare stuff, a hundred more of white linen, the finest that could be procured from Cairo, Suez, Cufa, and Alexandria ; a bed of crimson, and another of a different pattern and colour. Besides this, he sent a vase of agate, greater in width than in depth, of the thickness of a finger—on the sides there was sculptured in bas-relief a man kneeling on the ground, and in his hand a bow and arrow with which he was going to shoot at a lion ; and a richly ornamented table, which was supposed from tradition to have belonged to the great Solomon. The letter of the caliph ran thus :—

" HEALTH, IN THE NAME OF THE SOVEREIGN GUIDE OF THE RIGHT ROAD, TO THE POWERFUL AND HAPPY SULTAN, FROM THE PART OF ABDALLA HAROUN AL-RASCHID, WHOM GOD HAS PLACED ON THE THRONE OF HONOUR, AFTER HIS ANCESTORS OF HAPPY MEMORY.

" We have received your letter with joy ; and we send you this, proceeding from our council, the garden of superior minds. We hope that in casting your eyes over it you will perceive our good intention, and think it agreeable. Farewell ! "

The King of Serendid was rejoiced to find that the caliph reciprocated his own feelings of friendship. Soon after this audience I requested another, that I might ask leave to depart, which I had some difficulty in obtaining. At length I succeeded, and the king at my departure ordered me a very handsome present. I re-embarked immediately, intending to return to Bagdad; but had not the good fortune to arrive as soon as I expected, for Allah had disposed it otherwise.

Three or four days after we had set sail we were attacked by corsairs, who easily made themselves masters of our vessel. Some persons in the ship attempted to make resistance, but their boldness cost them their lives. I and all those who had the prudence to submit quietly to the corsairs were made slaves. After they had stripped us, and clothed us in rags instead of our own garments, they bent their course towards a distant island, where they sold us.

I was purchased by a rich merchant, who brought me to his house, gave me food to eat, and clothed me as a slave. Some days after, as he was not well informed who I was, he asked me if I knew any trade. I replied that I was not an artisan but a merchant by profession, and that the corsairs who had sold me had taken from me all I possessed. "But tell me," said he, "do you think you could shoot with a bow and arrow?" I replied, that I had practised that sport in my youth, and that I had not entirely lost my skill. He then gave me a bow and some arrows, and making me mount behind him on an elephant he took me to a vast forest at the distance of some hours' journey from the city. We went a great way into the forest, till the merchant came to a spot where he wished to stop, and made me alight. Then he showed me a large tree. "Get up in that tree," said he, "and shoot at the elephants that pass under it; for there are many of those animals in this forest: if one should fall, come and let me know." Thereupon he left me some provisions, and returned to the city. I remained in the tree on the watch the whole night.

During the first night no elephants came; but the next day, as soon as the sun had risen, a great number made their appearance. I shot many arrows at them, and at last one fell. The others immediately retired, and left me at liberty to go and inform my master of the success I had met with. To reward me for this good intelligence, he regaled me with an excellent repast, and praised my skill. We then returned together to the forest, where we dug a pit to bury the elephant I had killed. It was my master's intention to let the carcass rot in the earth, and then to take possession of the teeth.

I continued my new occupation for two months; and not a day passed in which I did not kill an elephant. One morning, when I was waiting for some elephants to pass, I perceived, to my great astonishment, that, instead of traversing the forest as usual, they stopped, then came towards me with a terrible noise, and in such numbers that the ground trembled under their footsteps. They approached the tree in which I had stationed myself, and surrounded it with their trunks extended, and their eyes all fixed upon me. At this surprising spectacle I remained motionless, and was so unnerved that my bow and arrows fell from my hands.

My terror was not groundless. After the elephants had viewed me for some time, one of the largest twisted his trunk round the body of the tree, and shook it with so much violence that he tore it up by the roots and threw it on the ground. I fell with the tree; but the animal took me up with his trunk, and placed me on his shoulders, where I lay extended more dead than alive. The huge beast now put himself at the head of his companions, who followed him in a troop; and he carried me to a retired spot, where he set me down, and then went away with the rest.

At length, after I had waited some time, seeing no other elephants, I arose, and perceived that I was on a little hill of some extent, entirely covered with bones and teeth of elephants. I now felt certain that this

The animal took me up with his trunk.

was their cemetery or place of burial, and that they had brought me hither to show it me, that I might desist from destroying them, as I took their lives merely for the sake of possessing their teeth. I did not stay long on the hill, but turned my steps towards the city, and, after walking for a day and a night, at last arrived at my master's.

As soon as my master saw me, he exclaimed: "Ah, poor Sindbad! I was anxious to know what could have become of you. I have been to the forest, and found a tree newly torn up by the roots, and your bow and arrows on the ground. After seeking you everywhere in vain, I despaired of ever seeing you again. Pray tell me what has happened to you, and by what fortunate chance you are still alive." I satisfied his curiosity; and the following day he accompanied me to the hill, and with great joy convinced himself of the truth of my story. We loaded the elephant on which we had come with as many teeth as it could carry, and when we returned my master thus addressed me: "Brother—for I will no longer treat you as a slave, after the discovery you have imparted to me, and which cannot fail to enrich me—may God pour on you all sorts of blessings and prosperity! Before Him I give you your liberty. The elephants of our forest destroy annually a great number of slaves, whom we send in search of ivory. Whatever advice we give them, they are sure, sooner or later, to lose their lives by the wiles of these animals. Providence has delivered you from their fury, and has conferred this mercy on you alone. It is a sign that you are especially protected, and that you are required in this world to be of use to mankind. You have procured me a surprising advantage: we have not hitherto been able to get ivory without risking the lives of our slaves, and now our whole city will be enriched by your means. I intend to give you considerable presents. I might easily move the whole city to join me in making your fortune, but that is a pleasure I will keep for myself alone."

To this obliging discourse I replied: "Master, may Allah preserve you! The liberty you grant me acquits you of all obligation towards me; and the only recompense I desire for the service I have had the good fortune to perform for you and the inhabitants of your city, is permission to return to my country." "Well," he replied, "the monsoon will soon bring us vessels, which come to be laden with ivory. I will then send you away, with a sufficient sum to pay your expenses home." I again thanked him for the liberty he had given me. I remained with him till the season for the monsoon, and during this interval we made frequent excursions to the hill, and filled his magazines with ivory. All the other merchants in the city filled their warehouses likewise, for my discovery did not long remain a secret.

The ships at length arrived, and my master, having chosen the one in which I was to embark, loaded it with ivory, making over half the cargo to me. He did not omit an abundance of provisions for my voyage, and he also obliged me to accept some rare curiosities of his country. After I had thanked him, I embarked.

We touched at several islands to procure supplies. Our vessel having originally sailed from a port of the mainland of India, we touched there; and, fearful of the dangers of the sea to Balsora, I took out of the ship the ivory which belonged to me, and resolved to continue my journey by land. I sold my share of the cargo for a large sum of money, and purchased a variety of curious things for presents: when I had finished my preparations, I joined a caravan of merchants. I remained a long time on the road, and suffered a great deal; but all these fatigues being at last surmounted, I arrived happily at Bagdad. I went immediately and presented myself to the caliph, and gave him an account of my embassy. The caliph told me that my long absence had occasioned him some uneasiness, but that he always hoped that Allah would not forsake me.

I retired well satisfied with the presents and honours he conferred on me; and then finally resigned myself entirely to my family, my relations, and friends.

TWICE IS TOO MUCH

OR, HOW THE CALIPH WAS TRICKED

Abu Hassan was a great favourite of the Caliph Haroun al-Raschid and his princess, Zobeide, who showed their favour towards him by giving him the beautiful slave Nouz-hatoul-aonadat for his wife.

For a year after their marriage Abu and his bride lived in great luxury, consuming the nicest and choicest meats, the most exquisite wines and all manner of delicious confectionery. At the end of a year they not only owed much money to the confectioner, but had spent all their wealth. They were ashamed to ask the Caliph and Zobeide for more money, as they had already received many rich gifts from them. They sold what treasures they had left, paid the confectioner his bill, and then sat down to think out how they could live. At first they were sorely embarrassed, but at length Abu said, "I have thought of a trick which will cheat money out of the Caliph and Zobeide, and will, moreover, so amuse them that we shall stand higher in favour than ever before. If only you will help me, Nouz-hatoul, our fortune is made!" He then told his wife of his plan. "We must die!" he said. "Die yourself," retorted Nouz-hatoul; "I shall not." "You are mistaken," said Abu. "We only *pretend*. First," he went on, "I will pretend to be dead, and you must go to Zobeide, pretending to be in great sorrow for my decease. The princess will be so moved that she will give you money to pay the expenses of the funeral, and also a piece of brocade to cover my body with. When you come back, you will then pretend to be dead, and I shall go with a similar tale to the Caliph and, I hope, receive similar gifts from him." Nouz-hatoul was so delighted with the plan that they at once began to carry it out.

Abu stretched himself on a carpet in the middle of the room, with his feet towards Mecca, and his wife wrapped him round with a sheet. She then pulled her hair about her face, and crying very loudly went off to the apartments of Zobeide, the princess.

She was at once admitted, and with many sobs and groans and beatings of the breast, told the story of her husband's sudden death. The princess was overcome with pity, and ordered the treasurer to give the poor widow a hundred pieces of gold and a piece of rich brocade. Nouz-hatoul thanked the princess and, appearing much comforted, went home. Laughing, she ran up to her husband and bade him rise and see how successful she had been.

Abu at once told his wife to lie down in his place, and promised that he would get at least as much out of the Caliph as she had won from the princess. And he did; for in less than an hour he came back with a hundred pieces of gold and a piece of rich brocade, given him by the Caliph to bury his "dead" wife with.

Now it had happened that when Abu went sorrowing to the Caliph with his tale of woe, that the Caliph was holding a council; but directly it was over he went to Zobeide's apartments to sympathize with her in the loss of her favourite slave Nouz-hatoul.

The princess was extremely puzzled. "You are mistaken," she said; "it is Abu who is dead. His wife was here not an hour since, sorrowtul indeed, but well in health." The Caliph laughed. "Madam," he answered, "this is a strange piece of obstinacy. Abu is alive, and came to me a little while since to tell me of his wife's decease." "I tell you Nouz-hatoul is *not* dead," replied Zobeide angrily. "It is Abu who is dead, and you will never make me believe otherwise." So the quarrel continued. Each was so sure that the Caliph wagered his garden of pleasures against Zobeide's palace of paintings that he was right.

At length the Caliph decided to settle the matter by sending his slave Mesrour to Abu's house to see what had really happened. Abu and his wife had expected such a visit, and were ready. Nouz-hatoul lay down as though dead, and when Mesrour entered he saw Abu weeping and moaning for his "dead" wife, who lay still under her winding-sheet. Mesrour said a few words of sympathy, and returned to the Caliph with the news that it was Nouz-hatoul who was dead.

Zobeide flew into a terrible rage. "I will never believe it," she cried, and at once sent off an old nurse to bring evidence that it was Abu who was dead.

Again Abu and his wife were on the look-out; so when the nurse entered their house she saw Abu lying still and "dead" under the piece of rich brocade, and the "widow" with tear-stained face moaning and weeping above the "corpse." The nurse returned gleefully to her mistress. "It is certain that Abu is dead, and Nouz-hatoul alive," she said.

Mesrour violently contradicted her, and laid a wager that he was right, while the quarrel between the Caliph and the princess came no nearer to being settled than it was before.

Finally the Caliph determined to go himself to ascertain the truth; so he and Zobeide, with Mesrour, the nurse and all their train, set off for Abu's house.

When she saw them coming, Nouz-hatoul was alarmed, but Abu was ready with a plan. "We will *both* be dead," he said. So when the Caliph and Zobeide entered there lay two corpses, each under a rich brocade, on the carpet in the middle of the floor.

"I have won," cried the princess. "Abu died

first, and his wife has since died of grief for him." "Not so," answered the Caliph; "Nouz-hatoul died first, and Abu died later." Then Mesrour and the nurse began quarrelling again, until the Caliph sat down near the corpses and said, "I will give a thousand pieces of gold to him that tells me which of these two died first."

There was a movement under Abu's pall and a voice said, "Give them to me, Commander of the Faithful, for I died first." Almost at once Nouz-hatoul leaped up and prostrated herself at Zobeide's feet, asking for pardon.

The Caliph and his princess burst out laughing at this unravelling of the mystery. Abu then told him the true story of the plot, and so delighted was the Caliph that he not only gave Abu the thousand pieces of gold, but held him in high favour from that time onward.

THE HISTORY OF CAMARALZAMAN, PRINCE OF THE ISLE OF THE CHILDREN OF KHALEDAN, AND OF BADOURA, PRINCESS OF CHINA

There was once an island, called the Isle of the Children of Khaledan. It was governed by a king, named Schah-zaman, who esteemed himself the most fortunate of men. One thing only disturbed his happiness; which was, that he was advanced in years and had no children. One day he had complained bitterly of this misfortune to his grand vizier, and asked him if he knew any remedy for it.

That wise minister replied, " If what your majesty requires of me had depended on the ordinary rules of human wisdom, you had soon had an answer to your satisfaction; but my experience and knowledge fall far short of your question. It is to God alone we can apply in cases of this kind. In the midst of our prosperities, which often tempt us to forget Him, He is pleased to mortify us in some instance, that we may address our thoughts to Him, acknowledge His omnipotence, and ask of Him what we ought to expect from Him alone. Your majesty has subjects," proceeded he, " who make a profession of honouring and serving God, and suffering great hardships for His sake; to them I would advise you to have recourse, and engage them, by alms, to join their prayers with yours, for the boon you crave."

Schah-zaman approved this advice, and thanked his

vizier. He immediately caused alms to be given to every community of these holy men in his dominions; and having sent for the superiors, declared to them his intention, and desired them to acquaint their devout men with it.

The king obtained of Heaven what he requested, for shortly after he had a son. To express his gratitude to Heaven, he sent fresh alms to the communities of dervishes, and the prince's birthday was celebrated throughout his dominions. The prince was brought to him as soon as born, and he found him so beautiful that he gave him the name of Camaralzaman, or "Moon of the Age."

When he had attained the age of fifteen, the sultan, who tenderly loved him, proposed to resign his throne to him.

"Sire," replied the grand vizier, "the prince is yet but young, and it would not, in my humble opinion, be wise to burden him with the weight of a crown so soon. Do not you think it would be proper to marry him first? Your majesty might then admit him to your council, where he would learn by degrees the art of reigning; and so be prepared to receive your authority, whenever you shall think fit to resign your high office."

Schah-zaman approved the advice of his prime minister, and summoned the prince to appear before him.

The prince, who had been accustomed to see his father only at certain times, was a little startled at this summons; when, therefore, he came into his presence, he saluted him with great respect, and stood with his eyes fixed on the ground.

The sultan, perceiving his constraint, addressed him with great mildness. "I sent for you, my son, to inform you that it is my intention to provide a proper marriage for you; what do you think of my design?"

The prince, on hearing this, became greatly agitated,

and, with much respect and many apologies, begged the sultan to excuse him for declining to marry on account of his youth.

Schah-zaman felt very sorry at the prince's refusal to accede to his request. He entertained, however, no feelings of anger, but admitted him to his council, and continued to heap on him his royal favours. At the end of another year he again pressed upon him the same question, and urged upon a compliance with his request. The prince answered with much more readiness than on the first occasion. "Sire, I find myself more and more confirmed in my resolution not to marry. The mischief which women have caused in the world, and which are on record in our histories, and the accounts I daily hear to their disadvantage are the motives which powerfully influence me; so that it will be in vain to solicit me upon this subject." As soon as he had thus spoken, he quitted the sultan abruptly, without waiting his answer.

Any monarch but Schah-zaman would have been angry at such freedom in a son, and would have made him repent; but he loved him, and preferred gentle methods before he proceeded to compulsion. He communicated this new cause of discontent to his prime minister. "Tell me, I beseech you, how I shall reclaim a disposition so rebellious to my will."

"Sire," answered the grand vizier, "patience cures all. May it please you to give the prince another year to consider your prosposal. If in this interval he return to his duty, you will have the greater satisfaction, and if he still continue averse when this is expired, your majesty may in full council observe, that it is highly necessary for the good of the state that he should marry; and it is not likely he will refuse to comply before so grave an assembly, which you honour with your presence."

The sultan, who so anxiously desired to see his son married, thought this long delay an age; however, though with much difficulty, he yielded to his grand vizier.

The sultan went next to the apartment of the mother of the prince, and told her, with much concern, how his son had a second time refused to comply with his wishes. "I know," he said, "that the prince has more confidence in you than he has in me, and will be more likely to attend to your advice. I therefore desire you would take an opportunity to talk to him seriously, and urge upon him, that if he persists in his obstinacy, he will oblige me to have recourse to measures which would give him cause to repent having disobeyed me."

From that time Fatima (this was the name of the prince's mother) had frequent conversations with her son the prince; and she omitted no opportunity nor argument to endeavour to induce in him a compliance with his father's wish; but he eluded all her reasonings by such arguments as she could not well answer, and continued unaltered.

The year expired, and to the great regret of the sultan, Prince Camaralzaman gave not the least proof of having changed his sentiments. One day, therefore, when there was a great council held, the prime vizier, the other viziers, the principal officers of the crown, and the generals of the army being present, the sultan thus addressed the prince: "My son, it is now a long while since I expressed to you my earnest desire to see you married; I have thought fit to propose the same thing once more to you in the presence of my council. It is not merely to oblige a parent that you ought to have acceded to my wish; the well-being of my dominions requires your compliance, and this assembly joins with me in expecting it. Declare yourself, then, that your answer may regulate my proceedings."

The prince answered with so little reserve, or rather with so much warmth, that the sultan exclaimed, "How, unnatural son! have you the insolence to talk thus to your father and sultan ?" He ordered the guards to take him away, and carry him to an old tower that had been long unoccupied ; where he was shut up, with only a bed, a little furniture, some books, and one slave to attend him.

Camaralzaman, thus deprived of liberty, was nevertheless pleased that he had the freedom to converse with his books, which made him regard his confinement with indifference. In the evening he bathed and said his prayers ; and after having read some chapters in the Koran, with the same tranquillity of mind as if he had been in the sultan's palace, he undressed himself and went to bed, leaving his lamp burning by him while he slept.

In this tower was a well, which served in the daytime for a retreat to a certain fairy, named Maimoune, daughter of Damriat, king or head of a legion of genii. It was about midnight when Maimoune sprung lightly to the mouth of the well, to wander about the world after her wonted custom. She was surprised to see a light in the prince's chamber. She entered, and without stopping at the slave who lay at the door, approached the bed.

She could not forbear admiring the prince, and kissed him gently on both cheeks and in the middle of the forehead without waking him, and took her flight into the air. As she was ascending, she heard a great flapping of wings, and knew it was a genie whose name was Danhasch who made the noise, one of those genie who resisted the power of the great Solomon, while she acknowledged his rule and authority.

"Tell me, wandering spirit," said Maimoune, "whence thou comest, what thou hast seen, and what thou hast done this night ?" "Fair spirit," answered Danhasch, "you meet me in a good time to hear something very wonderful. The country of China, from whence I come, is one of the largest in the world. Giaour, the present king, has an only daughter, the most beautiful creature that ever was seen. Neither you nor I could find sufficient eloquence to convey the most distant idea of her loveliness. Her hair is golden, and reaches below her feet ; her forehead is as smooth as the finest polished mirror ; her eyes are brilliant as lighted coals ; her nose is perfect ; her mouth small ; her cheeks vermilion ; her teeth surpass the finest pearls in whiteness ; her voice agreeable ; the most beautiful alabaster is not whiter than her neck. In short, there is not a more perfect beauty in the world.

"The fame of this princess's incomparable beauty has induced many powerful kings to demand her in marriage. But as the king her father has determined that his daughter shall not marry except with her own consent, all the ambassadors returned without success.

"At last one king, most wealthy and powerful, sent a solemn embassy to demand the hand of the princess. The king pressed his acceptance upon his daughter. The princess entreated him to dispense with her compliance, and on his commanding her to obey, she forgot the respect due to the king her father, and angrily replied, 'Sire, speak to me no more of this, nor of any other marriage ; if you persist in your importunities, I will plunge a poniard into my heart, and thus free myself from them.'

"The King of China, extremely irritated against the princess, replied, 'My daughter, you are beside yourself, and as such I must treat you.' In fact, he had her confined to an apartment in one of his palaces, and allowed her only ten old women to attend on her, the chief of whom was her nurse. Then he sent ambassadors to the neighbouring kings to inform them of his daughter's refusal to marry—and to make known in every court that if any physician would cure her distraction, he should obtain her in marriage as his reward. I entreat you, powerful Maimoune, to come and see this wonderful fair one. I am ready to conduct you to her."

Instead of replying to Danhasch, Maimoune burst into a loud fit of laughter, which continued for some time, and which very much astonished Danhasch, who did not know to what cause to attribute it. Having at last, however, composed herself, she said, "You would quickly change your opinion if you had seen the beautiful prince I have this moment left. He is indeed worth looking at, for never was such a gracious creature born." "May I inquire," replied Danhasch, "who this prince can be whom you speak of?" "Know," said the fairy, "that nearly the same thing has happened to him as to the princess thou hast been talking of. The king his father would marry him against his will. For this reason he is at this moment imprisoned in an ancient tower where I take up my abode, and where I have had an opportunity of seeing him."

"I will not contradict you," resumed Danhasch, "but you will give me leave, until I have seen your prince, to think that no mortal, either man or woman, can equal the beauty of my princess. The only means of deciding which surpasses the other in beauty, is to accept the proposal I have made you to come and see my princess, and afterwards to show me your prince." "There is no occasion for me to take so much trouble," said Maimoune; "there is another method by which we can both be satisfied. You know my abode in the ancient tower—there the prince is confined. Go bring thy princess and place her by the side of my prince on his bed. We can then easily compare them with each other, and thus settle our dispute."

Danhasch at once flew to China, and returned with inconceivable swiftness, bearing the beautiful princess on her couch fast asleep. Maimoune received her, and introduced her into the chamber of Prince

Camaralzaman, where they placed her on the bed by his side.

When the prince and princess were thus laid close to each other, a grand contest arose between the genie and the fairy as to which was the handsomest. They stood for some time admiring and comparing them in silence. Danhasch was the first to speak. " Now are you convinced," said he to Maimoune, " that my princess is more beautiful than your prince ? "

" How ? " cried Maimoune. " Thou must be blind not to see that my prince is infinitely superior to thy princess. She is beautiful, I confess ; but compare them well one with the other, and then thou wilt see that it is as I say."

" Were I to compare them for any length of time," replied Danhasch, " I should think no otherwise than I do. This, however, will not prevent me from giving up my judgment to yours, charming Maimoune, if you wish it." " It shall not be so," interrupted the fairy ; " I will never suffer a rebellious genie such as thou art to show me a favour. I will call an umpire : and if thou dost not consent, I win the cause by your refusal."

Danhasch had no sooner consented, than the fairy struck the ground with her foot. The earth opened, and there instantly appeared a most hideous dwarf, lame, blind of one eye, having six horns on his head, and his hands and feet hooked. As soon as the ground had closed again, he perceived Maimoune, and kneeling on one knee, he asked what she desired of him, as he was ready to obey her commands.

" Rise, Caschcasch," said she, " and cast your eye on that bed, and tell us truly which is the most beautiful, this prince, or this princess."

Caschcasch having examined them very attentively for a long time, without being able to make up his mind, " Mistress," he said to Maimoune, " I confess that I cannot tell which is handsomer than the other.

The more I examine them, the more each seems to me to have a like perfection of beauty. I propose that you submit them each to this test—that you wake them each in turn, and the one that expresses the strongest affection for the other shall be considered to be the less beautiful."

The proposal of Caschcasch was approved of. Maimoune then changed herself into a flea, and jumped upon the neck of Camaralzaman. She gave him so sharp a bite that he awoke, and put his hand to the place; but he caught nothing, for Maimoune, prepared for this, had jumped away, and taking her original form—invisible, however, like the other two genii to all but themselves—stood by in order to witness what would happen.

In drawing back his hand, the prince let it fall upon that of the Princess of China. He opened his eyes, and expressed great surprise at seeing so beautiful a woman by his side. He lifted up his head, and supported it on his elbow, the better to observe her. The great beauty of the princess excited sensations in his breast to which he had hitherto been a stranger, and he could not help exclaiming, "What beauty! what charms!" and saying this, he kissed her forehead, her cheeks, and her lips so fondly, that he must have broken her slumbers, except for the enchantment of Danhasch.

"There cannot be a doubt," he exclaimed, "but that this is the lady to whom the sultan my father wished to marry me. He has been much to blame not to let me see her sooner; I should not then have offended him by my disobedience. Who knows if he may not have brought her here himself, and may even now be concealed, in order to see how I conduct myself, and make me ashamed of my former decision."

The Princess of China had a very beautiful ring on her finger, and as the prince concluded this speech, he drew it off quietly, and put on one of his own in its place. And it was not long before, through the enchantment of the genie, he fell into as deep a sleep again.

Now Danhasch, in his turn, transformed himself into a flea, and bit the princess directly under her lip. She awoke suddenly, and, starting up, opened her eyes. How great was her astonishment when she saw the young prince.

"What!" she exclaimed, "are you the prince whom the king my father has destined for my husband? Would that I had known this before! I should then never have been imprisoned for a refusal to comply with his request."

Having said this, the princess shook Prince Camaralzaman in so violent a manner, that he must have awoke if Maimoune had not heightened his sleep by means of enchantment. She then took hold of his hand, and tenderly kissing it, perceived her own ring to be on his finger, and that she herself had on a different one. Having tried in vain to wake the prince, she lay down, and in a short time fell asleep.

When Maimoune perceived that she might speak without any danger of waking the Princess of China, she said to Danhasch, "Art thou now convinced that thy princess is less beautiful than my prince? But do you and Caschcasch take the princess, and carry her to her own bed." Danhasch and Caschcasch executed these orders, while Maimoune retired to her well.

When Prince Camaralzaman awoke the next morning, he looked on each side of him, to see if the lady whom he had seen in the night was still there; but when he perceived she was gone, he said to himself, "It is so: the king my father wished to surprise me; I am, however, happy that I was aware of it." He then called the slave, who was still asleep, and desired him to make haste and dress him.

After he had thus finished his usual occupations,

"Tell me truly," said he to the slave, "who brought the lady who slept in my chamber last night?"

"Prince," replied the slave, in the greatest astonishment, "I swear to you that I know nothing about the matter. How could any lady possibly get in, as I slept at the door?" "Thou art a rascal," replied the prince, "and art in league with some one to vex and distress me." Saying this, he gave him a blow, and then tied the rope of the well round his body, and let him down several times into the water. "I will drown thee," cried he, "if thou dost not tell me who the lady is, and who brought her."

"Prince," said the slave, trembling, "I cannot tell you in the state I am now in; allow me to change my dress." "I will," replied the prince, "but take care on thy return thou tellest all the truth."

The slave went out, and after having fastened the door on the prince, ran to the palace, wet as he was. The king was engaged in conversation with his grand vizier, and was complaining of the restless night he had passed, in consequence of the disobedience of the prince his son.

The minister endeavoured to console him, and convince him that the prince had justly merited the punishment he endured.

The grand vizier had hardly spoken, when the slave presented himself before King Schah-zaman, and related everything that Prince Camaralzaman had said, and the excesses he had been guilty of, and expressed his fears that he had lost his reason through his imprisonment.

The king, on hearing these sad tidings, exclaimed to the grand vizier, "This is, indeed, a new and unexpected affliction. Go, lose not a moment, and examine yourself this affair, and come and tell me what you discover." The grand vizier immediately obeyed. When he entered the chamber of the prince, he found him seated with a book in his hand, which he was reading with apparent composure. He saluted him; and then the prince addressed him, "O vizier, as you are here, I am glad to have an opportunity of asking you, who must know something about the matter, where the lady is who was with me in this chamber last night."

"Prince," said the grand vizier, "do not be surprised at the astonishment you see me in at this question. How can it be possible that any lady could have penetrated into this place in the night, to which there is no other entrance but by the door, at which a guard was set? I entreat you to collect your thoughts, and I am persuaded you will find it is only a dream, that has left a strong impression on your mind."

"I shall pay no attention to your arguments," resumed the prince, in a more elevated tone of voice: "I will absolutely know what is become of this lady. I saw her. She played the part allotted her vastly well. You know it all, I dare say; she has not failed giving you an account of the whole transaction." "Prince," resumed the grand vizier, "I swear to you, that all you have been relating was unknown to me, and that neither the king your father nor I sent you the lady you mention; we should never have had such an idea. Allow me once more to say, that this lady could only appear to you in a dream."

Upon this, he took the grand vizier by his beard, and said, "Go, tell my father that I will marry the lady whom he sent me last night." The grand vizier made a profound reverence on quitting him. He presented himself before Schah-zaman with an air of sorrow and said, "Sire, what the slave related to your majesty is too true." He then related all that had passed.

Upon this, the king went himself to the tower with the grand vizier. Prince Camaralzaman received his father with the greatest respect. The king sat down, and asked him many questions, to which he replied with perfect good sense. At length he said, " My son, I beg you tell me who this lady is who slept last night in your chamber." " Sire," replied Camaralzaman, " I entreat you to bestow her on me in marriage. I am ready to receive her from your hands, with the deepest sense of my obligation to you."

" You speak to me in a way, my son," said he, " that astonishes me beyond measure. I swear to you that I know nothing of the lady you name, nor of her visit."

" Sire," resumed the prince, " after the solemn assurance you have given me, I request you to hear me, and then judge if what I shall have the honour of relating to you can be a dream."

Prince Camaralzaman then told the king his father all that had passed in the night ; and as he concluded, he took the ring from his finger and presented it to the king.

" After what I have now heard, my son," replied King Schah-zaman, " I can no longer doubt that you did see the lady last night in your chamber. But where am I to seek her ? Come, my son, let us weep together ; you for loving without hope, I for seeing your affliction without the means of relieving it."

Schah-zaman took the prince out of his prison, and conducted him to the palace, where the prince fell quite ill from his despair, and the king shut himself up to weep with his afflicted son.

While these things were passing in the capital of King Schah-zaman, the two genii, Danhasch and Caschcasch, had reconducted the Princess of China to the palace where the king her father had confined her, and placed her in her bed.

The next morning, when she awoke, and perceived that Prince Camaralzaman was no longer near her, she called her women in a voice which made them all run quickly to her. Her nurse approached her pillow, and asked her what she desired. "Tell me," replied the princess, "what is become of the young man who slept in my chamber last night, and whom I love so tenderly." "You do this to joke us, my princess," replied the nurse; "will you please to rise now?" "I speak seriously," said the princess, "and I will know where he is." "But, my dear princess," rejoined the nurse, "you were alone when we put you to bed last night, and no one has entered this place that we know of."

The Princess of China seized her nurse's head, and slapped her. "Thou shalt tell me truly," cried she, "or I will murder thee." The nurse, getting out of her hands, instantly ran to the Queen of China, the mother of the princess. "Madam," said she, "the princess is out of her sesnes. You may judge of it yourself, if you will take the trouble of coming to see her."

The Queen of China immediately went to the princess. "Indeed, my daughter," said she, "a princess of your rank ought never to forget herself, or yield to anger. You well know, my dear child, that you are alone in your chamber, and that no man can possibly enter it."

The princess forgot the respect she owed to her mother, and answered, "Madam, the king my father and you have for some time urged me to marry; the wish to do so has at length taken possession of my breast, and I will absolutely either marry the young prince who slept in my chamber last night, or I shall die for love of him." On her saying this, the queen left her to acquaint the king of this new source of grief. The King of China immediately repaired to the princess. "What is this I hear?" exclaimed he. "Has any young prince slept in your chamber last night?" "That you may not entertain any doubts of my having seen this youth in my chamber last night, look, if you please, at this ring." She held out her hand, and the King of China knew not what to think when he perceived that it was the ring of a man. But as he had confined her originally because she was supposed to have lost her wits, he supposed that the same calamity had befallen her again. He therefore had her committed again to the tower, and sent ambassadors to intimate his misfortune at the courts of the neighbouring kings, and to give them notice that if any one could effect her cure, he should have her hand in marriage, and be made heir to the kingdom; but if he attempts the cure and does not succeed after his admission to the presence of so beautiful a princess, he must lose his head.

Several of the emirs * and astrologers of the court of the King of China and of the neighbouring potentates, animated by the double desire to be the husband of so fair a lady, and the heir of so splendid a kingdom, tried in vain to effect the cure of the princess, and paid with their heads the penalty of their ambition and their rashness.

Now, it so happened that the nurse of the princess had a son, named Marzavan. He had been brought up as the foster-brother, and had been nourished by one and the same breast as the Princess of China. They had in their childhood treated each other as brother and sister. Marzavan became a great traveller, and visited many countries. He had also devoted himself to the study of judicial astrology, and other occult sciences. About a year after the princess commenced her captivity, he returned to his own home; and on learning from the princess's nurse, his mother, the wonderful incidents of her illness, and her mysterious tale of the young man who left his ring on her finger, he expressed an earnest desire to be admitted to the presence of the princess, as he thought he might, by his knowledge of magic, explain the

* "Emirs: grand officers of the court—really the title implies 'Children of the prophet.'"—Sales's *Koran.*

16

marvel of which she had been the subject, and help towards her recovery. He did not wish to run the risk of losing his life, and so he entreated the nurse, his mother, to admit him to a secret interview with his foster-sister. After many consultations with her son, she determined to secure him the favour he desired; and one night, having obtained the favourable ear of the guard at the princess's door, she disguised her son in the dress of a female slave, and thus obtained for him a passage through the palace to the princess's chamber. Before the nurse presented her son to the princess, she went to her, and said, "Madam, this is not a woman whom you see—it is my son Marzavan, who is just arrived from his travels, and whom I have found means to introduce into your chamber, disguised by this dress. I hope you will allow him to pay his respects to you."

At the name of Marzavan, the princess expressed great joy. "Come forward, brother," cried she to Marzavan, "and take off that veil. It is not forbidden to a brother and sister to see each other uncovered." Marzavan saluted her with great respect; but without allowing him time to say anything, she exclaimed, "Surely, brother, you at least are not of the number of those who think me to be mad."

The princess then related to Marzavan all her history, and showed him the ring which had been exchanged for hers. "I have disguised nothing from you," continued she. "In what I have told you, I acknowledge that there is something mysterious, which I cannot comprehend, and this leads them all to suppose that I am not in my right senses; but they pay no attention to the other circumstances, which are exactly as I have related."

When the princess had related her history, Marzavan made a most respectful obeisance, and expressed his determination to go and visit the cities and countries of the world he had not yet seen, and to try and discover at some of their courts the prince whose ring was on the finger of the princess, that he might thereby promote her happiness and recovery. He set out on the following day.

Marzavan travelled from city to city, from province to province, and from island to island. At the expiration of four months he arrived at Torf, a populous maritime town, where he no longer heard of the Princess Badoura, but every one was talking of Prince Camaralzaman, whose history he found to be nearly similar to that of the Princess of China. Marzavan, with much joy, inquired in what part of the world this prince resided, and he was told the place. There were two ways to it, the longer by land, and the shorter by sea. Marzavan chose the latter, and embarked in a merchant vessel, which had a good voyage till within sight of the capital of the kingdom of Schah-zaman. But as the vessel was entering the harbour, it struck on a rock, went to pieces, and sunk in sight of the castle in which Prince Camaralzaman passed his life, and where his father, King Schah-zaman, was at that moment conversing with his grand vizier.

Marzavan threw himself into the sea, and swam to the castle of King Schah-zaman, where he was well received, and every assistance given him, according to the orders of the grand vizier.

On the next day, after his recovery from his fatigues, he was admitted to the presence of the grand vizier, who soon led the conversation to the afflicted son of his royal master, and related to Marzavan all the wonderful history of Prince Camaralzaman.

Marzavan felt convinced that this young prince was the person who had exchanged rings with the fair Princess of China, and he informed the vizier that he thought he could promise his recovery. He was admitted to the presence of the prince, who was lying on his couch, with his father in much sorrow weeping beside him. Scarcely had Marzavan entered the room than he exclaimed, " What a likeness! What a wonderful likeness! " He spoke of the likeness which he saw at once between the Prince Camaralzaman and the Princess Badoura. These words excited the curiosity of the prince, which was still more increased by some improvised verses which Marzavan repeated, in which he made some mysterious allusions indicating that he knew all his secret history. The king, perceiving an unwonted look of interest come across the pale countenance of his son, took Marzavan by the hand, and said, " God grant that you may restore me my son; " and then, with the grand vizier, left the chamber.

No sooner was Marzavan left alone with the prince than he approached his couch, and said, in a low and confidential tone, " Prince, the lady whom you love is well known to me. She is a princess, Badoura, daughter of Giaour, King of China. She loves you no less than you do her. You are as necessary to her restoration as she is to your own recovery. Try, therefore, and perfect your health, that you may the sooner regain strength to visit her. I will be your companion."

This discourse of Marzavan instantly produced a wonderful effect. Prince Camaralzaman was so comforted by this new hope, that he got up and entreated the king his father to permit him to dress himself. His countenance was full of joy.

The king embraced Marzavan, but did not inquire into the means by which so surprising a change was instantaneously effected. He ordered public rejoicings for several days, distributed presents to his officers and the populace, gave alms to the poor, and had all prisoners set at liberty. In short, nothing but joy and mirth reigned in the capital, which very soon spread its influence throughout the dominions of King Schah-zaman.

Prince Camaralzaman, having in a few days recovered his strength, pressed Marzavan to hasten his plans; and to prevent the King Schah-zaman interfering with their intended departure, they determined to ask leave to form a hunting party, and under that excuse to flee secretly to the court of the King of China. The next day, Prince Camaralzaman told the king his father how much he wished to take an airing, and begged him to allow him to hunt for a day or two with Marzavan. "I do not object to it," replied the king, "provided, however, that you promise me not to remain out longer than one night. Too much exercise at first might injure you, and a longer absence would be painful to me." The king then gave orders for the best horses to be chosen for him, and took care himself that nothing should be wanting for his expedition. When everything was ready, he embraced him, and having earnestly recommended him to the care of Marzavan, he let him depart.

Prince Camaralzaman and Marzavan reached an open country; and to deceive the two grooms that led the relay of horses, they pretended to hunt, and got as distant from the city as possible. At night they stopped at a khan, where they supped, and slept till about midnight. Marzavan, who was the first to wake, called Prince Camaralzaman, without waking the grooms. He begged him to give him his dress, and to put on another, which one of the grooms had brought for him. They mounted the horses of relay, and each leading one of the grooms' horses by the bridle, to hinder their following, set out at a quick pace.

The prince and Marzavan, well supplied with valuable jewels to defray their expenses, continued their travels till they arrived at the capital of China. Marzavan made the prince alight at a public khan for the reception of travellers. They remained there three days to recover from the fatigue of the journey. When the three days were expired, they went together to the bath, where Marzavan made the prince put on the astrologer's dress he had provided, and afterwards conducted him within sight of the palace of the King of China.

The prince, instructed by Marzavan in what he was to do, and furnished with every implement necessary for his assumed dress and character, approached the gate of the palace; and stopping before it, cried out with a loud voice, in the hearing of the guard and porters, "I am an astrologer, and I come to complete the cure of the illustrious Princess Badoura, daughter of the great and puissant monarch Giaour, King of China, according to the conditions proposed by his majesty, to marry her if I succeed, or to lose my life if I fail."

Now, it had been a long time since either physician, astrologer, or magician had presented himself, after so many tragical examples of people who had failed in their enterprise. This address, therefore, soon drew a vast crowd of people around Prince Camaralzaman. On observing his elegant figure, noble air, and extreme youth, every one felt compassion for him. "What are you thinking of, sir?" said those who were nearest to him; "what can be your motive for thus exposing to certain death a life which has only just commenced? Pray abandon this useless and fatal design."

The prince remained firm to his purpose; and calling out a third time the same words, the grand vizier came himself, and conducted him into the presence of the king. The prince no sooner perceived the monarch seated on his throne, than he prostrated himself, and kissed the earth before him. Of all the competitors for the honour of his daughter's hand, the king had not seen one he liked so well, and he felt great compassion for Camaralzaman. "Young man, I can scarcely believe that at your youthful age you can have acquired sufficient experience to cure my daughter. I wish you to succeed; I would bestow her on you in marriage with the greatest joy. But if you fail, neither your youth nor your noble air can save your life."

"Sire," replied Prince Camaralzaman, "I thank you. What would be said of me, if I were now to abandon the cure of so beautiful a princess? I entreat you to let me prove the infallibility of the art in which I am a proficient."

The King of China ordered the prince to be conducted to the chamber of the princess. In his anxiety to meet with the long-wished-for object of his affections, he so hastened his steps as to elicit from the officer of the palace expressions of surprise at his eagerness to meet a cruel and certain death. "Friend," said the prince, "the astrologers before me had not the confidence in their art that I entertain. I am certain of effecting the cure I have undertaken; but to convince you of my skill, and of my knowledge of the disease, which is half the cure, I will cure the princess without seeing her." On saying this, the prince drew out his tablets, and wrote these words:—

"*Prince Camaralzaman to the Princess of China.*

"ADORABLE PRINCESS!

"A heart-stricken prince would remind you of the fatal night when he gave you his heart during your sweet sleep. He even had the presumption to place his ring upon your finger, as a token of his love, and to take yours in exchange, which he sends you, enclosed in this note. If you will condescend to return it him as a reciprocal pledge of yours, he will esteem himself the happiest of men. But should you not comply, your refusal will make him submit to the stroke of death with so much the more resignation, as he will receive it for the love he bears you. He awaits your answer in your antechamber."

The officer of the king's palace went into the princess's chamber and presented the packet. The fair daughter of the king opened it with the utmost indifference; but as soon as she saw the ring, she ran to the door and opened it, and ran into the arms of the prince, and neither of them could scarcely speak for joy at their happy reunion. The nurse, who had run out with the princess, brought them into the chamber, where the princess returned her ring to the prince. "Take it," said she; "I keep yours, which I am resolved not to part with to the end of my life."

The officer of the palace, meanwhile, returned to the king. "Sire," said he, "all the physicians and astrologers who have hitherto undertaken the recovery of the princess, made use either of magic or of conjurations, or of perfumes or other things; he has cured her without even seeing her." The king, most agreeably surprised, went immediately to the apartment of the princess, whom he tenderly embraced; he embraced the prince also, took hold of his hand, and joining it to that of the princess, "Happy stranger," cried he, "whoever you may be, I keep my promise, and give you my daughter in marriage. But it is not possible to persuade me that you are what you appear to be." "I am," said Camaralzaman, "a prince by birth, the son of a king and queen; my father is called Schah-zaman, and reigns over the well-known Islands of Khaledan." He then related his adventures, and the miraculous origin of his love for the princess; that their affection for each other was conceived simultaneously, as was fully proved by the exchange of the two rings.

"So extraordinary a history," cried the king, "deserves to be handed down to posterity. I will have it written; I will make it public to the neighbouring nations." The ceremony of the nuptials was performed on that very day; and the most solemn festivities and rejoicings took place throughout the extensive dominions of China. Marzavan was not forgotten: the king granted him free access to the court: bestowed on him an office of honour and importance. In the midst of these nuptial festivities, Prince Camaralzaman had a dream one night, in which he saw King Schah-zaman, his father, on the point of death, saying: "This son, whom I have so tenderly cherished, has abandoned me, and he is the cause of my death." He awoke with a deep sigh, which made the princess inquire what occasioned his unhappiness.

"Alas!" cried the prince, "perhaps at this very moment that I am speaking, the king my father breathes no more." The princess, being persuaded that it would be her husband's wish to revisit his father, on the very next day went to the King of China and, making a respectful obeisance to him, requested the royal permission for the prince and herself to depart on a visit to the court of Schah-zaman. "Go," said the King of China. "I give my consent, on the condition that you both remain no longer than one year." The princess announced this consent to Camaralzaman, who was much rejoiced at it, and thanked her for this new proof of her affection towards him. They set off to return to the prince's native kingdom as soon as preparations could be made for their journey. After a month's travelling they arrived at a vast plain, planted with trees, which formed a very agreeable shade. As the heat was excessive, they halted in this beautiful spot. As soon as their tents were pitched, the princess, who had been resting in the shade, retired within hers. In order to be more at her ease, she took off her girdle. She then fell asleep through fatigue, and her attendants left her.

Prince Camaralzaman shortly afterward entered the tent, and as he perceived that the princess had fallen asleep, he came in and sat down without making any noise. While he was thus sitting, the girdle of the princess caught his eye. He examined the different diamonds and rubies with which it was enriched, one by one; and he perceived a small silk purse, sewn neatly to the girdle. Curious to know what it contained, he opened the purse and took out a cornelian, upon which there were certain unintelligible characters engraven. Now, this cornelian was a talisman, which the Queen of China had given to her daughter to insure her happiness, as long as she wore it about her.

In order the better to examine this curious engraving, Prince Camaralzaman went to the outside of the tent, when, as he was holding it in his hand, a bird made a sudden dart from the air upon it, and carried it away, to his exceeding great grief and astonishment.

The bird having flown away with his prize, alighted on a tree at a little distance, with the talisman* still in his beak. Prince Camaralzaman went towards him in the hope of his dropping it; but as soon as he approached, the bird flew a little way, and then stopped again. The prince continued to pursue him; the bird then swallowed the talisman and took a longer flight. The farther the bird got from him, the more was Camaralzaman determined not to lose sight of him, and obtain the talisman.

Over hills and through valleys did the bird lead the prince the whole day, always advancing farther from the spot where he had left the Princess Badoura. At the close of day, instead of perching in a bush, in which Camaralzaman might have surprised him during the night, he flew to the top of a high tree, where he was in safety.

The prince, mortified beyond measure, deliberated what he should do. Shall I return? thought he;

* "Talisman, a corruption of the Arabic word 'talsam.' It is a word applied to anything bearing mystical characters. The purposes for which talsam are contrived are various. They respectively preserve from enchantments, from accidents, from a variety of evils. They protect treasures from discovery, and being touched or rubbed, secure the presence of genii."—Lane's *Notes*, vol. ii., p. 203.

shall I repass the hills and valleys over which I came? Shall I not lose my way, and will my strength hold out? How could I present myself before the princess without her talisman? Disconsolate, fatigued, hungry and thirsty, he lay down, and passed the night at the foot of the tree.

The next morning Camaralzaman was awake before the dawn of day. The bird had no sooner quitted the tree than he got up to pursue him, and followed him the whole of that day with as little success as he had done on the preceding one, eating occasionally of the herbs and fruits he met with on his way. He did the same till the tenth day, always keeping his eye on the bird, and sleeping at night at the foot of the tree where it perched on its highest branches.

On the eleventh day, the bird constantly flying on, and Camaralzaman as constantly pursuing, they arrived at a large city. When the bird* was near the walls, he rose very high above them, and bending his flight to the other side, the prince entirely lost sight of him, and with him the hope of recovering the talisman of the Princess Badoura.

Afflicted and hopeless, he entered the city, which was built on the seashore, with a very fine harbour. Not knowing either where he was or where to go, he walked along the shore, till he came to the gate of a garden, which was open, when he stopped. The gardener, an old man, had scarcely perceived and recognized him as a stranger and a Mussulman, when he invited him to go in quickly and shut the gate. Camaralzaman did as he desired, and asked him why he had made him take this precaution. "It is," replied the gardener, "because I see that you are a stranger and a Mussulman; and this city is inhabited

* "The huma—a bird which flies always in the air, and never touches the earth. It is looked upon as a bird of happy omen, and that every head it overshades will in time wear a crown."—*Lalla Rookh*, p. 249.

for the most part by idolaters, who have a mortal aversion against Mussulmans, and try to lead them into temptation, if they are off their guard. But you must want food, so come and rest yourself." The gardener took him into his house, and after he had eaten to his satisfaction, asked him to tell him his history. Camaralzaman told him all that had happened, and inquired by what means he might get to the dominions of Schah-zaman, for he despaired of ever meeting again his dear princess.

The gardener told him that the city he was then in was a whole year's journey from the territories of Schah-zaman, but that by sea he might reach the Isle of Ebony, and thence find a passage to the Islands of Khaledan, and that once every year a merchant ship made the voyage to these ports. "If you had arrived some days sooner," continued he, "you might have embarked in that which sailed this year; but if you will wait till that of next year sails, and live with me, you are welcome to do so."

Prince Camaralzaman accepted the offer, and remained with the gardener. He worked in the garden during the day, and passed the nights in sighs, tears, and lamentations, for the loss of his Badoura. We will return to the Princess Badoura, whom we left sleeping in her tent.

The princess slept for some time, and on waking was surprised not to find her beloved husband. She called her women, and whilst they were assuring her that they had seen him go into the tent, but had not observed him leave it, she perceived that the talisman she valued so much was taken from the purse, and she could not divest her mind of the idea that the prince's absence was in some way connected with this talisman. When the night fell, and he did not return, she was overwhelmed with affliction. On the morrow she determined to carry out a design, which demanded courage unusual in her sex. She commanded her attendants not to say nor do anything that might excite the slightest suspicion. She then changed her dress for one of Camaralzaman's, whom she resembled so strongly that his people took her for the prince himself, on the following morning when she made her appearance, and commanded them to pack up the baggage, and proceed on their journey. When all was ready one of her women took her place in the litter, and she herself mounted a horse, and they set off.

After a journey of several months, the princess, disguised as Prince Camaralzaman, arrived at the capital of the Isle of Ebony. The intelligence soon reached the palace of the king.

King Armanos (for that was his name), accompanied by his court, received the princess as the son of a king who was his friend and ally, and conducted her to his palace, where he lodged her and her whole suite.

When three days were expired, King Armanos, being quite charmed with the princess, whom he still supposed to be really Prince Camaralzaman, proposed that he should postpone his return home, and should unite himself in marriage to his only daughter, the sole heiress of his dominion. Badoura was sadly perplexed at this offer ; but, having announced herself as Prince Camaralzaman, she determined to continue to act the part of the prince, and, fearful to offend King Armanos, assented to his proposal. She enjoined yet closer secrecy upon her women, and assured the officers of the prince that the Princess Badoura had given her consent to her husband's union with the daughter of Armanos.

The King of the Island of Ebony, overjoyed at having acquired a son-in-law with whom he was so much delighted, assembled his council on the morrow, and declared that he bestowed the princess, his daughter, in marriage on Prince Camaralzaman ; that he resigned his crown to him, and enjoined them to accept him as their king, and to pay him homage. When he had concluded, he descended from the throne, and made the Princess Badoura, disguised as the prince, to ascend and take his place, where she received the oaths of fidelity and allegiance from all who were present.

The new king was solemnly proclaimed throughout the city; rejoicings for several days were ordered, and couriers dispatched to all parts of the kingdom, that the same ceremonies and the same demonstrations of joy might be observed.

In the evening the whole palace was in festivity, and the Princess Haiatalnefous, for this was the name of the daughter of the King of the Island of Ebony, was conducted to the Princess Badoura, whom every one supposed to be a man, with a magnificence truly royal. The ceremonies being completed, they retired to rest.

And now the hour was come when Badoura could no longer conceal her true history from the Princess Haiatalnefous. She told her all the events of her life, and entreated her not to betray her secret, and to help her in acting the part of Camaralzaman, till the prince should himself arrive on his return to the dominions of his father.

"Princess," replied Haiatalnefous, "it would indeed be a singular destiny, if a union such as yours, conceived and preserved with so many miraculous adventures, should be of such short duration. I join my wishes to yours, that Heaven may soon reunite you. Be assured in the meantime that I will preserve the secret entrusted me. I shall rejoice to be the only person in this great kingdom who really knows you; while you govern it with the wisdom you have displayed at the commencement of your reign, I shall be fully satisfied with your friendship." After this conversation the two princesses tenderly embraced, and with a thousand demonstrations of reciprocal friendship they lay down to rest. From this time the Princess Badoura continued to govern the kingdom in great tranquillity, to the complete satisfaction of the king and all his subjects. While these things were being done in the Isle of Ebony, Prince Camaralzaman was still in the city of idolaters with the gardener who had offered him a retreat.

One day at the end of the year, shortly before the destined vessel was about to sail to the country of King Armanos, when the prince could not work as usual with the gardener, because it was a holiday on which the public law allowed no labour to be done, he became absorbed in deep melancholy, with the reflection on his sad destiny in the premature loss of his beloved Badoura. As he sat desolate in the garden his attention was attracted by the noise made by two birds perched on a tree near him. Camaralzaman observed that these birds fought desperately for several minutes, when one of them fell dead at the foot of tho tree. The conqueror bird resumed his flight, and soon disappeared. At the same moment two other birds of a larger size, who had seen the combat from a distance, arrived from a different quarter, and fell upon the victor in the late combat, who uttered dreadful cries, and made violent efforts to escape, but whom they deprived of life by pecking him with their beaks. They then flew away.

Camaralzaman gazed in silent admiration on this surprising spectacle. He approached the tree, took up the mangled remains of the bird, and found the talisman of the Princess Badoura. "Dearest princess!" he exclaimed, "this fortunate moment, in which I thus redeem what is so valuable to you, is a happy presage that I shall meet you in the same unexpected manner—and perhaps even sooner than I dare to hope." As he finished these words, Camaralzaman kissed the talisman, and, wrapping it up carefully, tied it round his arm. On the next morning, at break of day, the gardener begged him to root up a particular tree, which he pointed out to him, as being old and no longer bearing fruit.

Camaralzaman took an axe and set to work. As he was cutting a part of the root, he struck something which made a loud noise. He removed the earth, and discovered a large plate of brass, under which he found a staircase with ten steps. He immediately descended, and found himself in a vault, about fifteen feet square, in which he counted fifty large bronze jars ranged round it, each with a cover. He uncovered them all, one after the other, and found them filled with gold dust. He then left the vault, quite overjoyed at having discovered so rich a treasure; replaced the plate over the staircase, and continued to root up the tree, while he waited for the gardener's return. The gardener returned with a countenance which proved that he bore good news to Camaralzaman. "My son," said he, "rejoice; the vessel will sail in three days, and I have arranged about your passage and departure."

"In return," replied Camaralzaman, "I have to tell you news which will give you great pleasure. Take the trouble of following me, and you will see your good fortune." Camaralzaman conducted the gardener to the spot where he rooted up the tree, and made him go down into the vault, and showed him the jars filled with gold dust.

Hereupon a severe though friendly controversy arose as to whom these jars rightfully belonged, the prince and the gardener each being determined that the whole should belong to the other. The dispute was finally decided by their dividing the jars between them, twenty-five to each.

The division being made, "My son," said the gardener, "there are no olives in the Isle of Ebony, and those which are taken from here are in great request. As I have a good provision of them, gathered from my own garden, you must take fifty jars, and fill them half-way with the gold dust, and the other half with olives, up to the top, and take them to the ship when you embark."

Camaralzaman adopted this advice, and employed himself the rest of the day in filling and arranging the fifty jars; and as he feared that he might lose the talisman of the Princess Badoura by wearing it constantly on his arm, he put it in one of these jars, on which he set a mark, to know it again.

Whether from sorrow at the prince's departure, or from the infirmities of age, the gardener was taken very ill, so that when the captain called next morning to say the wind was fair, and he was about to embark, he was obliged to send the fifty jars to the vessel, and to say that he would follow immediately. As soon as the captain and seamen were gone Camaralzaman went to the gardener to bid him farewell, and to thank him for all the good offices he had rendered him; but he found him at the point of death, and he had scarcely obtained from him the profession of his faith as a good Mussulman, than he expired. The prince, having used the utmost diligence in performing the last offices of respect to the deceased, set out for the harbour, when on his arrival he found to his great grief that the ship, after the captain had waited for him three full hours, had set sail, and was already out of sight.

Camaralzaman was pained to the utmost degree to find himself obliged to wait another year before the opportunity he had lost would again occur. What mortified him still more was that he had parted with the talisman of the Princess Badoura, which he now gave up for lost. He proceeded to rent the garden of the landlord to whom it belonged, and to hire a boy to assist him; and that he might not lose the other share of the treasure, which came to him by the death of the gardener, he put the gold dust into fifty other jars, and covered them with olives, as he had done before, that he might take them with him next year, when the time came for him to embark.

While Prince Camaralzaman was thus doomed to another year of pain, sorrow, and impatience, the vessel continued its voyage with a favourable wind, and arrived without any misfortune at the capital of the Isle of Ebony.

As the palace was on the seashore, the new king, or rather the Princess Badoura, who perceived the vessel while sailing into port, with all its flags flying, inquired what ship it was, and was told that it came every year from the city of idolaters at that season, and that it was in general laden with very rich merchandise.

The princess, who in the midst of all the state and splendour that surrounded her, was constantly occupied with the idea of Camaralzaman, conceived that he might have embarked on board that vessel. Under pretence, therefore, of being the first to see and to choose the most valuable for herself, she ordered a horse to be brought her. She went to the harbour, accompanied by several officers, and arrived at the moment that the captain came on shore. She desired him to be brought to her, and inquired of him from whence he had sailed, if he had amongst his passengers any stranger of distinction, and, above all, with what his vessel was laden.

The captain answered all these questions. He assured her there were no passengers besides the merchants, and that they brought very rich stuffs from different countries, linens of the finest texture, painted as well as plain, precious stones, musk, ambergris, camphor, civet, spices, medicinal drugs, olives, and several other articles.

As soon as the Princess Badoura heard of olives, she said to the captain, " I will take all you have on board ; order them to be unladen immediately, that I may bargain for them."

" Sire," replied the captain to the princess, disguised

as Camaralzaman, " there are only fifty jars of olives, and they belonged to a merchant who remained behind. I had informed him of my departure, and even waited on him some time ; but as I found he did not come, and that his delay prevented my profiting by a favourable wind, I set sail." " Let them be put ashore," replied the princess : " this shall not prevent our making the bargain."

" Sire," replied the captain, " the merchant is very poor ; your majesty will confer a great obligation on him by giving him a thousand pieces of silver." " That he may be perfectly satisfied," said the princess, " and in consideration of his great poverty, you shall have a thousand pieces of gold counted out to you, which you will take care to give him." She gave orders for the payment of this sum, and desired that the jars be taken to the palace.

As night approached, the Princess Badoura retired to the interior palace, and went to the apartment of the Princess Haiatalnefous, where she had the fifty jars of olives brought to her. She had opened one, to taste them, and to eat of them herself, and poured some into a dish, when to her astonishment she found the olives mixed with gold dust. She immediately ordered the other jars to be opened, and emptied in her presence, by the women of Haiatalnefous ; and her surprise increased, as she perceived that the olives in each jar were mixed with the gold dust. But when that was emptied in which Camaralzaman had deposited the talisman, her emotions on seeing it were so strong, that she was quite overcome, and fainted away.

The Princess Haiatalnefous and her women ran to her assistance. When she had recovered her senses, she took up the talisman, and kissed it several times ; but as she did not choose to say anything before the princess's women, who were ignorant of her disguise, and as it was time to retire to rest, she dismissed them.

"Princess," said she to Haiatalnefous, as soon as they were alone, "after what I have related to you of my adventures, you no doubt have guessed that this talisman is mine, the very one that was the cause of the separation between my beloved prince and myself. I am certain its discovery will be the means of our speedy reunion."

The next morning, at break of day, the Princess Badoura sent for the captain of the vessel. "I beg you," she said to him, "to give me a more full account of the merchant to whom the olives belonged, that I bought yesterday. I think you told me that you left him behind in the city of idolaters; can you inform me what was his occupation there?"

"Sire," replied the captain, "I know it for certain he is a gardener. This made me say to your majesty that he was poor. I went to his garden to seek him, and spoke to him myself."

"You must set sail again to-day," said the princess, "to search for this young gardener, and bring him here, for he is my debtor. If you refuse, I will confiscate, not only all the goods which belong to you, and those of the merchants you have on board, but will also make your life and that of the merchants responsible for it. At this moment they are going by my command to place the seal on the magazines where they are deposited, and which shall not be taken off until you have delivered into my hands the young man I require. This is what I had to say to you. Go, and obey my orders."

The captain had nothing to reply to this command, and set sail on that very day.

The ship had a very good voyage, and the captain purposely managed to arrive by night at the city of idolaters. When he was as near land as he thought necessary, he did not cast anchor, but while the vessel lay to, he got into his boat and rowed to shore at a spot a little distance from the harbour, from whence he went to the garden of Camaralzaman, accompanied by six of his most resolute seamen.

The prince had not retired to rest. His sorrow prevented sleep. When, therefore, he heard late at night a knocking at the gate of his garden, he went to open it, when the captain and sailors, without speaking a word, seized and conducted him by main force to the boat, and took him to the ship, which set sail again as soon as they had re-embarked.

Camaralzaman, when once on board, asked the captain, whose features he recollected, why he dragged him away with so much violence. "Are you not a debtor to the King of the Island of Ebony?" inquired the captain in his turn. "I a debtor to the King of the Island of Ebony!" exclaimed Camaralzaman, with amazement. "I do not know him; I never had any dealings with him, nor ever set my foot in his dominions." "You must know that matter better than I can," replied the captain, "but you will speak to him yourself: however, remain here quietly, and have patience."

The vessel had as successful a voyage in conducting Camaralzaman to the Isle of Ebony as it had experienced in going for him to the city of idolaters. Although night had closed when they got into port, the captain did not delay going on shore to take Prince Camaralzaman to the palace, where he requested to be presented to the king.

The Princess Badoura was no sooner informed of his return, and of the arrival of Camaralzaman, than she went out to speak to him. Had she followed her inclination, she would have run to him, and discovered herself by her tender embraces; but she restrained her emotions, as she thought it for the interest of both that she should continue to sustain the character of king for some time longer before she made herself known. She contented herself with recommending him particularly to the care of an officer who was present, charging him to be attentive, and treat him well until the following day.

When the Princess Badoura had ordered everything that related to Prince Camaralzaman, she turned towards the captain, and restored all his merchandise, and dismissed him with a present of a rich and precious diamond, and bade him keep the thousand pieces of gold which had been paid for the jars of olives.

The next day, the Princess of China, under the disguise and authority of the King of the Isle of Ebony, after taking care to have Prince Camaralzaman conducted to the bath very early in the morning, and dressed in the robe of an emir, introduced him into the council, where he attracted the attention of all the nobles who were present by his majestic air and princely bearing.

After he had taken his place in the rank of emirs, according to her directions, "My lords," said she, addressing the other emirs, "Camaralzaman, whom I this day present to you as your colleague, is not unworthy of the dignity he occupies amongst you. I have had sufficient experience of his worth in my travels, to be able to answer for him, and I can assure you that he will make himself admired by you, as much for his valour and a thousand other good and amiable qualities, as by the superior greatness of his mind."

Camaralzaman was extremely surprised when he heard the King of the Isle of Ebony, whom he little suspected to be a woman, and his wife, call him by his name, and assure the assembly that he knew him, when he was himself convinced that he had never met him in any place.

When he left the council, the prince was conducted by an officer to a large mansion, which the Princess Badoura had ordered to be prepared for his reception. He there found officers and servants ready to receive his commands, and a stable filled with very fine horses, the whole suited to the dignity of an emir; and when he went into his closet, his steward presented him with a coffer full of gold for his expenses.

Camaralzaman would have been the happiest of men, but in the midst of all his splendour he never ceased to lament the loss of his princess, and to grieve that he could gain no information respecting her in a country where he concluded she must have passed some time, since he had been separated from her by an accident so unfortunate for both. He might have suspected something if the Princess Badoura had retained the name of Camaralzaman, but when she ascended the throne, she changed it for that of Armanos, in compliment to the former king, her father-in-law; so that she was now known only by the name of King Armanos the younger.

As the Princess Badoura wished Camaralzaman to be indebted to her only for their recognition, she resolved at length to put an end to her own torments, and to those she well knew he suffered. In fact, she had remarked that he frequently heaved deep sighs, which could only proceed from a recollection of herself. Besides which, the friendship of the nobles, the zeal and affection of the people, everything, contributed to persuade her that the crown of the Island of Ebony might be placed on his head without any obstacle.

The Princess Badoura had no sooner formed this resolution, in concert with the Princess Haiatalnefous, than she spoke to Prince Camaralzaman, in private, on the same day. "Camaralzaman," said she, "I wish to converse with you on an affair which will require some discussion, and on which I want your advice. As I think I cannot do it more conveniently than at night, come to me this evening."

Camaralzaman did not fail to repair to the palace at the hour appointed by the princess. When they were closeted together, the princess suddenly presented the talisman to Camaralzaman. "It is not long since an astrologer gave me this talisman," said she ; " and as I know you to be well informed in every science, you perhaps can tell me its peculiar properties." Camaralzaman took the talisman, and approached a light to examine it. He no sooner recognized it, than with a degree of surprise which delighted the princess, he exclaimed, " Ah, sire, you ask me the properties of this talisman ? Alas ! its properties are such as to make me die with grief and sadness, if I do not shortly find the most loved and amiable wife that was ever beheld under Heaven, to whom this talisman belonged, and which was the cause of my losing her. I will tell you the history, if you will have the patience to listen to it."

" You will relate it to me some other time," replied the princess ; " but I am very happy," added she, " to tell you that I know something concerning it ; wait for me here, I will return in a moment."

Saying this, the princess went into a closet, where she took off the royal turban, and having in a few minutes put on a woman's dress, together with the girdle she wore on the day of their separation, she returned to the chamber where she had left the prince.

Camaralzaman instantly ran to her, and embracing her with the utmost tenderness, " Ah," cried he, " how much I am obliged to the king for having prepared for me so unexpected and so pleasant a surprise."

" Do not expect to see the king again," replied the princess, embracing him in her turn, and with tears in her eyes ; " in me you behold the king. Sit down, that I may explain to you this enigma." Then the princess related her adventure.

On the next morning, the princess laid aside the royal robe, and resumed her own dress, and requested the presence of King Armanos, her supposed father-in-law, in her apartment.

When King Armanos arrived, he was very much

surprised to see a lady who was totally unknown to him.

"Sire," replied the princess, "yesterday I was king; to-day I am nothing more than the Princess of China, the wife of the true Prince Camaralzaman, who is the true son of King Schah-zaman. If your majesty will have the patience to listen to my adventures, I flatter myself you will not condemn me for imposing on you a temporary deceit for a salutary purpose."

When she had concluded, "Sire," added she, "if you will consent to give the Princess Haiatalnefous, your daughter, in marriage to Prince Camaralzaman, I will cheerfully resign the rank and quality of queen, which properly belongs to her, and will myself be content with the second rank. Even if this preference were not her due, I should have insisted on her accepting it, after the obligation I am under to her for having so generously kept the secret with which I entrusted her. If your majesty's determination depends upon her consent, I have already obtained that, and am certain she will be happy."

Upon this, King Armanos, turning to Prince Camaralzaman, said, "My son, I have only to inquire if you are willing to wed my daughter, and to wear my crown, which Badoura would well deserve to retain for the rest of her life, if she did not prefer resigning it through her love for you." "Sire," replied Camaralzaman, "though I do desire to revisit my father, Schah-zaman, the obligations under which you have placed the Princess Badoura and myself are so many that I cannot refuse your request."

The Persian Sultan Schah-riah could not but admire the prodigious and inexhaustible memory of the sultaness his wife, who had entertained him for a thousand and one nights with such a variety of interesting stories.

His temper was softened and his prejudices removed.

He was not only convinced of the merit and great wisdom of the sultaness Schehera-zade, but he remembered with what courage she had offered to be his wife, without fearing the death to which she knew she exposed herself, and which so many sultanesses had suffered within her knowledge.

These considerations, and the many other good qualities he knew her to possess, induced him at last to say to her: "I confess, lovely Schehera-zade, that you have appeased my anger. I freely renounce the law I had imposed on myself, and I will have you regarded as the deliverer of the many damsels I had resolved to sacrifice to my unjust resentment."

The sultaness cast herself at his feet and embraced them tenderly, with all the marks of the most lively and perfect gratitude.

The grand vizier soon learned this agreeable intelligence from the sultan's own mouth. It was instantly carried to the city, towns, and provinces, and gained the sultan and the beautiful Schehera-zade his consort universal applause and the blessings of all the people of the extensive empire of Persia.

PRINTED IN GREAT BRITAIN AT
THE PRESS OF THE PUBLISHERS

[*Continued*

NELSON'S FAMOUS BOOKS AT 2s. net

(*Continued*)

ALICE IN WONDERLAND. By LEWIS CARROLL. Illustrated by HELEN MONRO.

THROUGH THE LOOKING GLASS. By LEWIS CARROLL. Illustrated by HELEN MONRO.

JOHN HALIFAX, GENTLEMAN. By Mrs. CRAIK. Illustrated by BESSIE D. INGLIS.

TWO YEARS BEFORE THE MAST. By R. H. DANA. Illustrated by A. S. FORREST

ROBINSON CRUSOE. By DANIEL DEFOE. Illustrated by VICTOR COOLEY and W. B. ROBINSON.

THE OLD CURIOSITY SHOP. By CHARLES DICKENS. With a selection of the Original Illustrations.

OLIVER TWIST. By CHARLES DICKENS. Illustrated by G. CRUIKSHANK.

A TALE OF TWO CITIES. By CHARLES DICKENS. Illustrated by "PHIZ."

BLACK TULIP. By A. DUMAS. Illustrated by A. E. BESTALL.

MONTE CRISTO (The Chateau D'If). By A. DUMAS. Illustrated by HELEN MONRO.

THE THREE MUSKETEERS. By A. DUMAS. Illustrated by A. E. BESTALL.

ADAM BEDE. By GEORGE ELIOT. Illustrated by A. S. FORREST.

THE MILL ON THE FLOSS. By GEORGE ELIOT. Illustrated by BESSIE D. INGLIS.

SILAS MARNER. By GEORGE ELIOT. Illustrated by SYBIL TAWSE.

JACKANAPES AND OTHER STORIES. By Mrs. EWING. Illustrated by HONOR APPLETON.

CRANFORD. By Mrs. GASKELL. Illustrated by HEBER THOMPSON.

ROBIN HOOD AND THE MEN OF THE GREENWOOD. By HENRY GILBERT. Illustrated by H. M. BROCK and WALTER CRANE.

STORIES OF KING ARTHUR'S KNIGHTS. By HENRY GILBERT. Illustrated by T. H. ROBINSON.

THE VICAR OF WAKEFIELD. By OLIVER GOLDSMITH. Illustrated by C. E. BROCK.

[*Continued*

NELSON'S FAMOUS BOOKS AT 2s. net

(*Continued*)

GRIMM'S FAIRY TALES. Illustrated by R. MOORWOOD and H. ROUNTREE.

UNCLE REMUS. By J. C. HARRIS. Illustrated by RENÉ BULL.

TANGLEWOOD TALES. By NATHANIEL HAWTHORNE. Illustrated by RUTH MOORWOOD.

TOM BROWN'S SCHOOLDAYS. By THOMAS HUGHES. Illustrated by E. E. BRISCOE.

THE HEROES. By CHARLES KINGSLEY. Illustrated by HELEN MONRO.

HYPATIA. By CHARLES KINGSLEY.

THE WATER BABIES. By CHARLES KINGSLEY. Illustrated by ANNE ANDERSON.

WESTWARD HO! By CHARLES KINGSLEY. Illustrated by HELEN MONRO.

HEREWARD THE WAKE. By CHARLES KINGSLEY. Illustrated by A. M. TROTTER.

TALES FROM SHAKESPEARE. By CHARLES and MARY LAMB. Illustrated by F. G. MOORSOM.

THE CHILDREN OF THE NEW FOREST. By CAPTAIN MARRYAT. Illustrated by HONOR C. APPLETON.

MASTERMAN READY. By CAPTAIN MARRYAT. Illustrated by A. S. FORREST.

MR. MIDSHIPMAN EASY. By CAPTAIN MARRYAT. Illustrated by A. S. FORREST.

TALES OF MYSTERY AND IMAGINATION. By EDGAR ALLAN POE. Illustrated by A. M. TROTTER.

OLD PETER'S RUSSIAN TALES. By ARTHUR RANSOME. Illustrated by DMITRI MITROKHIN.

IVANHOE. By Sir WALTER SCOTT. Illustrated by F. E. HILEY.

KENILWORTH. By Sir WALTER SCOTT. Illustrated by F. E. HILEY.

THE TALISMAN. By Sir WALTER SCOTT. Illustrated by F. E. HILEY.

BLACK BEAUTY. By ANNA SEWELL. Illustrated by DOUGLAS RELF.

THE BLACK ARROW. By R. L. STEVENSON. Illustrated by A. M. TROTTER.

[*Continued*

THOMAS NELSON AND SONS, LTD.
London, Edinburgh, Paris, Melbourne
Toronto, and New York